"YOU STILL DON'T TRUST ME, DO YOU? YOU THINK I MIGHT TAKE OFF AGAIN," HE MURMURED.

Sighing lightly, she shrugged. "You have to admit that might happen. What if you get as bored with the shop as you did with teaching?"

"That's where you're wrong, Gracie," Daniel said softly. "I never got bored. Restless maybe, but now I know what I want."

"Well, we'll just have to wait and see about that, won't we?"

"Gracie," he muttered, "what will it take to make you believe I'm here to stay?"

"Stick around about ten years and I might begin to believe it."

"You can be a hard woman, honey."

"Not really. Just not gullible," she responded flatly, stopping his hand as it stole around her waist, and stepping out of his reach.

A CANDLELIGHT ECSTASY SUPREME

ASKING FOR TROUBLE

Donna Kimel Vitek

A CANDLELIGHT ECSTASY SUPREME

Published by
Dell Publishing Co., Inc.
1 Dag Hammarskjold Plaza
New York, New York 10017

Dell ® TM 681510, Dell Publishing Co., Inc.

Candlelight Ecstasy Supreme is a trademark
of Dell Publishing Co., Inc.

Candlelight Ecstasy Romance®, 1,203,540, is a registered
trademark of Dell Publishing Co., Inc.

ISBN: 0-440-10334-7

Printed in the United States of America

First printing—September 1984

To Our Readers:

Candlelight Ecstasy is delighted to announce the start of a brand-new series—Ecstasy Supremes! Now you can enjoy a romance series unlike all the others—longer and more exciting, filled with more passion, adventure, and intrigue—the stories you've been waiting for.

In months to come we look forward to presenting books by many of your favorite authors and the very finest work from new authors of romantic fiction as well. As always, we are striving to present the unique, absorbing love stories that you enjoy most—the very best love has to offer.

Breathtaking and unforgettable, Ecstasy Supremes will follow in the great romantic tradition you've come to expect *only* from Candlelight Ecstasy.

Your suggestions and comments are always welcome. Please let us hear from you.

Sincerely,

The Editors
Candlelight Romances
1 Dag Hammarskjold Plaza
New York, New York 10017

"I wondered if any of us would ever see you again," drawled Grace, sounding as matter-of-fact as possible. "When you didn't come back last year after your sabbatical leave was over, I figured you never would. Are you just passing through now?"

"No, I'm back to stay."

"Oh?" Her eyebrows lifted. "You mean you're going to try to get back on the faculty?"

A hint of a smile touched Daniel's mouth as he shook his head. "No, the university's replaced me, and since there's not a great demand for philosophy professors these days, it's a good thing I have no desire to go back. The ivory tower's not for me. I'd never be content just talking about living the simple life and getting back to nature again. It's better to live it."

"Ah, then your pilgrimage was a success, I guess? You found the true spirit of America or found yourself, whichever one you were looking for?" Grace asked more sharply than she meant to. She glanced away from him as his smile faded and his jaw hardened. A certain tightness quickened in her chest and tried to squeeze her heart as a heavy silence commenced between them. She hadn't meant to ask him that, especially in that tone of voice. Instead, she had wanted to treat him as politely as one would a casual acquaintance, although he had once been much more than that. She wished she could act as if he were hardly more than a stranger, yet how could she possibly do that when exactly two Aprils ago they had been lovers? She had imagined herself wildly in love, had even believed they might have a future together. Then, in June, he had left, and she had felt horribly lost without him until she had been able to convince herself that they had been ill suited for each other from the beginning. And she had found great comfort in that, but now he was back so unexpectedly that she wasn't truly prepared to cope with seeing him again, and the old memories, best forgotten, threatened resurrection. She swallowed with some difficulty. He

9

didn't look very different. His thick light-brown hair was a bit longer, perhaps, and just brushed the back of the opened shirt collar rising up from beneath his crew-neck sweater. Taller than average, his muscles stretched tautly over his large frame, he looked more like a professional athlete than a philosopher, and that look simply enhanced his appeal, the appeal she was totally aware of when he reached out to lift her chin with one finger.

"Allison told me about Gran," he said quietly, his previous impatience apparently forgotten. "I'm sorry, Gracie."

Grace had to fight back the tears. He had always known what could make her vulnerable, but in this instance she knew intuitively that his sympathy was quite sincere. She nodded. "She never was really well after that first heart attack. Mom and Dad asked her to live with them in Chattanooga, but ... Well, you know how much she loved this old house; she couldn't stand the thought of leaving it, so I gave up my apartment in Knoxville to come stay with her."

"And was that hard on you?"

"You know the answer to that because you knew Gran," Grace said with a sad but very fond smile. "And she was determined to be as active as possible until ... She was an inspiration and ... I want you to know she was always happy when I got a letter from you. She liked you very much, but I guess you knew that."

"I hoped she did, because I liked her very much too. A fine lady," Daniel replied gruffly while he searched the depth of her smoke-gray eyes, eyes that had always held a fascinating hint of mystery. Yet he detected less mystery now and more honest bereavement. He released her chin to touch the tendril of silky black hair that had fallen forward to graze her left cheek. "I just hope she knew how much she meant to me."

"She did. And thank you for always adding a personal note to her in your letters. They always made her beam."

"Although I didn't write as often as I meant to?"

"Yes. The letters you sent were enough to satisfy her."

"And how about you?" Daniel asked, stepping closer. "Did those infrequent letters satisfy you too?"

"Sure," she lied, stepping back to once more put a safer distance between them. "I know that traveling from place to place didn't give you much time to write, so I was glad to hear how you were once in a while."

"You didn't always answer."

"Because I figured you'd already moved on."

"I was in Pierre, South Dakota, for the past year. It must have occurred to you that I was going to stay there for a while?"

"How the devil should I know what you were going to do?" she exclaimed softly. Fortunately she was distracted by the kitten before she could thoroughly express her confusion. The loudly meowing kitten had stretched up on her hind legs to rake her forepaws over the calf of Grace's bare right leg. Grace winced. She bent down to gently lower the kitten back onto the ground, quietly admonishing, "Watch it, Little Bit. Those claws of yours are like razors."

"Nice kitten," Daniel commented. "But what happened to Muffin?"

"She died, about a month after Gran. I think she missed her. And of course she was nearly twelve years old."

"And you were so lonesome without her that you found yourself a new kitten?"

"Something like that," Grace confessed, smiling ruefully. "This old house just felt so empty. So I went to the animal shelter and found Little Bit. She was the smallest kitten there and . . . "

"You just couldn't resist her?"

"Well, she did come out of that awful cage right to me," she explained, ignoring his amused indulgent tone. "After that, I had to bring her home."

That faint smile lingered on his lips as he brushed the

11

back of his hand against her left cheek. "You've always been tenderhearted in some ways, Gracie but . . ."

He was interrupted by a burst of rather demanding barking, and grateful for the timely diversion, Grace turned her attention to the van. "You have a dog."

"Umm, and she's obviously getting impatient. Mind if I let her out?"

"Go ahead. I'll hold the cat so she won't get chased."

"Maybe you'd better, although Buster doesn't usually chase cats."

"Which doesn't necessarily mean she likes them."

"No, I wouldn't go so far as to say that," Daniel said wryly. "Mainly, she just tolerates them and at least knows better than to chase one when I'm around."

Scooping up Little Bit to be on the safe side, Grace watched Daniel walk over and open the sliding side door of the van. A sleek red Irish setter tumbled out all awriggle, acting for all the world like she had been imprisoned her entire lifetime instead of a mere five minutes. She was a lovely animal, her coat lustrous, her eyes big and brown and brimming with adoration as she nuzzled her nose against Daniel's hand while he looked back at Grace, who quizzically shook her head. "Whatever made you give such a pretty dog a name like Buster?"

Daniel laughed. "Wait until you get to know her better. Then you'll see the name fits. She can be very rowdy sometimes."

As if determined to court danger, the kitten swiftly wiggled free of Grace's light grasp, leapt down, and landed on the ground on all fours with typical feline ease and agility. Without hesitation, she scampered toward the dog.

When Grace started after her, Daniel lifted a restraining hand. "It's okay. Sit and be nice, Buster," he quietly commanded.

Reluctantly, the setter obeyed. Her tail thumped only once with a lack of enthusiasm, and her eyes darted in every direction except down as the purring kitten rubbed

12

back and forth against the dog's legs. Buster shifted rest-lessly on her haunches but stayed. Grace exchanged a bemused smile with Daniel.

"I thought she'd be scared. But she is a very young kitten, no more than six weeks old at the most. Maybe she's just lonely for another animal."

"It looks that way, but Buster doesn't seem exactly thrilled with the situation."

"But she's being very nice about it. You're a good girl," Grace softly praised and went over to scratch behind the dog's silken ears. She could understand how ill at ease Buster probably felt because Daniel's surprise visit was making her feel much the same way herself. In a way, it was good to see him again, yet his presence was making her tense. Nearly two years ago, when he had first gone away, she had missed him terribly, and though she had long since gotten past that stage, she was still wary of him. She breathed deeply and tried to relax because she could see that he didn't seem to be in any hurry to end his visit. And she could hardly keep him standing out in the barn-yard forever. Giving him a polite smile, she inclined her head toward the house. "Would you like to come in and have coffee?"

"Fine, thanks. And after that I want to take you out to dinner."

Her eyes met his. "It's nice of you to ask, but I've got beef stew on the stove simmering."

"Gran's secret recipe, by any chance?"

She nodded, then decided to appear to be a sophisticate even if she didn't feel particularly sophisticated in that instant. Pride wouldn't allow her to let him know how uneasy he was making her, so she issued the invitation. "You always did love Gran's stew. I remember now. So why don't you stay and have dinner with me? I'm sure I can even find something good for Buster to eat."

His slow answering smile carved attractive indentations in his cheeks. "We gladly accept."

Together, they followed the flagstone path that led to the side porch. Daniel gazed out over the rolling meadow to the right. It was freshly carpeted in spring's new grass and adorned with patches of golden buttercups and dark purple violets. Beyond the pasture a thicket of pines followed the gentle contours of the hills.

"Beautiful place," he murmured. "Nothing seems to ever change here."

"Things look the same, but there is some difference. Gran sold all the land except for five acres surrounding the house," Grace told him. "After Grandpa went out of the dairy business and even after he died, she wanted to hold onto every acre. But then, last year, she changed her mind and sold to Mr. Bates, who owns the dairy farm just down the road."

"Is he one of your clients? Eric mentioned that you're the accountant for a few dairymen around here."

"Uh-huh, three others besides Mr. Bates. And I handle the accounting for a few of the small businesses in Alpine Springs."

"How do you like being in business for yourself?"

"I enjoy it. It's nice to have my office here at home and the freedom to arrange my own schedule."

"That surprises me," Daniel said tonelessly, a frown notching his brow as he looked down at her. "I thought you preferred the security of working for an established accounting firm. Nothing would have made you quit your nine-to-five job two years ago when I left."

"That was then; this is now," she replied just as tonelessly, detecting the undercurrent of tension that shot up between them but choosing to ignore it while coolly meeting his gaze. "Circumstances change. When Gran got sick, she needed someone here to stay with her, but she couldn't afford a full-time nurse or even a companion. I decided to go into business for myself so I could work out of an office here and be with her at the same time. Luckily, I found clients and it all worked out."

"Sometimes, fate takes a hand."

"And exactly what does that cryptic remark mean?"

"It means you would never have tried to set up your own business if you hadn't been forced to."

"Okay, maybe I wouldn't have, but there's nothing wrong with being cautious."

"Unless you make caution an obsession, which you always did."

"Don't bring up old arguments, Dan," she muttered through clenched teeth, eyes flashing. "That's not the way to be a gracious dinner guest."

Low laughter rumbled up from deep in his throat. "Ah, blackmail. In other words you're saying if I try to drag up the past, you aren't going to give me any of that delicious stew, right?"

Irritated at him for laughing, she sighed. "Something like that."

"Then I propose a truce," he countered, giving her one of his most winning smiles while catching her right hand up in his. "I have my heart set on that stew, so how about it, Gracie?"

He could have easily been a successful con artist. Or even an award-winning actor—except for one thing. Grace knew he wasn't acting. He had never been pretentious. Instead he had always come across as genuine and sincere, which was why she had almost always found him irresistible. And she couldn't resist now. A truce was such a little concession. She would make it. There was no way she could tell him he was no longer welcome for dinner . . . unless he tried to renew any of their old arguments.

"Okay, truce," she agreed, but withdrew her hand from his when the pleasantly rough texture of his fingertips grazing her palm became too pleasant and a shiver danced up and down her spine. She preceded him across the wooden porch to open the screen door and step into the cozy kitchen, which still had its original wood-beamed ceiling but also had the modern conveniences. Little Bit,

15

deserting her newfound friend and hoping for a delicious handout, shot inside too and meowed hungrily when Grace stirred the stew and the appetizing aroma wafted through the room.

Advising her to have some patience, Grace glanced at the screen door, then at Daniel, who sat at the antique walnut worktable sipping the coffee she had poured for him. He raised one eyebrow and she asked, "Is Buster housebroken?"

He nodded.

"Then for goodness sake, let her in. I can't stand to see her sitting outside, staring in with those sad brown eyes, like an orphan shut out in the cold."

"Another example of how tenderhearted you can be sometimes," he softly said, chuckling and tugging gently at a strand of her hair as he passed her at the stove to go open the door and allow Buster to join the party.

Dinner was stimulating and entertaining. Happily able to relax to a great extent, Grace truly enjoyed it. Of course, Daniel had always been an exciting companion, knowledgeable in many varied subjects and an original conversationalist, so he was never boring. They kept their discussion general and impersonal, agreeing on some issues, disagreeing on others. Occasionally, she felt that their two years apart hadn't really come between them, that they were as close as they had once been. She shook off that feeling, knowing very well that Daniel possessed a natural ability to win over almost anyone, even the most hardened cynic. There was simply something about him. Charisma, perhaps. But, no, it was even deeper than that. He was so sure of himself without ever being cocky and conveyed such an inner strength that it was nearly impossible to imagine that he might ever put on an act just to impress somebody. And he cared, not as much as Grace had once wanted him to, but he did care, which made him very special indeed. He could be serious; he could be funny. There had been times when he had huskily and

16

poetically compared her to a summer's day one moment, and in the next moment, he wrestled with her on the bed, playfully tickling her until she was helplessly giggling. He had never been predictable, except in his tenderness, and remembering all of this, Grace looked down at her plate and mentally chided herself. It was very foolish to waste even one thought on the old days.

After dinner she stacked the dishes in the sink, declining Daniel's offer to help tidy the dining room and kitchen. The two of them, faithfully accompanied by both the dog and cat, went into the parlor, where he sat down on the comfortable antique blue velvet sofa and lifted his feet onto the well-used ottoman after she settled herself in the matching chair opposite him.

"This is a wonderful house," he commented a few moments later, breaking the silence. "Exactly how old is it?"

"A hundred and twenty-three years and sturdy as ever. With an occasional coat of paint and general repairs, it'll probably outlast both of us," she said, then grinned and lifted a silencing hand when he started to speak. "You don't have to say it. I've heard it a million times: 'They don't build houses like they used to.' "

Daniel grinned back. "Do you really believe I'd say anything that mundane even if it is true?"

"You might. Nobody's perfect, not even you," she retorted. Slipping her feet out of her canvas espadrilles, she tucked them up beside her on the chair cushion. "You mentioned starting a business. What kind?"

"An organic nursery. Plants grown from seed without any chemicals. Guaranteed. It seems to be the coming thing, and it certainly makes sense. I've been working with John Powell in his garden shop in Pierre for the past year, and he has no lack of customers, so I decided to come back here and open my own place. I'll be able to make a profit while finding satisfaction in what I'm doing."

"A lot of people are beginning to worry about the effects of chemical fertilizers and pesticides," Grace mused

17

aloud, then nodded. "You should get plenty of customers from the suburbs, and there's the university faculty. It really could be a very sound business venture."

"Glad you think so, because I'm looking for an investor," he casually announced. "And Allison said you happen to be looking for a sound investment right now. Perfect timing, isn't it?"

Her hand came to a halt midair as she started to smooth her skirt, and she stared at him rather blankly. "You're *not* serious?"

"Yes. I am."

He wasn't kidding! With that realization, angry resentment flew all over her, and the hand she had dropped onto her lap clenched into a fist as her stare became a glower and her lips twisted derisively. "Is that why you came to see me?" she asked sharply. "Just because you're looking for someone to invest in this business scheme of yours?"

"You know better than that, Gracie," he stated with near-infuriating calm. "I'm here because I wanted to see you. I would have come whether or not you were interested in making a sound investment, but since I can offer you one, it wouldn't make sense if I didn't."

Slapping a wayward wisp of hair back from her neck, she almost snorted. "Forgive me for being so blunt, but do you think I'm crazy or something?" she said, her voice ice-edged, unusually hard. "Sure, Gran left me some money and I am looking for a sound investment, *but* it wouldn't be very wise of me to gamble my inheritance on you. Oh, your idea's great; an organic nursery would probably be a success. But how could I be sure you'd stick around to run it? It would be just like you to catch another case of the wanderlust and take off again to live with some flower children in a commune where all of you can spend all your time finding yourselves, or whatever it is you've been doing for the past two years."

"Don't be judgmental and don't exaggerate. It doesn't become you, Gracie," Daniel said, only the momentary

18

glint in his narrowing eyes reminding her that he could show a quick temper on occasion. But he usually controlled it, and he managed to control it now as he surveyed her intently. Faint rose color had bloomed in her cheeks. She had spirit, which he had to admire, even though "spirit" translated to sheer stubbornness in her half the time. Prolonging his silence, he lowered his feet from the ottoman, leaned forward on the sofa, and rested his elbows upon his knees, capturing and holding her gaze. "You know very well that I haven't been a penniless drifter for nearly two years. At first, I moved from place to place fairly often, but I never lived in a commune—nothing could appeal to me less. Everywhere I went, I found work and a decent place to stay. And I wasn't looking for myself. I've known exactly who I am for several years, but a university campus tends to become a world within itself. I wanted to find out how some of the people in the outside world live. I did and it's been an education, so don't try to make me seem irresponsible for leaving or I might be tempted to retaliate by calling you a stick-in-the-mud."

"I'm not a stick-in-the-mud! I . . ."

"I asked you to go with me, practically begged."

"And I asked you to stay!"

"I wish you had gone with me."

"It's a good thing I didn't, since Gran had her first heart attack less than four months after you left and she really needed me."

"You could have come back to take care of her. That, I could have understood."

"I could never go in the first place. I wasn't like you; I . . . just needed the security of a home base. I was twenty-three, and keeping my job as an accountant at Jones and Latham was important to me. I had to stay here."

"I still wish you'd gone with me," he persisted, a semblance of a smile touching his firmly shaped mouth. "I missed you. Did you know you were one of the best students I ever had?"

"Oh, come on, don't hand me that." She tried to dismiss his words with a careless flick of her wrist. "What you really mean is that I was one of the most willing *female* students you ever had."

"Willing? *You?* Oh, no, you certainly weren't overly willing. You took a great deal of convincing before—"

"And you knew exactly how to convince me! How was I supposed to resist the youngest, most dynamic associate professor on campus?" she murmured. "Sometimes, I think the biggest mistake I ever made was enrolling in your evening enrichment class."

"Do you?" he inquired, his low-timbered voice taking on an appealing huskiness, his gaze imprisoning. "But we did have some wonderful times together, Gracie. Didn't we?"

Too wonderful to bear remembering. The look in his dark green eyes was both disturbed and disturbing, and she hastily glanced away for an instant until her wildly skittering heart began to resume a more normal beat. Then she shrugged, hopefully with something closely approximating nonchalance. "But that was in the past, and I see no point in discussing the relationship we had so long ago. We were talking business, Dan."

Nodding brusquely, he relaxed back on the sofa. "Business then. I'm still looking for an investor, and you're still looking for a good investment, so what do you think? Interested in my offer?"

"I don't . . ." she began, then broke off, feeling he was in no mood to take a simple no for an answer. "How much money do you need?"

"Fifty thousand, more or less."

"What sort of terms?"

"What sort of terms would you want?"

She pretended to mull that over for a minute. "Forty percent for you, sixty for me," she finally said, certain he would never be willing to accept a deal like that. "And I would have to be actively involved in the business. That way, if you happened to decide to skip town again, I'd have enough experience to keep the shop going."

"Fifty-fifty. That's the best I can offer, Gracie," he immediately replied, his tone solemn and sincere. "I'm going to be putting up ten thousand of my own money and managing the shop because at the moment I'm the only one with the experience. But, if you want to be actively involved, that's fine with me, although I won't 'skip town again,' as you so quaintly put it."

Seemed as if she had painted herself into a corner. She really hadn't expected him to suggest a fifty-fifty split, since the whole thing was, after all, his idea, one that was very timely. Many people were already into organic gardening—yet . . . She shook her head. "I don't think . . ."

"Think it over some more. I didn't expect you to give me an answer tonight," he quietly assured her. "I only want you to take a few days to consider it."

Grace sighed inwardly. His out-of-the-blue arrival, their verbal sparring, and this intriguing proposal had all combined to make her unusually weary, and she felt a growing need for some time to herself. "All right, I'll consider it," she agreed, then gratefully glanced at Buster, who awoke on the cold hearth, found the kitten sleeping cozily beside her, and jumped up to beat a hasty retreat toward Dan. And she seemed more than a little dismayed when Little Bit roused herself to follow hot at her heels. Shaking her head at the sight of the odd couple, Grace grinned. "Buster may not be far away from a nervous breakdown."

"Cats aren't generally her greatest admirers," Daniel drawled, scruffing the dog's neck when she laid her nose upon his right knee. "No wonder she's confused."

Smiling at the skittish setter, she nodded agreement but could think of nothing else interesting to say to further the conversation about the dog and cat. That topic seemed to have run its course, perhaps because it isn't easy for ex-lovers to make idle chitchat. A long silence commenced. She began to feel increasingly uneasy again and aware that the only sound in the parlor was the ticking of the grandfather clock. She glanced at the time. Nearly nine. The hours since Daniel had arrived had passed quickly until now, when every second seemed to be dragging by. Looking at him, she found him watching her closely. With a faint fleeting smile she removed a small bundle of white lace-edged organza from the sewing basket by her chair.

"Mind if I work on this while we . . . talk?"

"Not at all," he said, his gaze wandering over her slowly. "What are you making?"

"A christening gown."

He quirked one eyebrow. "You didn't mention being pregnant, so I assume you're making it for someone else's baby."

"No, it's not for somebody else's child." She calmly countered his teasing tone, then grinned at his sudden deep frown. She held up the diminutive garment. "See, it isn't for a real baby at all. Too small. It's a doll's dress. And, no, before you ask, I don't still play with dolls. I help fix up the ones donated to the Christmas Stocking program for underprivileged children."

His frown dissolved. "That must be very satisfying."

"I enjoy it. Besides, Gran did it for years, and I thought it would be nice to keep up the tradition."

"But I'm sure you don't spend all your spare time making dresses for dolls," he commented, his tone slightly altered. "What about men, Gracie? Are you seriously involved with anyone?"

Glancing up from the bit of lace she was stitching onto the tiny tucked yoke, she almost wished she could have answered yes to his question. That would have been an outright lie, however, and since she'd never been a convincing liar, she told the truth. "No serious involvement, but I've gone out fairly often in the past few months. Before, with Gran not well, I wanted to be with her as much as possible. How about you? Who's the woman in your life right now?"

"How could I have a woman in my life when, according to you, I've been flitting from place to place for nearly two years?"

"You just told me that you spent the past year in Pierre, South Dakota."

"Ah, so you do realize I settled down for quite a while and didn't spend all my time drifting around?" he said wryly. "I believe we're making progress."

"I don't really consider staying in one place for a year settling down, but that's beside the point. You must have gotten involved with someone in Pierre. You always had something of a reputation on campus as being a ladies' man."

He laughed. "So did Dean Gann, although he has several grandchildren and a wife who would kill him if he even thought about another woman. You never believed the rumors you heard?"

"Not really," she conceded, concentrating on taking a few more even stitches to avoid looking up at him. "But there were some women."

"I never claimed to be a monk. But there were fewer women than you probably think and only one other long-term relationship that didn't last as long as ours."

Unfortunately, she had hoped theirs would last forever. But it hadn't. Her shoulders rose and fell in a shrug. "Well, that's all water under the bridge now, anyhow. We just weren't . . . aren't compatible, Dan. You have sort of a vagabond spirit, and I'm . . ."

"Afraid to take chances?" he finished for her when she paused to search for the exact descriptive word.

"I'm more a homebody," she coolly corrected. "If you think I'm a timid—"

"Oh, I know you're not timid. Just overcautious at

23

times, but that's different. And I think that can be changed," he said mysteriously, only adding a simple smile to his words when she quickly looked up from her sewing with a questioning expression. He offered her no answer, consulted his wristwatch, and rose lithely to his feet. "Better go. I enjoyed dinner. You make delicious stew, as good as Gran's always was."

Murmuring her thanks, Grace set aside the christening dress, got up, and escorted him and Buster out into the hall to the front door where the dog stood poised at the screen, obviously eager to get out and escape the persistent attention of the too friendly kitten. After picking up Little Bit when she scampered over to join all of them, Grace faced Daniel. "Where are you staying?"

"Eric and Allison offered me their guest room until I find a place."

"Nice of them. Tell them I said hello."

Nodding, he looked down at her. Her smoky eyes, darkened by her long thick lashes, directly met his. Her creamy skin nearly shimmered in the soft glow of the outside lamplight, and he recalled how warm and smooth-textured it had once been to his touch. Desire stirred in him, but he merely leaned down to lightly kiss her cheek. "It's good seeing you again, Gracie."

When he stepped back, she managed a slight smile. "You too."

"Just give me a call when you've had time to think over my proposition."

"Yes. I'll be in touch soon."

They said good night. After watching him walk across the veranda, down the the steps, and disappear in the shadows beneath the magnolia trees, she closed the heavy old mahogany door and turned the key in the lock. Stroking the cuddling kitten, she nearly smiled. Although her heart had done a silly little somersault when Dan kissed her, it had soon resumed a regular pace. Seeing him again had not been as traumatic as she had once feared it would be. Of course, remnants of some of the old feelings were still there, but she had been able to control them. She was proud of herself. Yet . . . she was also rather relieved that he'd put an early end to the evening.

Three nights later Daniel returned to the farmhouse at Grace's invitation. While they walked into the parlor together, he removed his tan safari jacket, then he laid it across the back of the sofa before sitting down.

She sat on the chair and spoke without fanfare. "I have some questions about the garden shop."

"I expected you to." Reaching inside his coat, he removed a long envelope and handed it over to her. "Maybe this will answer some of them. Cost estimates for the shop itself, if we can't find a suitable place to rent and have to build. Also cost estimates for inventory, insurance, taxes, and so on."

Grace carefully perused the information he had brought her and found no discouraging figures in any part of it. Still, she was not quite ready to commit her money—or herself. Folding the sheets, she tucked them back into the envelope, then tapped the corner against her chin while looking thoughtfully at him. "What about suppliers? This trend toward organic gardening has just recently become very popular. It must not be easy to find seedlings and shrubs that have been organically grown?"

"It's not as easy as finding nonorganic shrubs and seedlings, no. But I know of several reliable suppliers that John Powell dealt with, so we'll have no problem there."

"Good. And what do you think of the idea of having the shop right here, out next to the barn? I thought about converting the barn, but I think it would be less expensive to construct a new building, including a greenhouse. That way, we won't have to pay rent, and this is a well-traveled road. And with the right amount of advertising, we'll bring the customers in. What do you think?"

"I think we have much more in common than you want

25

to believe, since I was going to suggest the same thing myself," Daniel said. "This seems like the perfect location unless it would conflict with zoning laws."

"That shouldn't be a problem. I know someone who knows someone who works in the county zoning office, and he said we should have no trouble getting a permit to build a garden shop here. After all, it's not like we want to put up a factory. And there are no neighbors close enough to be bothered."

Daniel smiled at her enthusiasm. "Sounds like I have a partner."

Smiling back, she nodded. "As soon as we have a lawyer draw up an agreement, you will."

"Why are you doing this?" he abruptly asked, searching the depths of her widening eyes. "Because I told you you're afraid to take chances and this is your way of proving that you're not?"

"Hardly. I'm no fool. And I don't feel a need to prove anything to you," she retorted. "But I've been checking around the past three days, and this seems like a good deal. Besides, I called Dad this morning and asked his advice, and he said if the numbers looked good, it could be a very good investment. He knows about these things, and I respect his opinion, so I'm saying yes, Dan, only because I expect to make a handsome profit."

His smile returned and deepened. "Always so practical-minded, Gracie."

"Good thing too. I'll be the perfect balance for you if you decide to be impractical anywhere along the line, which could certainly happen, considering your past record."

He chuckled good-naturedly. "I have no doubt we'll make a terrific team. Your seriousness *will* be a balance for my 'vagabond spirit,' as you called it. And vice versa."

His willingness to laugh at himself had always been an endearing quality, one she couldn't hope ever to resist. She smiled again, despite herself. "You're an impossible man, but since we're going to be partners, I think we should drink to our new business. That's why I bought a bottle of champagne today. I'll get it."

As swiftly and agilely as a pouncing leopard, he moved to catch hold of her left wrist as she got up. He turned her round to him, his green eyes fastening on hers as he murmured, "The champagne can wait a minute. But I think it would be very foolish for us to shake hands right now. So how about a kiss to seal our bargain?"

She detected the faint but familiar lime scent of his after-shave and noticed the strength conveyed in the firm line of his jaw and the sensuality of his carved lips, nicked by a tiny scar in one corner of his mouth. For an instant, she ached to touch a fingertip to it and ask him again how he had gotten it. He would never tell her before. Yet she resisted touching and asking and instead nodded and turned her cheek up to him. "All right, one kiss," she agreed calmly, but when he curved a hand round her neck and his thumb beneath her chin turned her face toward his and his mouth descended on hers, her breathing ceased momentarily. Firm warm lips parted hers with tender insistence, and as he drew her close, the vital heat of his lean body seemed to radiate deeply into her. For an insane moment she kissed him back, but when his arms started to go around her, her senses were restored, and she pushed him away with a none-too-gentle force.

"We may be partners," she uttered tersely, ignoring the thrill still vibrating in her. "But not that kind, ever again."

His narrowed gaze held hers. "If that's the way you want it."

"It is."

He wondered if she was telling the truth but was wise enough not to say so. Instead he inclined his head. "That's the way it'll be then."

"Good. Just so you understand. I'll get the champagne now," she said stiffly, and left him. Out of his sight a moment later she walked into the kitchen and touched her

27

fingers to her lips. She wished he hadn't kissed her like that; he had aroused too many memories, memories she had believed were already forgotten. But they weren't, and he was still a very appealing man. But she could handle him. Theirs would be strictly a business relationship. Yet, even as she reassured herself, a tiny voice in the farthest corner of her mind whispered that she might be asking for trouble by getting involved with Daniel again, in *any* way whatsoever.

CHAPTER TWO

Grace and Dan had dinner with Allison and Eric Kingston the next evening. Grace had happily accepted Allison's invitation because she'd always enjoyed being with the couple since Dan had introduced her to them more than two years ago. Even after Daniel had left Knoxville, she and Allison had kept in close touch, so she had every reason to believe the evening would be a comfortable one. It began that way; dinner was relaxing, enlivened by interesting conversation. And, thankfully, no one mentioned Grace and Dan's romantic relationship or, rather, their present lack of one. It was only after the four of them went into the living room of the Kingstons' house on Faculty Row that Eric suddenly turned quite somber and gave Grace a puzzled look.

"I must say I'm surprised at you for deciding to get involved in Dan's new plan," he announced, rubbing his bearded jaw. "In fact, we were hoping you'd try to talk him out of it. He should go back into the lecture hall where he belongs, don't you think? You know what a fine teacher he is."

"Yes, I do know," she readily conceded, glancing at Daniel. When she saw something akin to amused resignation play over his lips, she spread her hands in an expressive gesture for Eric's benefit. "But if he doesn't want to go back to teaching, he shouldn't. It's as simple as that."

29

"Not quite," Eric argued, his tone only half teasing. "What the devil does a philosophy professor know about running a business?"

"A great deal, after being involved in the day-to-day operation of a garden shop for the past year," said Grace flatly. "From what he's told me, I'm perfectly satisfied that he knows how to run this particular kind of business. If I didn't believe that, I wouldn't be investing in it."

"Maybe you're hoping for too much. Dan's no entrepreneur and—"

"And you're beginning to sound a little pompous and overprotective," she interrupted, though with a grin. "Dan's thirty-three, certainly old enough to make his own decisions. So am I. And, although you are thirty-seven, I think you're still too young to qualify as a father figure to either of us."

"You'll have to learn to ignore him," Daniel spoke up. He was sitting beside her on the sofa, lounging back, perfectly relaxed. "Eric and I have this unspoken agreement. I don't mind when he starts handing out advice, and he doesn't mind when I never listen."

"I just hope you don't live to regret not listening," Eric persisted. "Seems to me both of you are taking a big chance."

Catching Grace's eye, Daniel smiled rather secretively. "Gracie and I have decided there are worse things than taking a few chances. Like being too afraid to try anything new and different. Right, Gracie?"

"Frankly, I don't feel like this is such a great gamble," she answered evasively, acting as if she hadn't received his private little message. "Why all the worry, Eric? Many people are getting interested in organic gardening, and we'll have the first exclusively organic shop in this area. I'm sure we'll have many customers. It may be a little slow at first."

Eric grimaced. "It may be dead."

"Dear, I think you could try to be a bit more diplomatic," Allison quickly put in, smiling apologetically at Grace and Daniel. "I hope you two understand why Eric's being so blunt. He . . . and I just don't want you to get involved in something that might prove to be a big disappointment."

"Exactly," her husband added. "These days, with the unbelievable number of small business failures, it seems too damned risky for you two to invest all your money and energy in such an iffy venture."

"How's the baseball team doing this year?" Daniel inquired quietly, a certain set of his jaw and his tone indicating that as far as he was concerned this particular discussion was closed.

And it was. With a fatalistic shrug Eric dropped the subject and didn't refer to it again. Once more the evening became relaxing and so enjoyable that Grace wondered aloud where the time had gone when she looked at her watch and discovered it was close to eleven o'clock. After she said the typically prolonged friendly good nights to the Kingstons, Daniel walked her outside to her car, helping her arrange her lightweight cashmere shawl round her shoulders to ward off the chilly night breeze. The fresh scent of spring was in the air. Streetlamps placed at intervals cast the narrow road and faculty houses in a bluish-white light. Wrapping her shawl more securely around her, Grace stood by the driver's door, tucked her purse beneath her arm, and looked at Daniel, whose tall lean form was silhouetted in the blue-white glow. In shirt sleeves he casually shifted his weight to one foot while slipping a hand into a pocket of his trousers.

"You must be cold. Why don't you go back in now? I'm fine. And thank you for walking me out," she told him.

"I don't see why we have to talk to each other like we're strangers," he responded as he took one long stride to move closer to her. "You shouldn't be so standoffishly polite with me, Gracie, since we were lovers once and will be business partners soon."

31

"Speaking of that," she said evasively, "our lawyers are getting together to draw up our agreement the first of next week, which means it should be ready for us to sign by Thursday or Friday. After that, we might want to hire another attorney to represent our business interests. Don't you think so?"

"Sounds fine to me, if you'll feel more comfortable with a neutral lawyer."

"I didn't say that exactly. I only meant—"

"I'm still surprised you agreed to my proposition, since it's fairly obvious you don't trust me very much."

"Oh, but I trust you enough to get the garden shop started and to teach me everything you know about running it. Even if this does turn out to be a whim for you, you'll be here long enough to do that. If you leave later, I'll be able to buy your half of the business and keep it going."

His faint smile was barely detectable in the dim lamplight as he shook his head and lifted a finger to lightly tap her chin. "Your faith in me would move mountains, honey," he joked, then dropped his hand. "But despite your lack of faith in me personally, you have changed. You sounded very confident about our new venture when you were talking to Eric. I doubt you would have sounded nearly as confident two years ago, in the same situation."

"I don't know about that. This is a sound investment. Oh, I could let the money I inherited from Gran sit safely in the bank and draw a little interest on it. But this is a good deal. I know that."

"I'm glad."

"Dan," she began, and started to reach out a hand toward him, but thought better of it and instead wrapped her arm around her waist. "Do you have to listen to many of Eric's sermonettes like the one we heard tonight?"

"One a day, at least. But Eric means well," he said, chuckling. "So does Allison. But both of them have been on the faculty for over ten years and it's the only life they

32

know and they love it. That makes it hard for them to understand that I have no desire to go back to teaching. I enjoyed it while I did it, but things have changed now."

"I know they mean well, because they care, but isn't all their negativism a little depressing?"

"Gracie, Eric and Allison are diplomatic compared to some of my other former colleagues," he told her, his accompanying shrug almost devil-may-care. "Some of them are so entrenched in the academic world that I seem like an outrageous renegade, and they tell me so."

"Then they're being ridiculous!"

"Oh?" Daniel drawled, surveying her face intently. "And *you're* the one I expected to call me impractical and irresponsible."

"I . . . well, I did think you were irresponsible when you went off on your trek of self-discovery," she said honestly. "But . . . this is different. Now, you want to settle down at least long enough to start what should be a thriving business. You don't need old acquaintances doing everything they can to try to discourage you, so maybe you should try to find a place of your own—off campus—as soon as you can."

"I'm looking. And I'm glad you brought up the subject." Stretching out one arm, he leaned comfortably against her car's doorjamb. "I've been thinking of adding some space to the shop for living quarters, if you have no objections. The rent I'd save could go toward our profits."

After a long moment of hesitation she began, "Well, I don't know if—"

"Maybe you'd rather not have me as such a close neighbor?"

"It's not that," she declared, responding to the slight hint of challenge she imagined she detected in his words. "I was just wondering if you'd really want to work and live in the same place. It might get very monotonous."

"I'd rather live in a place where I could look out the

33

window and see a meadow instead of an adjoining apartment building. Wouldn't you?"

She could only nod in agreement or be an obvious liar, so she had no real choice except to say, "If you really want to live behind the shop, I don't mind, but it's going to be some time before we get the building finished. What about in the meantime? I still think you'd be better off getting a place of your own."

"Easier said than done, unfortunately. The waiting lists for people wanting apartments are very long. And since I don't want to sign a long-term lease, that makes things doubly difficult. Besides," Daniel added, pointing toward Buster, who had followed them from the house and was now snoozing on the still-warm asphalt driveway, "most apartment complexes won't accept pets. And Buster and I have been together for nearly a year and a half. I'd hate to have to give her away now."

"Oh, no, you can't do that." Grace looked over at the sleeping dog. "She'd be lost without you, and you'd miss her so much too."

"But I can't impose on Allison and Eric's hospitality much longer. I'm going to have to take whatever I can get pretty soon, even if it means giving Buster up."

"But—"

"Of course, there is one other possibility, a very slim one, I admit," Daniel continued. "You're out there in that old house, rattling around, with all those extra rooms. You could rent one of them to me. I'd even be willing to take turns with you doing the cooking, and you know I'm a fairly good cook."

Grace silently caught her breath. "Yes, I know you are. But to rent you a room—"

"What's the matter, Gracie?" he softly interrupted, touching her shoulder, then curving one of his large hands around the slender column of her neck. "Surely you're not afraid for us both to live in the same house?"

"I'm not afraid of you, Dan," she blithely said. "Why on earth should I be?"

"I know you're not afraid of me. But that's not what I asked. Would you be afraid for us to live together under the same roof?"

"Afraid, no. But I'm not sure it would be a wise arrangement. I like my privacy."

"So do I. And it would be a sensible arrangement, especially when we start building the shop, since I picked up some construction experience during the past two years and plan to do some of the work myself. It certainly would be more convenient for me to walk a few hundred yards to work every morning instead of having to drive over from town. Besides"—Daniel smiled almost boyishly—"your place would be perfect for Buster."

With a wry grin Grace looked at the dog. "Are you sure of that? Isn't there a good chance she'd become neurotic, having to put up with Little Bit's worship full-time?"

"Living with a doting kitten would be a small price to pay for open fields to run in and woods to explore. She's an outdoor dog. It would be a shame to confine her to an apartment, even if I manage to find one where I'll be able to keep her."

Grace lifted her eyes heavenward. "Why do I have this feeling you're trying to use my affection for animals to get me to do what you want?"

He pretended to be hurt by the very suggestion. "Do you really think I'd ever try to manipulate you like that?"

"Yes."

"Well, is it working?" he asked, his hopeful tone comically exaggerated. "Or should I switch tactics?"

"Don't bother."

"Does that mean you've decided to rent me a room then?"

"No. It does *not* mean that at all," she said, lightly laughing in the semidarkness. "I've never considered taking in boarders, so I want some time to think about this.

35

And while I'm thinking, it would be a good idea for you to keep looking for an apartment."

"I'll go on trying to find one, of course," Daniel assured her but shook his head. "Seems a pity, though. Don't you get lonely out there in that big house, especially knowing your nearest neighbors are so far away?"

She shrugged. "I've lived alone before."

"In apartments. This is different."

"Sometimes, I do feel a little uneasy," she conceded. "And I wish the neighbors were a little closer."

"It must be hard to get to sleep sometimes, upstairs in your bedroom with only a tiny kitten for protection."

"You can be a devil, Dan," she accused, laughing again. "If you're trying to make me have nightmares tonight, you're not going to succeed. I don't need any protection. I always lock all the downstairs doors and windows, and if anyone ever tried to get in, which is highly unlikely, I'd hear them because I'm a very light sleeper. I might get a little uneasy sometimes, but I'm never really what you'd call scared."

"Maybe not," he said, gently touching her hair as his deep-timbred voice suddenly became more solemn. "But I don't like the idea of you being in that isolated house all alone."

He meant that, and she was oddly touched by his concern. Yet when his fingers left her hair to graze her left cheek, she tensed, stepped back, and opened the car door. She slipped inside. After smoothing her skirt, she searched for her key in her purse. "I have a busy day tomorrow," she told Daniel as he leaned down to look in at her. "I have to go now."

"Wait. Buster," he called, then whistled. He opened the back door of Grace's car and shooed the dog in, onto the backseat. "Take her with you. She's a good guard dog. At least, she has a ferocious bark, which should scare off any would-be intruder."

"Oh, but, Dan, I don't need—"

36

"Take her," he softly commanded. "You'll be doing me a favor; she's getting restless, fenced in Eric's backyard, and needs some time in the country."

"But I—"

"See you tomorrow," Daniel said, quietly closing her door before she could utter another word. Then he tossed up one hand in a wave and strode back toward the front door of the Kingston house.

Several minutes later, as Grace headed southeast out of Knoxville, Buster wriggled forward, over the gear console and into the front passenger seat, where she sat erect and watched the countryside swoosh by out the window. Glancing over at her, Grace shook her head. Reaching out, she stroked the setter's silken ears and wondered if Daniel would ever be, in any way, predictable.

Buster stayed at the farmhouse, and a week later Daniel moved in. He claimed he couldn't find an apartment that he liked which also accepted pets. Grace couldn't really doubt the truth of what he said. Nice apartments in Knoxville were never easily found, especially during the regular school year at the university, which hadn't yet ended. And besides, Grace admitted to herself, though not to Dan, Buster's presence in the house was wondrously reassuring. She didn't bark excessively but would let loose with a dangerous-sounding guttural growl whenever she heard a reasonably strange noise. It only took a few nights for Grace to come to depend on her alertness and therefore sleep quite a bit sounder. But the setter missed Daniel terribly. That fact became increasingly obvious every day he visited. When he left, Buster whimpered and had to be held back from chasing after his van, then went around with a woebegone look and a drooping head for an hour or two. Still, it wasn't strictly out of sympathy for the dog that Grace finally agreed to let Daniel move into the house, giving him the last bedroom in the east wing, the one farthest away from her own; it was her belief in her own sophistication that enabled her to agree with his proposition. She decided it didn't matter that they had once been lovers. They were business partners now, and it made sense for him to live close to the shop they would soon be building, since he planned to do some of the work on it himself.

Saturday afternoon, one day after Grace and Daniel had signed the agreement their lawyers had drawn up and he had moved into the farmhouse, she heard the friendly beeping of a car horn in the driveway. Smiling, she switched off the small computer with which she kept track of her clients' accounts, scooted her swivel chair back, and got up to hurry out of the cozy downstairs anteroom she had converted into an office. Out on the white-columned front veranda a moment later, she waved to the occupant of the white sedan that slowed to a stop by the boxwood hedge that bordered the yard. She ran lightly down the stone steps to greet the tall, spindly, gray-haired man who spryly got out of the car.

"I'm so glad you could make it," she fondly welcomed him, giving his hands a brief squeeze when he took hold of hers. She tilted her head in the direction of the barn where Daniel was stepping off the dimensions of the garden shop, a roll of blueprints tucked under one arm. "Come on, I want you to meet my partner."

The elderly man easily keep pace with her as she walked across the barnyard to the open space beyond. Looking up, Daniel saw them approaching and came forward to meet them.

Grace made the introductions. "Jim, Daniel Logan. Dan, this is Jim O'Donnell. He used to be one of my clients, and his daughter still is since he retired and she took over running their bakery in Alpine Springs." As the two men greeted each other with a handshake, she went on. "Jim's a volunteer in a program that brings retired businessmen together with people just starting out, like us, so I asked him to come over and talk about our plans for the shop. He can give us a lot of valuable tips."

"I'm sure he can," Dan agreed, tapping the roll of blueprints against his palm and nodding toward the house. "Why don't we go inside and you can have a look at these plans. Gracie and I would appreciate any suggestions you can give us."

Later, after the three of them thoroughly examined the blueprints at the wood worktable in the kitchen, Jim said that he liked everything, but he did offer a good idea. "You probably should increase the size of your side storage room," he advised, outlining that area on the paper with one fingertip. "Lack of storage space can be a big headache. And if you plan for plenty in the beginning, you won't have to go to the expense of adding on to the building as the business grows."

Grace smiled at the older man and gave him a wink. "Now, that's what I like to hear. Honest to goodness optimism."

"Every reason to be optimistic, since you're planning to offer the public something it wants and that no one else around here offers," Jim replied. "And although you're going to have to compete with Thad Compton's Garden Centers, there won't be any other competitors. He's monopolized this business for years, so there's certainly plenty of room for you to come in, especially since his shops don't offer much at all to anyone interested in organic gardening. Oh, your business is going to grow all right; I know a sure thing when I see it."

"Keep telling Gracie that," Daniel joked. "She may need to hear it often if we get off to a slow start."

"Speaking of starts, what do you have in mind for your grand opening?" Jim inquired. "Or is it too early to think about that?"

"No." Long legs outstretched, Daniel leaned back in his chair and thoughtfully strummed his fingertips against one muscular thigh. "As a matter of fact, the contractor who gave us the lowest estimate for building the shop said he could probably have it finished in five or six weeks, if there isn't an unusual amount of rainy weather before he can get it roofed in. And he can start as soon as we get the building permit."

"Which we'll be able to do after the commissioners' board meets next Tuesday night," said Grace. "We're not expecting any problems, because there's already a craft and ceramic shop less than a half mile down the road, so it's obvious the board's willing to allow a few small businesses to locate around here."

"It's not too early to start planning the opening. Any suggestions?" Daniel asked Jim.

"Make it festive. Have free coffee and donuts, balloons for the kids, a couple of door prizes. Gimmicky, I know, but the public likes to be wooed, and your main objective is to get the customers in the shop the first time, then get them to come back by giving them good value and excellent service. Most important—don't make any promises you might not be able to keep."

"In other words, don't guarantee that every seedling and shrub we sell will grow and flourish, because that depends mainly upon the person who takes it home to plant it and how he or she takes care of it," Daniel said with a knowing smile. "Yes, I learned that lesson while I worked with my friend in South Dakota. We had a few customers who thought putting a plant in the ground was all they had to do, although most plants need some care to survive. We can only tell the customers what kind of care to give. There's nothing we can do if they decide to ignore the advice."

"Exactly. Once a lady bought poppy-seed strudel from me on a Friday, then came back in the shop the next Tuesday saying, 'We had your strudel for breakfast this morning. It was stale.'" Remembering the episode, Jim laughed and threw up his hands. "Was it my fault she didn't serve it for four days? It was baked fresh the day she bought it." Slapping his thin thighs, he shook his head, then stood up. "Well, enough of this reminiscing. I promised Dottie I'd be home by five, since we're going out this evening. Saturday's our night to go dancing. Wouldn't miss it." He smiled at Grace and Daniel, who also rose to their feet. "You two seem to have everything pretty much under control, but I'll be available if you ever need me. Just give me a call."

"We probably will. Your experience is going to come in handy," Daniel said in all sincerity, shaking Jim's hand once again.

After walking Jim to his car, Grace returned to the side porch, where Daniel stood in the kitchen, leaning casually against the doorjamb as he looked outside. He swung the screen door open for her to enter, and she stepped across the threshold, commenting, "Jim's a nice man, isn't he?"

"Very nice. I like him," murmured Daniel, who caught hold of her hand as she walked by. His forest-green eyes fixed on hers. "You still don't trust me, do you? That's why you asked Jim for his help."

"Not his help, really. Just advice and a little guidance sometimes. Like you said, his forty years of business experience will come in handy. He knows so many things we haven't had a chance to learn yet."

"I know he does. But I wonder if that's your prime reason for involving him," Daniel pressed on perceptively, drawing her nearer. "Maybe you just want to be protected to some extent because you think I might take off again?"

Sighing lightly, she shrugged. "You have to admit that might happen. What if you get as bored with the shop as you did with teaching?"

"That's where you're wrong, Gracie," he said softly. "I never got bored. Maybe a little restless. Mainly, I decided it was time to find out how other people live, and I just happened to discover a life-style I enjoy more than I did my old one. Now, I know what I want."

"We'll just have to wait and see about that, won't we?"

41

"Gracie," he muttered, "what will it take to make you believe I'm here to stay this time?"

"Stick around about ten years, and I might begin to believe it."

"You can be a hard woman sometimes, honey."

"Not really. Just not gullible," she responded flatly, stopping his free lean hand as it stole around her waist, and stepping away, out of his reach. "Better get back to my computer. And it's your turn to make dinner tonight. Remember? I expect something special, so you don't have any time to waste."

Daniel made no reply, but when Grace turned around and strolled out of the kitchen, she imagined she felt his gaze following her every step of the way.

About three hours later Daniel stepped into the opened doorway of Grace's office, bowed from the waist with a grand flourish, and announced, "Dinner is served, miss."

"Terrific. I'm starved," she answered, shutting off the computer and putting her shoes back on. Smiling, she preceded him along the hall, then stopped outside the wide-opened double doors of the dining room, where a walnut table covered with lacy linen shimmered in the glow of the lights in the antique candelabra centered upon it. She looked at him. "Well, I expected something special but not as special as this."

"This is merely the beginning, miss," he intoned, his somber impersonation of a proper British butler remarkably convincing as he pulled out a chair for her and she walked over to sit down in it. He bowed again, his lean tan face expressionless. "Now, I intend to prove what a culinary genius I am."

He certainly proved he was an excellent cook, at least, as he served a green salad with his own recipe for bleu cheese dressing, followed by sole amandine, rice pilaf, and asparagus tips, along with a delicately delicious sparkling white wine. He soon dropped the pseudo-British accent, and they chatted amicably throughout the meal, sometimes discussing their garden shop, sometimes talking about much more general topics. By the time he poured them both a cup of freshly brewed coffee, Grace was totally relaxed.

"Mmmm, that was good," she murmured. "Can I expect a meal like this every time it's your turn to cook?"

"Not exactly," he said. "I plan to make chili Monday night."

She smiled at him. "Oh, but you make great chili too. I remember."

"Do you?" he asked softly.

"Yes," she answered, and some secret message in his emerald eyes made her sit up straighter in her chair, then finally push it back and stand up. She started to pick up his plate and her own. "Well, since you cooked, I have to wash the dishes."

"Later," he whispered, his strong hands lightly grasping her wrists. He pulled her down upon his lap. "*Gracie.*"

"Dan, no, I . . ." she began, but her attempted protest was silenced, then forgotten as his warm, feathering lips touched her own.

"I have to kiss you, really kiss you," he muttered roughly against her mouth. "In candlelight, how am I supposed to be able to resist?"

And how was she supposed to be able to resist him? In that crazy heart-stopping instant she discovered that she couldn't resist as the heat of his flesh permeated into her skin and her softly curved body was molded against the long and harder length of his. Her senses reeled. It was too much wine, she tried to tell herself, but deep in her soul she knew it was simply him, his clean lime scent, the very feel of him that made her fingers spread apart to move over his broad chest and made her mouth open sweetly beneath the possessive pressure of his.

For several long dangerous moments she was overwhelmed by memories of the intimate hours they had once spent together, of the exquisite pleasures they had shared,

43

and of the closeness to him she had felt after their love-making. Caught up in the past, as if she were reliving it, she returned Daniel's intensifying kisses, her slender fingers tangling in his thick brown hair as his hands shaped her waist, then her back. It wasn't until he cupped her breasts in his palms and a jolt like a live current of electricity shot through her that she came to her senses and struggled in his embrace, suddenly more afraid of herself than she was of him. She pulled herself upright, pushed his arms away, and scampered off his lap.

"I told you it isn't going to be that kind of partnership," she reminded him, her voice tight as she quickly gathered up their dishes. "I'll clean up in the kitchen." And as she left the dining room, his answering silence seemed to gather like a dark, storm-threatening cloud around her. And she had to wonder if she had been tremendously foolish to allow him to move into her house.

CHAPTER THREE

Tuesday night Grace had a visitor after dinner, a male visitor, Brian Price. She had been out with him a few times, and when he had called that morning asking to see her that evening, she had agreed. She wasn't going to be busy anyhow because she and Dan had decided it was useless for both of them to attend the county commissioners' public meeting where their application for rezoning would be approved. So Dan went alone, leaving the farmhouse before Brian arrived.

Grace entertained Brian in the parlor, where they sat together on the sofa, talking. They hadn't seen each other socially in several weeks, and she was happy to be with him again. As a loan officer in the Alpine Springs bank where she had an account, he knew many of the people she did, and he was very nice. Although she suspected he wished their relationship would become more serious, he never pressed her.

"Well, how are the plans for the garden shop coming along?" he asked after they had chatted for an hour or so. "Making any progress?"

"Oh, yes, things are going along fine," she told him, an enthusiastic sparkle appearing in her eyes. "After we get our application for rezoning approved tonight, we'll be ready to start building."

"And when am I going to meet this partner of yours?"

Grace looked at the grandfather clock. "I expect him anytime. As soon as the commissioners' meeting ends."

"Oh?" Brian frowned slightly. "That's disappointing news. I thought we were going to have the whole evening to ourselves."

"We've had most of it" was her soft reply as he moved a little closer to her on the sofa cushion.

Outside, Daniel parked the van by the barn, got out, closed the door quietly, and murmured a greeting to Buster, who tore off the side porch and pranced happily out to meet him. He looked at the unfamiliar car parked in the drive, then remembered Grace had been expecting a friend to drop by. Daniel raked his fingers through his hair, wondering if he could avoid giving her the bad news until after her visitor left. Lost in thought, he walked across the yard and took the side steps up to the veranda two at a time, the crepe soles of his desert boots making no sound on the wooden planking. He moved past the parlor window, happened to glance inside, then stopped dead in his tracks while the blond man on the sofa with Gracie laid a hand upon her shoulder and leaned forward to kiss her.

Daniel uttered an explicit curse beneath his breath, his jaw tightly clenched. Although Gracie made no move to touch the man, she willingly touched her lips to his, yet it was less the kiss itself and more her faint smile when it ended that did something to Daniel, something unpleasant. His quick temper threatened a violent eruption. It took a mighty strength of will to cool it to a mere simmer, then to show no outward evidence of his feelings when he went to the front door and knocked.

Excusing herself, Grace went out into the hall to answer, and when she saw Daniel standing on the other side of the screen, she was surprised. "I didn't know you were back. Didn't hear the van come in," she said, noting the slight lifting of his brows. "I've told you to just walk in. You didn't have to knock."

46

Swinging the door open, he stepped into the foyer. "I thought I'd better this time."

"It wasn't necessary," she reiterated, eyeing him speculatively, wondering if there had actually been a hint of censure in his tone or if she had simply imagined she had heard something like that. The bland expression on his suntanned face was absolutely unreadable, and his eyes inscrutably dark. She motioned toward the parlor. "Come in and meet a friend of mine."

"I don't want to disturb you."

"You're not," she insisted, and after he silently nodded, she led him across the hall, where she introduced him to Brian and they greeted each other politely.

"Well, Dr. Logan," Brian began after everyone was seated, "I understand you were a philosophy professor?"

"Please call me Dan. And, yes, I was."

"But now you're going to try your hand at commerce?"

Resting his chin on steepled fingers, Daniel only nodded.

"I'm the loan officer at First American Bank in Alpine Springs, and if there's ever anything we might be able to do to help you, please give us a call," Brian suggested, then smiled. "Hope that didn't sound too much like a radio commercial."

"Not at all, and we appreciate the offer," Daniel replied sincerely. "Gracie and I are going to have to set up an account for the shop very soon and we'll probably be in to see you."

"It may even be this week sometime," Grace added before asking Daniel, "Now that we have the place re-zoned, when will the contractor be able to start building?"

"As far as that's concerned, I'm sorry to say we ran into a little roadblock tonight," he told her calmly. "The board postponed making a decision about our request."

Her forehead wrinkling, she faced Brian. "But your friend who works for the county said she couldn't see any

47

reason why the board wouldn't approve it very quickly, didn't she?"

"Yes. She told me she could foresee no problems whatsoever."

"They postponed their decision," Grace murmured, turning back to Daniel. "You mean they didn't even have our request on their agenda for this evening?"

"Oh, it was brought up for discussion, and it looked as if they were going to approve it in short order . . . until someone spoke up in opposition, saying he feared the commissioners would be endangering the rustic charm of this area if they spot-zoned this property and allowed a business to be built."

"Endangering the rustic charm of the area?" Gracie softly exclaimed. "A garden shop is hardly an eyesore. There's nothing much more basic and natural than plants."

"I pointed that out to the board and also reminded them they had already allowed a craft shop to be located just down the road, and they seemed very receptive to my comments. But they still voted to postpone their decision until their next meeting."

"Who was the man who spoke in opposition?" asked Gracie. "I've talked to all the neighbors, and none of them had any objections to our plan. I just can't believe it was any of them. What was his name?"

"Clark Harrison, and he's very articulate."

Thinking hard, Grace tapped a fingertip against her lips. "Harrison, Harrison?" She tossed up one hand, shaking her head. "No, I've never heard of him. I'm sure he doesn't live around here."

Beside her, Brian coughed quietly to gain their attention. He grimaced. "I've heard of Clark Harrison, and he has every reason to be articulate. He's a high-priced lawyer. I've had some dealings with him at the bank because one of his most important clients is our largest depositor, Thad Compton."

48

"Thad Compton," Grace repeated, looking swiftly at Daniel. Their eyes met in instant mutual understanding, but now that she knew the truth, she was no less confused. She gestured uncertainly. "But that just doesn't make any sense. Why should Compton try to stop us from starting our business?"

"You know the answer to that," Daniel said, resting back in his chair and nonchalantly linking his fingers together across his midriff. "He doesn't want any competition."

"What competition? After all, his garden centers are so well established in this area he doesn't have to worry about us. I think we'll take away some of his customers but not enough to really hurt him. Even though the interest in organic gardening is growing, there are still a lot of people who have never given it a thought and probably never will."

Daniel's gaze held hers. "Even so, there are people in the world who feel a tremendous need to protect what they consider their turf. It looks as if Thad Compton may be one of them. Maybe he believes he's the ruler and guiding force of this little empire he's created and isn't willing to let go of any part of it, no matter how small."

"You've obviously met Compton," Brian spoke up, then seemed rather taken aback when Daniel shook his head no. "Well, you've sized him up. I have to admit he isn't the most pleasant person to deal with on occasion. He's a big fish in a little pond and seems to enjoy wielding power. And he does have powerful connections."

"What are you saying?" Grace inquired worriedly. "That he might have enough power to influence the board's decision?"

Brian uncomfortably shifted on the cushion. "I wouldn't want to go so far as to say that."

"But you think it's possible?"

"Gracie, it's pointless for Brian or either of us to try to

predict the board's decision," Daniel intervened. "We'll just have to wait and see what they decide."

"But—"

"I think I'll go on up to bed now," Dan announced, rising up from his relaxed position to stand with the effortless lissome strength of a big cat. Smiling apologetically, he entended his right hand to Brian. "I didn't mean to intrude anyway, and I'll leave you two alone now."

"That's all right," the shorter man hastily said, jerking his head around to stare at Grace with a startled expression as he jumped to his feet too. "I need to be going anyhow."

Daniel spread open his hands. "If you insist . . ."

"I have an early day tomorrow, so I'd better be on my way."

"I'll walk you to the door," Grace murmured, casting a withering glance at Daniel for his uncharacteristic lack of tact as Brian said good night and started out of the parlor. She went with him, switching on the veranda light, then stepping outside with him. When he stopped to look at her, she smiled. "I'm glad you came. It was nice seeing you again."

"You should have told me you were living with Dan," Brian said stiffly. "I had no idea—"

"And you've obviously got the wrong idea now," she interrupted, her tone no-nonsense. "I'm not living with Dan. I mean, he lives here but he rents a room because that was the most convenient arrangement businesswise."

Brian grasped her right hand between both of his. "And that's the truth?"

"I'm not in the habit of lying."

"I know you're not," he assured her, apparently satisfied by her honest answer. But he hesitated for a moment before a long list of his doubts tumbled out. "What about this Compton situation? He does have a lot of influence around here. And Dan? I mean, he's very nice, but will he ever be capable of running a business? He was a philosophy professor, after all, and sometimes these deep thinkers just don't know how to be practical."

"Oh, come on, don't categorize him. So he was a philosophy professor. That doesn't mean he can't possibly be a practical person too."

"Maybe not," Brian persisted. "But I still think you'd be wise to reconsider this partnership with him. I'd hate to see you involved in a deal that could be doomed to failure from the start if he doesn't know what he's doing."

Her spine stiffened. She slipped her hand from between his. "But Dan does know *exactly* what he's doing. If I didn't believe that, do you think I would ever have agreed to be his partner?"

"You certainly leap to his defense fast enough."

"Because I happen to know him better than you do."

"How much better?" Brian questioned sharply, but when she simply uttered a strained good night and started to turn away, he caught her by the elbow. "I didn't mean that the way it sounded."

"I hope not."

"I just don't want you to take a bad risk. And with Thad Compton opposing you, you could have real problems on your hands."

"Dan and I will handle Mr. Compton."

"I hope you can," Brian said, releasing her with a shrug. "And if I've said anything to make you angry, I'm sorry. Do you forgive me?"

She nodded. "I want us to stay friends."

"And friends are all you've ever wanted us to be, isn't it?"

She nodded again. "Yes, I think it is."

"Friends, then," Brian said softly, his smile resigned as he took the first step down off the veranda. "I'll be in touch."

"Good," she called after him, her tone unmistakably genuine because she truly valued his friendship.

When she walked back into the house to the parlor, she

51

found Daniel pouring brandy into two cut-glass tumblers. He looked up at her as she came in. "I hope glasses are okay. I couldn't find any snifters."

"There aren't any. I've never gotten around to buying them," she said, settling herself at one end of the damask sofa. "Gran never needed any, since she only drank elderberry wine . . . except on the very rare occasions when she'd have a shot of bourbon, neat."

Daniel smiled. "A grand old soul."

"Yes," Grace agreed, smiling at her loving remembrances too. When Dan brought over her brandy, she took it while he sat down on the ottoman close to her feet. She took a tiny sip, then lightly sighed. "Well, what are we going to do about the board of commissioners?"

"Wait for their decision. Of course, we have an attorney too, and he'll be representing us at the next meeting."

"And what if they decide to deny our request?"

"If that happens, and I don't really think it will, we'll just have to look for another location for the shop."

"Would it be that simple, Dan?" she asked. "It sounds like Thad Compton could make things very difficult for us. Brian seems to think we might be getting in over our heads tangling with him."

"I got that impression," Dan said tersely, the remnant of his earlier smile vanishing. Suddenly, his eyes glinted like ice shards, impaling her as he added, "And are you so afraid of taking chances that you're going to panic every time someone like Brian utters a discouraging word?"

"I'm not panicking," she shot back, his abrupt flare of anger fueling the vast store of resentment that had been gathering up in her for two years. She was damned tired of him treating her as if she were a spineless coward, which she certainly wasn't. Thoroughly fed up, she put her glass down with a firm thud on the table beside her and stood to glare down at him. "I just happen to be a little concerned about this whole situation, and if you can't understand why, you're some kind of jackass! And since you can't seem to do anything except make insulting comments, I'm going to bed. I've had enough."

"Just a damn minute," he yelled, jumping up to catch hold of one of her slender wrists. With something less than gentleness, he pulled her back around to face him, his features hardening as he looked at her. "Before you go anywhere, tell me all about your Brian. You said you weren't involved with anybody, but now I wonder. Exactly what is he to you?"

"A friend," she retorted, trying to free herself from his grip but without any success at all. She took a deep, sharp breath that drew in her cheeks. "And I have to tell you, Dan—you're acting very foolish."

"You think so? Then explain why you and Brian seemed a lot more than just friends when I saw you kissing less than a half hour ago."

Flags of furious crimson color unfurled on her face, and she snatched her wrist out of his lean long fingers. "I had no idea you were a peeping tom!"

"I just happened to look in the window when I walked across the veranda."

"I don't care what you did. Just remember this: we're business partners, that's all. You have no right to try to interfere in my personal life," she stated, the gleam in her eyes as fiery as the glint in the depths of his. Spinning around, she marched out of the room, head held high. "I'm going upstairs. Before you come up, lock all the doors, please."

And, watching her go, he rammed his hands into his trousers pockets, where they curled into tight, heavy fists.

Ten minutes later Daniel followed Grace upstairs. He walked past her room, started toward his own, then stopped to retrace his steps and knock lightly on her door.

"Gracie," he called. "I'd like to talk to you again, reasonably this time."

53

"Just a second," she called back, and after a brief moment added, "All right, it's unlocked."

Daniel went in as she was pulling an apricot cotton duster snugly around her over a matching nightgown. Her shining hair cascaded over her shoulders while she looked down to slip her feet into her slippers. Then she lifted her head and faced him with neither a smile nor a frown. Motioning him into the easy chair, she sat down on the edge of her four-poster bed with its country-quilt coverlet. "What is it you want to talk about now?"

"What I said about you panicking—forget it. I was overreacting, I guess."

"And I overreacted a little myself," she conceded. "After what happened at the board meeting tonight, we're both just uptight."

Leaning forward, elbows resting on his knees, he searchingly surveyed her delicately featured face. "You're not going to let people like Eric and Allison and Brian Price discourage you though, are you? I'd like to know you're on my side in this."

She stared at him with much confusion. "But you know I am. What other side could I be on, since we're in this together?"

"There may be some rough times. Starting a new business isn't easy," he warned. "You're going to have to trust me and believe in yourself and in the shop, especially at first."

"You sound like you think I might want out of our deal."

"Do you?"

"No!" She shook her head emphatically. "I decided to make this investment because it's a good one, and I don't intend to quit trying to make our shop as profitable as possible. Heavens, Dan, you've called me stubborn often enough, so how can you imagine I won't be stubborn about this too? I will be. Or maybe tenacious is a better word. Whatever, I plan to see it through."

He gave her a slow, lazy smile. "That's what I wanted to hear."

"Good." Poised on the edge of the bed, she started to get up. "Since that's settled, it is pretty late and—"

"There is one more thing we need to discuss," he remarked. "The name of our shop. I've been giving that some thought. What about Dan and Gracie's Garden Shop?"

She cut her eyes over at him, fighting a grin but losing. "Why should your name be first? What's wrong with Gracie and Dan's?"

He shrugged. "If you're going to quibble about it, maybe we should try something totally neutral. How about Nature's Garden Shop?"

After repeating the words silently, she nodded. "I like that. It's perfect, really."

"That's it then. All right?"

"Yes," she agreed. But when Daniel sat back as if he had no intention of leaving her room soon, she felt it necessary to make the first move. Standing, she pretended to yawn behind her hand. "Well, like I said, it is late, and I think it's time for us to go to bed."

"What a provocative thing to say," he murmured, his voice a deep-throated rumble as he reached out and swiftly drew her between his long legs. "I hope that was meant as an invitation."

Was he teasing or serious? Deciding instantly to treat his words as a joke, she laughed softly. "You know the answer to that."

His narrowing gaze ranged slowly over her from head to toe. Her body was vaguely outlined in the glow of the lamp behind her which filtered through her thin gown and robe. He pulled her closer. "It was an invitation, then."

"It wasn't and you know it."

"Gracie," he whispered. "You're a lovely woman."

His masterful hands shaping her waist and his lean caressing fingers warming her skin through two sheer layers of fine fabric caused her heart to beat too ridiculously fast, and her pulses begin to pound. She stiffened. "Dan, I told you not to do this again or—"

"No, you told me not to kiss you. I'm not kissing you now. And you didn't say I couldn't tell you just how beautiful you are, which is all I'm doing at the moment."

"No, that's not all you're doing. You're . . ." she began.

Placing a finger against her lips, he shushed her and murmured, " 'Come live with me and be my love,/And we will all the pleasures prove.' "

"Sorry," she muttered, shaking her head. "Reciting poetry to me isn't going to work anymore, Dan."

"Then, how about this?" Rising swiftly to his feet, he swept her up in his arms, deposited her on the bed, and leaned over her, his green eyes containing a devilish twinkle. "Tickling was usually more effective anyway. Always loosened you up enough for you to discard all your inhibitions."

Despite the keen thrill of excitement that ran through her, she stilled his hands as they descended in an arc toward her ribs. "No, that's not going to work either," she said, her tone perfectly flat as she forced a hopefully indulgent smile to her mouth. "And I want you to go so I can get some sleep."

"That's what you really want?" he asked, his gaze darkly unfathomable. "You're sure?"

"I'm sure," she responded, although deep in her heart she wasn't quite that certain. With a trace of a smile flitting over his lips, he stood and turned away, and she sat up on the bed, wrapping her arms round her middle as she watched him walk across her room, open her door, and shut it behind him on his way out.

A minute later in his own room at the opposite wing of the farmhouse, Daniel sat down on the window seat to untie the laces of his suede desert boots. He took the right one off, and for a split second he felt a terrific urge to hurl it at the opposite wall but didn't. Instead, he allowed it to drop to the floor with a dull thud and turned to stare out at the inky star-studded sky. He combed his fingers through his thick brown hair, giving his faint reflection in the glass a sardonic smile. He was a former philosophy professor, supposedly a laid-back fellow who could take anything in stride with a calm, objective attitude. And he could do that to some extent but only up to a point, and tonight that point had been reached. He had felt far from calm and objective when he had seen Gracie and Brian Price kissing. The memory of that scene still irked him considerably. As a matter of fact, the very thought of her with another man made him madder than hell.

CHAPTER FOUR

"It's a rotten shame, that's what it is. But I can't say I'm surprised by the news," Jim O'Donnell told Grace and Dan the following Tuesday. He drew his fingers down across his jaw. "Same thing happened to me back in '41, not here in Alpine Springs though. It was the first bakery I owned, in southern Ohio. The minute we opened for business, we were harassed and intimidated by the family of the owner of another bakery in the same part of town. Got to the point where I had to sleep in the shop every night for two or three months with all the lights blazing so we wouldn't have to come in and find all the windows broken in the morning."

"Surely it won't be that bad for us," Grace said hopefully. "It's one thing to protest a rezoning and another to start destroying property. I don't think Thad Compton is going to go that far, do you?"

"How did you handle the harassment, Jim?" Dan asked, discreetly avoiding an answer to her question. "Or were you able to?"

"It wasn't easy, but we stuck it out," said the older man, a gleam of pride in his eyes. "I wasn't about to let an idiot like that run me out of business, so we put up with all the aggravation and the vandalism and even made it through the time he slashed his prices to the bone to try to get all my customers away from me. He could afford to do that.

58

I really couldn't but did anyhow—we had several lean weeks when I lowered every one of my prices to match his. I was selling baked goods for a lot less money than it cost to make them."

Grace tugged at a strand of her hair. "How did it turn out in the end?"

"He gave up. Saw he had competition whether he liked it or not and decided to live and let live, I guess. He just stopped bothering us after a while, and I expect we'd still be there in that same location if Dottie hadn't wanted to move to Alpine Springs because most of her family lives around here."

"Then you won ultimately," Dan said. "That's encouraging."

"I meant it to be, but I'm warning you that you might have a price war on your hands the day you open the shop."

"We don't have to worry about that yet. First things first," Grace reminded both men. "First, we have to convince the board to let us locate the shop here."

Jim clucked his tongue against the back of his teeth. "And Compton has Clark Harrison representing him. I've heard he's just this side of being shady—he'll do about anything for a dollar. I hope you two have found yourselves a good lawyer."

"We think so. He was recommended, and we see him later this afternoon," said Dan. "Maybe you've heard of him too. Walter Morton?"

Jim's lined face brightened. "Walt? Wonderful. He's a fine man, honest as the day is long. You couldn't have picked anybody better in the county. And he knows exactly how to handle Harrison; he usually beats him whenever they come up against each other in court."

Grace breathed a relieved sigh. "That is good news."

"I feel better about the whole thing now," Jim admitted, lifting himself out of a comfortable old wood-slatted rocker on the side porch. Saying he had to go, he shook Dan-

59

iel's hand and lightly tapped Grace's cheek. "Just give me a call if you need me for any reason."

Standing together on the porch steps, they watched him drive away, then waved good-bye to him as he turned out onto the blacktopped road. When the swirls of dust he left on the drive in his wake settled, they looked at each other.

With a half smile, Dan touched her cheek, featherstroking the hair-roughened back of his hand over it as he quietly assured her, "It's going to be okay."

"I know," she answered, truly believing.

He was right. A week later, after the attorneys, Clark Harrison and Walter Morton, presented both sides of the issue to the county commissioners, the board decided to approve the rezoning request. It was a close vote, however, four to three, which caused Grace several nervous moments as she sat beside Daniel near the back of the public meeting hall. In comparison, he was perfectly relaxed and gave her a teasingly "I-told-you-so" grin when the fourth commissioner said the decisive yes to their request.

"Thad Compton apparently doesn't control the whole county, thank goodness," she commented later after she and Dan and Walter Morton had driven over to Knoxville for an impromptu victory celebration. In the restaurant, she twirled the delicate stem of her wineglass between her fingers. "I wonder if he had anything to do with three of the commissioners voting against us."

"I certainly wouldn't rule that out as a very strong possibility," Walter said, pleating his small cocktail napkin. "Luckily, four of the board members realized your request was too reasonable for them to logically deny. But, knowing old Thad and his people, I suspect all the commissioners were wined and dined or buttered up a little somehow during the past two weeks."

"At least four of them weren't influenced by it," said Grace, relieved. "And now we'll be able to start building right away."

"You can build, yes." Removing his glasses, Walt

60

rubbed the bridge of his nose. "But let's not make the mistake of assuming this is the last we'll hear from Thad. As I said, I know him, and he's not a man who gives up easily."

Grace looked over at Daniel. His eyes met hers over the rim of the beer mug raised to his lips; he took a long, slow sip, then lowered the heavy glass stein. A faint but confident smile tugged up the corners of his mouth. "If he tries to set up any more stumbling blocks for us, he'll soon find out we don't give up easily either," he stated simply. "Do we, Gracie?"

Recognizing the personal challenge conveyed by his direct gaze, she quickly accepted it. "No, we don't." She smiled at Walt. "Just ask Dan. He'll tell you in no uncertain terms how stubborn I can be. Probably more stubborn than Thad Compton's ever thought about being. He isn't going to stop us from having our shop."

"That may not keep him from trying to though," Walt cautioned, but immediately grinned conspiratorially at both of them. "But we'll handle anything he wants to throw at us."

As it turned out, Grace and Dan faced another unexpected hurdle the very next day when the contractor who had verbally agreed to build the shop was suddenly no longer able to fit that project into his schedule. Grace and Dan suspected it was another one of Thad Compton's little ploys, but they had no proof, so Dan went to Knoxville and found a reliable contracting firm quite happy to get the business. By Friday morning a crew was out at the farmhouse clearing the area beside the barn. About four in the afternoon Grace took a break from her work in her office and picked up Little Bit, who had been either winding around her ankles or sleeping at her feet all day. Even before she walked out the kitchen door, the kitten squirmed out of her arms and shot out as quick as lightning underneath the side porch, her big round eyes and slightly arched back saying clearly that she didn't appreci-

61

ate the loud rumble and roar of the bulldozer being used to level the ground. Buster, on the other hand, didn't seem much bothered by the racket. She stayed faithfully at Dan's side while he checked the dimensions of the land already cleared. Tucking her red blouse more securely beneath the waistband of her ivory skirt, Grace walked across the barnyard to join them. Then Dan looked up, saw her coming, and started over to meet her. Clad in jeans and a light blue chambray shirt, his tanned skin bronzed in the bright glow of the sun, he smiled a welcome as they met.

"How's it . . . How's it going?" she had to begin again, forced to raise her voice in order to be heard over the noise. "Any problems?"

He shook his head. "Should be finished with this in about an hour. And I've been promised the trencher will be here early Monday so they can dig the footings and maybe get them poured by the afternoon. Tuesday morning by the latest."

Nodding approval, she gave him the thumbs-up signal.

He cupped her left elbow in his large gentle hand and turned her toward the two ancient oaks still standing in the plot of raw, smoothly shaved ground. "I told him not to knock those down," he yelled. "They're too pretty to go; we can arrange the parking area around them."

"They'll make the shop look less stark," she agreed enthusiastically. "More rustic, in keeping with the surroundings."

"They do take up space though," he reminded her, surveying the building site with a critical eye before adding, "I'm going to tell Clyde to level off about thirty more feet for parking."

The lilting sound of Grace's answering laughter was lost in the bulldozer's roar, but her sparkling features adequately conveyed her upbeat mood. "Always the optimist, aren't you? You really think we're going to be overrun with customers?"

"Sure." The finely chiseled contours and planes of his face gentled as he smiled back at her. "Don't you?"

"Could very well be. I hope so," she shouted, placing her palms for an instant over her ears. "Enough of this. My throat's beginning to hurt from hollering. And, anyway, I need to get back to my debits and credits."

"Mind taking Buster with you?" Dan requested, shaking his head, albeit fondly, at the dog standing as close to his right leg as possible. "She's been sticking to me like glue all day, and I'm a little tired of tripping over her."

"Here, girl," Grace called. As the setter trotted slowly along beside her, reluctantly leaving Dan behind, she reached down to stroke Buster's sleek head. "You don't care much for that bulldozer, do you? Well, at least you're not crouching under the porch like the cat. I bet you'd both feel better if I gave you some of the chicken left over from lunch. Come on, then, I'll even let you both into the kitchen for a few minutes."

Before Grace reached the house, however, she stopped as a long, shiny baby-blue car, one of the most expensive models, swept up the drive and slowed to a stop near the front veranda in the shade of a magnolia tree. She waited expectantly as a man in his early forties, wearing a sport coat the same color of baby blue, stepped out of the flashy sedan to stroll in his Gucci loafers over to where she stood. Buster barked twice, and she hushed her as the unknown visitor glanced around then settled his gaze on Grace. He smiled broadly. "Miss Mitchell?"

"Yes."

"Allow me to introduce myself," he said, his voice rather booming. "Pete Royce, manager of Compton's Garden Center out on Highway 411. Just passing by and thought I'd stop and say hello."

Although Grace was naturally suspicious, she decided it couldn't hurt to start out friendly. Perhaps Compton and his cohorts had had a change of heart. She smiled pleasantly. "It was nice of you to come, Mr. Royce."

"Pete. Call me Pete, please, little lady."

"If you'll call me Grace," she murmured. No one had called her "little lady" since she'd been about ten years old, and she thought it was foolish of him to address a grown woman in that manner, but it wasn't worth the effort to tell him so. She continued to look expectantly at him, waiting for him to say exactly why he had come.

He didn't immediately. He beat around the bush for a while. "This is a fine old house. The wife and I have always admired it. Ever thought about selling?"

"Never."

"Looks like a young girl like you would rather live in an apartment in Knoxville or even Alpine Springs, where there's more action. It must be boring for you out here in the country."

"Not boring at all. It's quiet, but I happen to like quiet. I'm very happy here."

"This place used to be a big dairy farm, didn't it?" he asked unnecessarily, and as she nodded, he went on, "And now, I hear you're thinking about opening some other kind of business." He glanced back at the bulldozer leveling the site. "Are you really going to start building?"

"Yes, indeed, as soon as possible."

Pete Royce shook his head. "I'm wondering if you've really thought this thing out, honey. What I mean is, aren't you afraid this so-called great interest in organic growing could be just another one of those crazy fads, here today, gone tomorrow?"

"I'm not afraid at all," she declared, shifting her weight to one foot. "More and more people are beginning to shy away from the use of so many chemicals."

His answering smile nearly turned into a disparaging smirk. "Some people are making mountains out of molehills in my opinion. Chemicals have been around for a long time now. What harm have they done?"

"That's the very question that's begun worrying people," Grace said succinctly. "But I'm sure you didn't come here for a debate about the environment or public health, did you?"

Royce laughed a bit too heartily to be convincing. "You're right, I didn't. I just stopped by to give you a little advice. You see, I've got twenty years experience managing a garden center, so I know the ropes. And you can't imagine how many things can crop up and keep a business from succeeding."

"But you're going to tell me some of them right now, aren't you?"

"It's the least I can do to be helpful. I'll just give you a few examples of what I mean. For instance, you could have problems with shipments of your supplies. Or you could find it's more difficult to buy advertising space than you imagine. Or, well, you could run into all sorts of problems, if you know what I mean."

Were those veiled threats? Grace had a hunch they probably were. There was something too smooth and slick in Royce's manner, and there was a false note in his voice. He nearly made her skin crawl, but she revealed no outward evidence of her growing distaste for him and continued to stare evenly at him.

"Of course, your biggest problem will be the stiff competition," he added, producing a truly disgusting ingratiating grin. "Compton's Garden Centers have been the only garden shops in the county for years, and you're going to find it impossible to get much of a foothold in the business."

"Is that a threat or just your personal opinion?" Dan suddenly broke in from behind, stepping in between Grace and Pete Royce.

Still wearing that idiot grin, Pete Royce held up his hands before slipping them into his back trouser pockets and rocking back on his heels. "Why in the world would I even think of making threats? I have no reason to do that. No, you got me all wrong. I was merely sharing some of my experiences with the little lady. Isn't that right, Grace?"

"So you said," she drawled. "Actually, Dan, I get the distinct impression Mr. Royce is one of those people who constantly babbles about the importance of free enterprise but wants that freedom to be limited to himself and a few others."

For an instant Royce's expression froze as if he had lost some of his overconfidence, but he soon recovered to issue forth another smarmy smile. "This sure is a misunderstanding. If I gave you that impression, I didn't mean to. No, ma'am. I just wanted to point out some of the realities of the business world, in case you hadn't really thought of some of the problems that can come along."

His face stony, Dan took one step nearer the other man, which compelled Royce to take one backward. "We're aware of the potential problems," he said, his voice hardening. "We certainly don't expect starting a new business to be a bed of roses. But we have every intention of succeeding."

"You are Dr. Logan, aren't you, Grace's partner?" Royce inquired. "I'm just assuming you are."

"I'm Dan Logan."

"And I'm pleased to meet you. Both of you. You seem like fine people. That's why I'd hate to see you getting into something over your heads."

"Your concern is touching," said Dan sardonically as he then virtually dismissed the man with a slight gesture of his hand. "But I'm afraid you're going to have to excuse us. We're busy right now."

"Of course, of course, I understand." Pete Royce practically oozed fraudulent charm as he ran his hand over the styled pompadour of his black hair. He turned to walk toward the long sedan. "But I certainly hope to see you folks again soon."

"You won't if we see you coming first," Grace muttered so quietly that only Dan heard. And as Thad Compton's lackey turned his car around and drove along the drive toward the highway, daring to wave back at them on his way out, her lips twisted slightly with disdain. "What a snake in the grass."

"Certainly not one of your genuinely lovable, easygoing good ole boys," Dan readily agreed. "Although he was trying hard to seem like one."

"Whatever happened to Southern gentlemen?"

"There are still some of us left," Dan told her, his smile lightly teasing, his tone gentle. He raised a hand to touch the curve of hair sweeping across her right temple. "Don't put us all in the same category with . . . Royce? Isn't that what you called him?"

"Yes, Pete Royce, manager of Compton's Garden Center on Highway 411," she explained. "And he seems to be proof positive that Thad Compton plans to keep on trying to discourage any competition."

"It does look that way," Dan agreed. "But we halfway expected him to, anyway."

Silently, she nodded. Almost of its own volition, her left hand found his right, and she was reassured when his lean fingers tenderly squeezed hers.

Two nights later Grace's peaceful sleep was shattered by the loud crash of shattering glass, followed immediately by another and punctuated by Buster's frenzied barking. Shooting up straight in bed, she pressed her hand between her breasts, her heart thundering. For a moment she was too befuddled to move, but when she heard Daniel's door open then apparently bang against the chest of drawers in his room, she scurried off her bed, leaving robe and slippers behind as she sped out into the hall. She met Daniel at the landing just as Buster, still barking, hit the bottom of the stairs and sprang at the front door in the downstairs hall, pawing at it to be let out. Little Bit, rudely awakened too, as she had slept in the upper hall outside Grace's room, streaked to safety beneath the walnut table

67

opposite the top of the steps. A deep frown creased Dan's brow, and he lightly grasped Grace's bare upper arms.

"You all right?" he immediately asked.

"Y-yes. But what the devil was that?"

"I don't know . . . yet."

"I think I heard glass breaking. Maybe a branch fell down and hit a window."

"Two branches, two windows? There isn't even any wind tonight," Dan reminded her. "I'll go down and have a look."

"I'll go with you," she said instantly.

"No, stay here."

"I'm going," she insisted with an obstinate set to her chin as she meet his emerald eyes, wide awake and determined. "You can't stop me."

"Dammit, do you have to be so stubborn?" Their gazes locked for a millisecond, long enough for him to understand that she wasn't going to give in. "All right then, but stay behind me."

She had no choice. Barefoot, navy pajama bottoms slung low on his lean hips, he agilely went down the steps two at a time as she followed. At the foot of the stairs, she waited while he went to open the door for Buster, who catapulted herself out into the darkness of the night, barking faster and louder as she went. Dan switched on the veranda light, peered out, and saw nothing. He went back to where Gracie waited, nearly shivering in her short white nightgown, her arms wrapped around her trim midriff. He looked around. "Where do you think the noise came from?"

She took a deep breath. "The parlor . . . I think."

"So do I." He walked over to the double sliding doors, pushed them open, and reached in to put on the light. Stepping into the empty room, he saw the shards of glass littering the floor in front of the west and south windows. On the polished hardwood floor lay two rough-edged rocks, one about two feet more off center than the other.

Dan stopped, looked down at it. "Someone doesn't have much of a pitching arm."

"Damn them," Grace softly swore, stepping past him to bend over the antique spinning wheel in front of the west window. One of the hurled rocks had glanced off the wood, leaving in its wake a deep, splintered scar. "Look what they did. I hope I can have it repaired."

"I think you probably can," said Dan, assessing the damage. "I'm just glad no one was in here during this . . . little attack."

"Yes, thank goodness," she murmured, forgetting the spinning wheel completely. "By . . . attack, do you mean you think maybe Thad Compton had something to do with this?"

"I can't think of a more logical explanation."

Neither could she, and they didn't speak for the next ten minutes while she found cardboard for him to temporarily replace the broken windowpanes. Outside, Buster had quit barking, but when she loped nosily across the veranda again to scratch at the screen, low woofs still rose up gruffly in her throat when Daniel let her inside. He patted her head.

"Nothing, eh, girl. Well, I didn't expect them to stay out there and wait for you," he said. He looked over at Grace. "Would you get her some food? I think it would be a good idea for her to stay out the rest of the night, in case we have visitors again. Her growling will chase anybody off."

"Maybe we should call the sheriff."

"I think we can wait until morning. Not much the authorities can do anyway."

A few minutes later, after Grace returned from the kitchen with Buster's bowl filled to the rim, she watched Daniel put the dog outside, then close and lock the front door. When he came over to her, she smiled wanly. "I think we'd better try to get some more sleep now."

Agreeing, he followed her up the stairs, but as they

69

reached the landing and said good night, both starting to go their separate ways, he quickly turned back to catch her by the hand. "Gracie," he murmured, his darkening gaze roaming over her face. "Sure you're all right?"

"I'm fine," she declared.

But she lied. Forty-five minutes later, after tossing and turning in her bed and coming no closer to falling asleep, she sat up with a sigh of utter frustration, then swung her legs off the side of her bed to wriggle her feet into her slippers. After picking up her lightweight robe, she tiptoed out of her room, along the hall, and down the stairs into the kitchen, where she poured a generous amount of milk into an enamel saucepan, placed it on the stove, and turned on the burner. Minutes later she stirred cocoa into a steaming mug of milk, and when Dan suddenly appeared in the doorway, she wasn't really surprised. He was an extremely perceptive man; he'd obviously sensed her disquieted mood before they had gone back to bed. Smiling faintly, she raised the mug she was holding.

"Care for some hot chocolate?"

Accepting her invitation, he sat across from her at the wooden worktable, but during the half hour that passed, they talked very little. It was enough to share the coziness of the kitchen, especially after he reminded her that Buster was stationed outside, her alert ears attuned to any strange sound.

At last when they decided once more to try to get more sleep, they walked together back upstairs.

"Well, good night again," she said. "With any luck we won't be up until morning."

"You're feeling better then? Relaxed?"

"I wouldn't go so far as to say that," she admitted. "I guess I still feel a little edgy."

"Oh?" His hands came out to span her waist; his slowly growing smile was deliberately provocative. "I have a remedy for that edginess. Invite me to spend the night in your bed with you, and we'll both be able to get rid of all our tensions."

Suddenly, his outrageous teasing relaxed her completely, and she lightly laughed. Her dark gray eyes were sparkling as they looked into his. "You're an impossible man, Daniel Logan. Aren't you ever going to stop being a flirt?"

"Never," he claimed. "Wouldn't you be disappointed if I stopped flirting with you?"

"Don't flatter yourself," she said. But after he leaned down from his considerable height to brush a lingering kiss over her right cheek, she found herself responding by feathering her lips against his. Then he released her, and they went in opposite directions to their respective rooms. And, a minute later, almost at the same moment her head touched her pillow, she fell back asleep, a tiny smile lingering upon her lips.

71

CHAPTER FIVE

"You mean someone actually broke your windows? Pitched rocks through them?" Allison Kingston exclaimed. Invited with her husband for dinner at the farmhouse, she stared disbelievingly at Grace across the kitchen, where they were adding final touches to the forthcoming meal. Finally remembering the head of lettuce she held, Allison put it down in the large wooden salad bowl on the counter. "But that's incredible, especially if what you suspect is right and some of Thad Compton's people did it. That makes it all the more disturbing. Weren't you terrified?"

"Well, I wasn't exactly thrilled. It's not much fun to be awakened that way in the middle of the night," Grace said truthfully, checking the lamb chops. "But after my heart stopped pounding, I was pretty much all right."

"And what about Dan? Did he explode? I know that sometimes he can't control that quick temper of his, and he must have been mad as the devil."

"Not as mad as I was when I saw that a rock had hit the spinning wheel and knocked a chunk out of it," Grace wryly replied. "No, actually, Dan didn't come close to losing his temper. He was angry, of course, but exploding wouldn't have helped matters. The damage was already done. All we could do was leave Buster outside to guard the house the rest of the night and call the sheriff's depart-

72

ment the next morning to report an act of vandalism. A deputy came out, and we told him what had happened, but he found absolutely no clues to show who might have been responsible. There wasn't anything else we could do. That was the end of it."

Allison gave her a worried frown. "Are you sure it was?"

"The end of that particular episode anyway," Grace qualified. "But I wouldn't be too surprised if something else happened."

"Then aren't you afraid? I mean, if this Compton person is out to stop you and Dan, maybe you should carefully reconsider opening this garden shop."

"No way. We've committed ourselves, and we won't back down now. Obviously Compton and his people are worried that we will make a success of the business, which is all the more reason for us to keep going. We couldn't possibly quit now. When you and Eric got here, you saw the shop's cement floor has already been poured and the builders have started framing up the walls. After getting this far, we can't let a few veiled threats or even two broken windows make us throw in the towel."

"But you must not feel very safe."

"I'm not really scared," Grace assured her friend while transferring the chops to a warming platter. "Why should I be, with Buster as a guard dog and Dan here every night?"

"Why did he move in here?" Allison asked, turning one hand in an uncertain gesture. "I'm not trying to be nosy, but are the two of you . . ."

"Lovers again?" Dan spoke from the doorway leading into the kitchen. Leaning against the jamb, he included both women in his lazy smile while shaking his head in answer to the question he had finished for Allison. "Unfortunately, we're not. This is strickly a business partnership. But those are Gracie's terms, not mine."

His tone was endearingly mischievous, and Grace gave him a tolerant smile. "Did you want something, Dan?"

"Only to know if I could give you a hand."

"Thanks, but you'll have your chance when it's time to wash dishes and clean up in here. Right now, Allison and I are doing just fine. Tell Eric dinner will be served in about five minutes."

Still smiling, he nodded and disappeared. Grace turned to Allison, found herself being seriously observed, and shrugged lightly.

"He was joking, wasn't he?" Allison asked at last. "He had to be. I can't imagine you two living in the same house and not being . . . Only two years ago you were in love with each other."

"We thought we were. He walked away from me easily enough, and I let him go, so obviously we weren't really," Grace murmured. "And now that makes everything different."

"Everything?" her friend persisted. "But there still must be that old chemistry between you?"

Grace silently drew in a long, deep breath. That was a question she had no desire to answer, and to avoid it, she glanced at her watch. "We promised them dinner in five minutes. How's that salad coming?" she asked, and was unreasonably relieved when Allison kindly dropped the subject and started filling the wooden bowl with lettuce leaves again.

Later, after the Kingstons ended their visit and Dan finished tidying the kitchen, it was nearly eleven o'clock. Grace was sitting in an antique rocker in the parlor, putting fine stitches in a blue-checked doll's sunsuit when Dan strolled into the room, the sleeves of his cream rugby-style shirt still pushed up above his elbows, exposing the tanned muscularity of his forearms. She looked up at him. "Finished?"

"Finally. The next time we have dinner guests, I'll cook and you can clean up afterward," he said, but with a trace

74

of a grin. "Did you have to use every pot and pan and dish in the house?"

"I wanted to make it something special."

"You succeeded, but to me, Gran's beef stew would have been special too and simpler, with fewer dishes to wash afterward."

As he dropped down on the sofa across from her, she smiled while rethreading her needle. "Is that a hint? Would you like me to make Gran's stew soon?"

"I wouldn't mind."

"Okay, tomorrow night's your turn to make dinner, and Friday's mine again. I'll make it then."

Long legs outstretched and crossed at the ankles, he nodded, his gaze never leaving her face as he abruptly asked, "What did you and Allison talk about in the kitchen after I came back in here with Eric?"

Pretending to concentrate primarily on knotting the new length of thread, she lightly shrugged. "Oh, just this and that."

"Gracie," he softly commanded. "Be more specific."

"You and me," she said, seeing no good reason to lie to him. "Allison can't quite understand how we're managing to keep our relationship so businesslike."

"She's not the only one. I can't understand that either."

Grace swallowed with difficulty as his deep melodious voice became more gruffly-timbred, issuing a vague warning signal that jarred her nerves. Her fingers shook slightly, and she took an untidy stitch in the sunsuit, decided it was time to make a hasty retreat, and faked a yawn. "Oh, excuse me," she murmured, standing. "Suddenly, I'm so sleepy. I'd better get to bed."

"No. You're not really sleepy, and I can't let you go yet," Daniel said, reaching out as she started past him to clasp her hands in his. With almost no effort at all, he pulled her to him, then down upon the sofa, gathering her close in his arms until she was half reclining upon his taut thighs. His eyes imprisoned hers while he touched her

75

hair, her cheeks, the naturally delicate arches of her dark eyebrows. And when she tensely started to struggle in his firm embrace, he leaned down his head to graze a kiss over her left ear and whisper, "I want you, Gracie, as much now as I ever did."

"*Don't,*" she breathed when he caught her thick hair up in one hand, pulled it aside, and softly blew at her heated nape. Appalled by the force of the tremor that rushed deeply within her, she struggled once more, moving her head back and forth in denial. "Dan, *no!*"

"Oh, yes, Gracie, yes," he whispered, his warm mouth descending swiftly to take possession of hers, his sensitive hands gliding up from her waist over her back, his fingers massaging and coaxing her exquisite flesh.

A soft moan swept forth from her, parting her lips beneath his, and as the tip of his tongue pushed slowly inside her mouth to taste the sweet nectar of hers, uncertainty vanished and she became evocatively soft against him. Her ability to think rationally ceased to exist, and as his tongue toyed with hers, hers parried his.

"Gracie," he groaned, wrapping his strong arms around her slender shapely form, trembling himself as their bodies seemed to forge together in a hot melting surge of feeling that seemed electrically charged. His firm lips plundered the tender full shape of hers as he repeated again and again, "Gracie, Gracie."

Her breasts yielded to the contours of his broad chest, and as he kissed her time after time, each kiss deepening, she began to want nothing more in the world than to be closer and closer to him. Her own arms wound upward around his strong neck. She kissed him back with a fever she hadn't experienced in two long years.

Oh, yes, Allison had been right. The old chemistry was still there between them, as dangerous and volatile as it had always been in the past, igniting wildfires that raged through both of them. She surrendered to the need for warmth and closeness that was far stronger than her rapidly fading will to resist. Her supple body yielded to the firm lineation of his. She slipped her fingers through his thick hair. Her lips played over his, softly and sweetly. As he touched her, she touched him, adoring the feel of hard muscle flexing beneath her skimming fingertips.

"Gracie, open your mouth. More. Yes," he huskily said, his minty breath filling her throat when she complied. His impassioned kiss deepened, and as she ardently responded, their tongues met and entangled in an erotic dance that quickened his breathing as much as hers.

"*Dan,*" she whispered, a shiver of delight racing over her when he released her mouth only to bury his face in her scented hair and nibble her earlobe. The even edge of his teeth teased the delectable morsel of flesh before he began lacing kisses along the ivory column of her neck and into the hollow at the base of her throat. She moaned softly again, pleasured by the sensations he was bringing to exquisite life in her. Taking his face between her hands, she urged his mouth back up to hers, revelling in the firm sensuous shape of his lips as they tenderly possessed the softness of hers. It was as if they were starved for each other and had been magically transported to a world all their own. Cradled in his arms, Grace tucked her knees against his side, and when he lowered one hand from her waist, she allowed it to follow the gentle swell of her hips, the graceful sweep of her right leg, then retrace its path upward to slip beneath her skirt's hem. He caressed her silken shapely thigh, making her tremble even as she eased her own fingers beneath his shirt to move them in slow, feathering circles across his midriff and around to the small of his back.

"Honey," he gruffly uttered, "I've missed you."

"No, you haven't, not really."

"I can't begin to tell you how much."

She shook her head, unable to truly believe him. After all, he had willingly left her. "You just think that's the right thing to say right now because you want—"

"You. Yes, more than I've every wanted anyone," he murmured, lowering her down upon the sofa to sit next to her on the cushion. His eyes were smouldering green coals as they held hers. "But I'm not lying, Gracie. I've missed you like hell." His hands encircled her waist, his thumbs easing slowly back and forth against the undersides of her breasts. "If I didn't miss you, why did I dream so often about touching you like this again? Why did I long for your warmth?"

Gazing up at him, she had trouble swallowing, because his words could have been her own. After he had gone away two years ago, she had been plagued by dreams of him night after night, unrelenting, especially at first. And she had experienced a cold emptiness in her life without him to make her feel vitally alive and warm. If he was really telling her the truth . . . if he had missed her even half as much as she had him . . .

"Believe me now?"

"I . . ."

"Believe me," he gently commanded, bending down to brush his lips against hers. Outlining their bow shape with the tip of his tongue until she was trembling once more, he cupped the weight of her breasts in his palms and felt them swell responsively to his touch. "And you missed me too. You can't deny it."

He was right. She couldn't. And his masterful caresses and coaxing kisses were inducing a tingling lethargy that was spreading throughout her entire being. When his fingers pressed lightly into her cushioned flesh, her breasts throbbed, and she was caught up in a tide of intensifying pleasure. Winding her arms upward around his neck, she pulled him closer, her eyes fluttering shut as her mouth met his again.

With a low groan he sought all the honeyed sweetness within, then drew her tongue in over his. The partial weight of his torso pressed her down into the springy sofa

78

cushions, and the feel of her rounded curves beneath him caused passion to gather in a feverish force in his loins. "Sweet, you're so sweet," he murmured, breathing in the delicate scent of her breeze-fresh perfume. They shared kiss after lingering kiss, their lips and tongues seeming to forge together in melting heat. His fingers swooped through her luxuriant mane of hair to cradle the back of her head and hold her fast while possessing her mouth hungrily.

Her heart hammered; her pulses raced with a frantic beat. She felt the shudder than ran over his long body when her hand skittered over his bare back beneath his shirt, fingertips probing the bone structure of his strong spine. Adrift in a glorious reawakening of the senses, she didn't resist, couldn't even think about trying to resist, as Dan slowly unbuttoned her blouse, opened it, then pushed it off her creamy shoulders. Her eyes flickered open. Above her, he watched the rapid rise and fall of her breasts, the fierce glint in his eyes easily readable despite his half-closed lids. He smiled tenderly and slid his fingers beneath the straps of her bra, lowering them before moving down to the front closure, unhooking it, and slowly peeling the lacy cups aside.

Uprising mounds of satiny feminine flesh tipped with rose-tinted peaks seemed to invite his mouth to taste them. "You're so beautiful," he whispered unevenly. "You always were. And I remember how I loved to touch you here." His fingertips toyed over and around one hardening crest. "And here." He caressed its twin. "And you loved for me to touch you like this."

She had. She still did. Loved it too much perhaps. But his pleasantly rough fingers felt so wonderful upon her sensitized skin that she brought her hands up to cover his, pressing his palms harder into her warm, resilient flesh.

"Gracie," he said, a tidal wave of raw need rising in him. Encouraged by her ardor, he let himself flow with it, and his lips descended to ply hers until suddenly, a flash of movement followed by a light thump on the cushion beside her head diverted his attention. Surprised, he looked up as Little Bit voiced a series of plaintive meows, even as she purred with the hum of a boat engine. "Great timing, cat. Come back later."

When Dan started to kiss Grace again, she turned her head aside, her entire body tense. Thank goodness for the kitten. Her arrival had come just in time to give her an opportunity to come to her senses. Desire quickly died as she realized precisely what she was inviting for herself— more pain, more disillusionment, more seemingly endless sleepless nights if she dared resume an intimate relationship with Dan and he decided someday to go wandering off again. She had endured that experience once, and it had taught her a lesson—she couldn't risk having to go through it a second time.

"Gracie, what's wrong?" he questioned softly. "Honey, I—"

"Oh, Dan, this is absolutely insane," she muttered, scurrying out from under him to sit pressed against the far armrest of the sofa, away from him while she rehooked her bra, closed her blouse, and buttoned it, trying valiantly to disguise the shakiness of her fingers. "I know I led you on and I'm sorry for that. I—I don't know what came over me."

He did. As much as he had wanted and needed her, she had wanted and needed him, until that damn cat had intruded. He glared at the kitten. For a moment he was tempted to give it a swift kick, but of course he didn't. He could never have done that, and instead he reached over to lightly stroke Little Bit's eagerly arching back. She was an innocent animal who had no idea how much frustration she had caused him by her untimely appearance. A very faint resigned smile touched his hard mouth as he gave the cat a final pat then turned his gaze toward Gracie.

"I wish you'd explain," he quietly said. "Why is it so insane for us to want each other again?"

"It . . . just is." She shrugged with as much aplomb as she could muster. "And I wonder if it's a smart idea for us to go on living . . . in the same house together."

"Are you telling me to leave?" he asked. "Are you sure you want me to go and leave you alone here, after that rock-tossing incident the other night?"

Confusion roiled up in her, and she glared at him. "You can't blackmail me by reminding me of that. I'm not afraid. I've lived here for months by myself."

"But that was before anyone had reason to try to intimidate you. Now things are different, and you're not a foolhardy woman. You must feel safer with Buster and me around, in case something else happens. Don't you, Gracie?"

She heaved an inward sigh, wishing she could say no but incapable of an outright lie. He was absolutely right. She'd never been a foolhardy person and was practical enough to realize that Dan's presence in the house was immensely reassuring, considering recent events. She looked quickly away from him and stood.

"It's late," she stiffly announced. "I'm going up to bed now."

"Does that mean I'm not being evicted?"

"We'll see. I'll have to think about it" was her deliberately noncommittal answer as she turned to walk briskly out of the parlor. Upstairs, she stripped off her clothes, put on a nightgown, and went to bed. But it took a long time for her to finally fall asleep.

Grace invited Brian Price to dinner two nights later, knowing Dan wouldn't be there because he had a late appointment to keep in Knoxville. But it was scarcely more than ten minutes after she and Brian had carried their coffee from the dining room into the parlor when

Dan arrived home early and strolled in to say hello to them.

"I don't want to interrupt anything. Just thought I'd let you know I'm back," he casually proclaimed, tapping a long white envelope against his left thigh. "I'll leave you alone now. We have a few problems to discuss about our insurance on the shop, Gracie, but they can wait until later."

"Problems?" A frown knitted her brow. "What kind of problems?"

"Oh, nothing we can't wait and talk about tomorrow. I'm sure we can work everything out."

"Everything? What exactly is the problem?"

Daniel spread his hands. "I don't think Brian would be interested in hearing. It'd be better for us to talk about it later, privately."

Next to Grace on the sofa, Brian moved restlessly. "Since the two of you need to discuss business, why don't I just run along?"

"But, Brian, you don't have to—"

"It's okay," he said, quickly getting up. "Sound's like something important, so I'll go and let the two of you discuss it."

He was right; it did sound like Dan had something important to tell her, and she made no further protest while walking Brian to the front door, offering an apology for the abbreviated evening. Accepting it, he gave her a light good-night kiss and left. She hurried back to the parlor, and when she found it empty, she went into the kitchen, where Dan was pouring them both cups of fresh coffee.

"What's wrong?" she asked at once. "What kind of problems are we having?"

Beckoning her to the table, he placed the cup and saucer before her, then settled onto the opposite chair. "I told you we could talk about this in the morning."

"Talk about what? What's the matter?"

"Nothing's wrong, Gracie. I didn't say there was," he replied after taking a cautious sip of the steaming brew. "I simply meant we might have a problem deciding what kind of policy to choose. Of course, we want enough coverage to compensate for our losses if the shop is destroyed. And we want adequate insurance for minor damages, less deductions naturally. But I thought it was important for us to decide whether or not we want flood insurance."

She nearly choked on a swallow of coffee. *"Flood insurance?* Why in the world should we need flood insurance when the nearest creek is almost a mile from here and we're uphill from it?" She glared at him suspiciously. "You did this deliberately, didn't you? You know we don't need flood insurance. You just pretended to have something very important to talk to me about to get rid of Brian!"

Spreading his hands, he maintained a perfectly innocent expression. "But you said you wanted to be completely involved in every aspect of the business, so I assumed you'd want to help decide what would be adequate insurance coverage."

"Sure you did. Dammit, Dan, I didn't see many other people while Gran was sick, and I'm just beginning to have a social life again. I'm not going to let you interfere in it."

"But, Gracie, I'd never dream of interfering."

She had a feeling he was playing games with her, and she didn't appreciate it one bit. Pushing her hair back over her shoulders, she rose from her chair. "Since you don't really have anything serious to discuss, I'm going to bed."

"We are going to have to talk about the kind of insurance we want sometime, though."

"Fine, but surely it can wait until tomorrow?"

He nodded, then caught her hand when she started past him, his face unreadable as he looked up at her. "I have

83

to be honest, Gracie. I wasn't at all sorry to see Brian go."

He was impossible. An outrageously impossible man. Pulling her hand free of his, she turned and marched out of the kitchen toward the stairs, valiantly fighting a near-primitive desire to go back and throttle him.

Still seated at the table in the kitchen, Dan slowly stirred his coffee. He was smiling.

CHAPTER SIX

Five evenings later Dan fulfilled his obligation to provide dinner by taking Grace to a restaurant instead of cooking at home. They returned to the farmhouse after nine, and as they pulled up the long drive, the frame of the shop was dimly illuminated by the beams of the van's headlights. Gazing in that direction by chance, Grace gasped and reached over to touch Dan's arm.

"Oh, no, look!"

When he turned his head and saw that the wall studs along a thirty-foot section of the shop had been broken in half, he slammed the heel of one hand hard against the steering wheel. "Damn, our 'friends' have paid us another visit."

"This is really getting ridiculous," she complained, scowling. As soon as Dan braked to a stop, she opened the passenger door of the van, hopped out, and was walking around to his side when Buster loped across the barnyard to meet them. Grace patted her head when she nuzzled her shiny back against her thigh. "At least they didn't harm the dog, and I guess they could have been tempted. I'm sure she must have barked at whoever did this."

"Unfortunately no one was here to hear her," Dan said, pushing his door shut before bending down for a brief moment to stroke the setter's ears. Straightening, he crossed his arms over his broad chest and stared at the

85

damaged building. "Of course, this wouldn't have happened, tonight anyway, if they hadn't known we weren't here."

"Are you saying you think we're actually being watched?"

"It's a good possibility."

"Oh, I don't like this at all," she murmured, clasping her hands tightly together in front of her to still their sudden slight trembling. Her eyes darted this way and that. The very thought that some unknown person or persons might have started spying on Dan and herself gave her cold shivers. Unconsciously, she moved a bit closer to his side. "If Compton really has someone watching us, he's more worried about us than I thought. But I still don't know why he is."

"He obviously thinks he has a right to protect his little empire," muttered Dan, marked sarcasm hardening his deep voice as he gestured toward the shop. "Why don't you go in and call the sheriff's department while I go take a closer look at what they did."

When he strode away from her, she followed in a hurry and caught up with him. "I'll go with you. Then we can both go inside to call the sheriff."

Dan stopped to look down at her upturned face shimmering in the soft light of a full cream-colored moon. "I don't want you to go with me, Gracie," he said. "I think Buster would still be barking if anyone were still here, but there's a slim chance I might be wrong. And just in case I am, you'll be much safer in the house."

Despite the fact his features were tautly drawn and determined, she shook her head. "No," she insisted, "I'm going with you."

His hands shot out to take hold of her shoulders, which he lightly squeezed. "For God's sake, do you always have to be so stubborn?" he nearly growled, a trace of that quick temper making an appearance. "Just this once, will you do what I ask without arguing. Go to the house and call the sheriff. And take Buster with you."

"But—"

"Gracie, go. Please."

It was that softly intoned "please" that persuaded her. She went, and by the time she finished calling to ask for a patrol car to be sent, Daniel walked into the house. Enormously relieved to see him, she met him in the hall-way. "A deputy will be here in a few minutes." When he nodded and led her into the parlor to the sofa, she sat down, poised tensely on the edge of a cushion while he chose to remain standing. "Well, what exactly did they do this time?" she asked. "How much damage?"

"All the two-by-fours in that one section will have to be replaced. I'll order what I need from the lumber yard tomorrow and get started right away."

"This is crazy." Crossing her legs, Grace spiritedly swung her suspended foot back and forth in sheer frustra-tion. "If Thad Compton is behind all this, I'd love to give him a piece of my mind."

"And if he is, he could obviously use any pieces anyone was willing to donate to him," Dan joked, smiling softly at her. "Because he's certainly not showing much intelli-gence now."

She had to smile back. His jesting comment helped ease some of her tension, and she began to feel a little more relaxed.

A minute or so later, the sheriff's deputy arrived, the same one who had come out the morning after the win-dow-smashing incident. After Dan took him outside to see the damage done to the shop, they returned to the parlor, where the deputy sat on the edge of a chair and jotted down some notes in a leather-bound report book. After a minute he quit writing and looked up to give both Grace and Dan a commiserating smile.

"You folks are having more than your share of trouble lately," he said. "Have any idea why?"

"We have an idea," Dan answered. "It seems someone doesn't want us to build our shop and open it for business."

"Hmmm, and what kind of shop is it going to be? I don't remember you telling me the last time I was here."

"It's going to be a garden shop," Grace told him, an uncharacteristic resentment darkening her features. "And we've been given the distinct impression that Thad Compton and his people aren't very pleased about having any competition."

"Thad Compton?" Deputy Watson repeated, his tone dismayed. Moving restlessly in his chair, he dropped his eyes and quickly scrawled a few words in his report book. "You think Thad Compton could be behind these acts of vandalism? Do . . . uh, do you have any proof?"

"No proof . . . yet," Dan replied. "But you asked if we had any idea who was responsible for the problems we're having. And we have good reason to believe it's Compton or someone who works for him."

"Yeah, but that's not much to go on. Not even enough for you to sign a complaint. Now, if you'd seen whoever broke your windows and wrecked part of your building out there, we'd maybe be able to get somewhere."

"We didn't. We couldn't possibly identify anybody."

"That makes it tough," Watson muttered, shaking his head. "Real tough."

Daniel leaned forward in his own chair, long lean hands clasped together between his knees. "We did have a visit from a manager of one of Compton's garden centers, and some of the things he said were obviously veiled threats. His name's Pete Royce."

"Royce. Pete Royce. The dude who drives the powder-blue Cadillac? A real hotshot," the deputy added beneath his breath as he wrote it down. Once more he looked up and sighed regretfully. "But if Royce didn't make any outright threats, you can't even file a complaint against

88

him. And if you could, that wouldn't necessarily connect him to Thad Compton."

Grace and Dan exchanged glances before she said, "We know that, but we can't help suspecting Royce and Compton, since nobody else has any reason to harass us."

Deputy Watson shrugged uncomfortably. "I guess it might have been some bored teenagers who vandalized your house and shop. It's getting close to the end of the school year, and they always start getting restless along about this time. They might've done it just for kicks."

"They might have, but we seriously doubt restless teenagers are responsible for what's happened here," Dan declared flatly. "But we also realize that we don't have enough evidence to implicate Compton or Royce. We would like to know that someone from the sheriff's office will patrol this area more often than usual, in case we have any more trouble."

The young deputy jumped to his feet, slipping his report book into a back pocket of his uniform trousers, looking immensely relieved that nothing more had been asked of him. He smiled at Grace and then looked at Dan. "I'll tell the sheriff you've requested the extra patrols, and I'm sure he'll authorize them. That's what the department's here for—to protect all the county citizens."

He sounded so earnest that Grace had to smile at him when he departed, but when Daniel returned from showing him to the front door, she raised darkened, troubled eyes to meet his as he came across the room to join her on the sofa. "Well, what do you think?" she asked him. "Does Thad Compton wield so much power in this county that even the sheriff and his men are afraid of him?"

"Maybe. Maybe not. I wouldn't even begin to make a guess," he admitted. "But at least Watson doesn't seem very impressed by Pete Royce."

Grace sighed. "No, but that doesn't mean he isn't afraid of him and the power behind him, Thad Compton."

Capturing and holding her shadowed gaze, Dan

89

reached for her hands, his strong fingers exerting a gentle pressure around the slender length of hers. "Maybe Compton does have some influence in the sheriff's department," he said, his low-timbred voice almost a whisper. "But, even if that's true, we're not going to give up, Gracie. We're going to win in the end."

It was as if his vital strength of will transmitted itself through the pores of her skin to augment her own. Smiling faintly, she nodded. This time she believed with heart, mind, and soul, and no doubts remained to haunt her.

Happily, nothing unpleasant happened during the week that followed. Daniel and Grace did decide, however, that they should build a larger greenhouse than originally planned. The only problem was that they didn't have enough extra money left in their business account to finance the expansion. They needed a loan. Grace called Brian Price and told him they wanted to borrow ten thousand dollars, and when he acted as if that would be no problem at all, she graciously expressed her appreciation and agreed to come to his office with Daniel two days later so they could co-sign the loan agreement.

Friday morning Dan opened the door to Brian's office at the bank and followed as Grace walked inside. After a kiss that barely brushed her cheek and a heartily effusive handshake for Dan, Brian politely pulled up two chairs for them before settling in his own behind his modern desk. Abstract paintings hung on the stark white walls added a vivid splash of color to what was otherwise a rather plastic decor. At least the plants scattered here and there were live instead of artificial, and they added considerable vitality to the office.

For nearly twenty minutes Brian seemed quite content to indulge in casual chitchat. At last, though, Dan leaned forward a few inches in his chair to say, "We know you must have a busy schedule, and we don't want to take up too much of your time. About our loan, we'd like to discuss the specific terms."

Brian tugged at the knot of his tie, coughed, and re-crossed his legs. "Well, hmmm, I regret having to tell you that your application for a loan has been turned down," he mumbled. "I'm sorry. When I talked to you last week, I thought it would probably be approved but . . . there are problems that make it impossible for the bank to lend you ten thousand dollars."

Grace was stunned. Tightly clutching the navy purse she held in her lap, she stared at Brian. "What kind of problems are you talking about?"

"For one thing, Dan is currently unemployed."

"Of course he is. He's busy getting the shop completed, even helping with the actual building himself," she coolly replied. "Besides, you knew last week that he isn't employed right now, but that didn't seem to bother you then. And I still don't see why it makes a difference, since I'd be co-signing the loan and my accounting business is providing a very good income."

"Oh, that's quite true, but I'm afraid that factor wasn't strong enough to allow for approval," Brian intoned, fidgeting with a pencil on his desk top. "I have to abide by bank policy."

"Exactly what is this bank's policy?" Dan calmly asked.

"It's going through some changes, as a matter of fact. Money's tight, as I'm sure you know. And bank policy isn't allowing for as many loans to small businesses."

To Grace his excuses had a false ring to them. She sat up straighter in her chair. "It's not as if Dan and I are asking for the entire amount of money it's going to take to start our business. In fact, we already have enough to start it. We only wanted the loan to be able to build a larger greenhouse. I'm surprised that wasn't taken into consideration."

"It was considered, oh, certainly. But bank policy—"

"Please, don't tell us about bank policy again," Grace

requested. "You're beginning to sound like a recorded message."

Brian looked at Dan, as if seeking moral support. "I do regret this," he repeated. "I hope you understand."

A hint of a rueful smile moved Dan's lips. "Bank policy. We know. We'll simply have to apply for a loan at Knoxville National. I'm sure we'll have no trouble getting a loan there. I've dealt with them before."

"What's really going on here?" Grace abruptly questioned, and knew beyond a shadow of a doubt something was when Brian blushed. "Did *you* turn down our loan application personally?"

Glumly, he nodded. "Making these decisions is my responsibility."

"But this time you didn't make the decision alone, did you? Someone put pressure on you because Thad Compton would have been very displeased if this bank had given us our loan. Right?"

Brian said nothing. He didn't need to. His expression made the answer to her question perfectly clear. He didn't look very proud of himself, and Grace could understand why he didn't. Feeling a little sorry for him, she looked at Dan, and as she started to rise to her feet, he stood also. Hopping up, Brian hurried around his desk to escort them to the door but still didn't utter a word.

Dan extended his hand to him. "Sorry it didn't work out."

"So am I," Brian muttered, then he faced Grace at last, wearily shrugging. "There just wasn't anything I could do about the situation."

"I guess not," she said without much conviction, told him good-bye, and walked out the door.

A moment later when she and Dan had stepped out of the bank onto the sidewalk, she sadly shook her head. "He sold out."

"Being a little hard on him, aren't you?" Dan challenged, taking her arm as they crossed Alpine Spring's

Main Street. "To be such a practical lady, you're sounding very idealistic. If the manager of the bank pressured him to turn down our loan, he probably would have been risking his job if he had approved it instead."

"I don't think I'd care to keep a job where I had to violate my principles at the drop of a hat," she declared, stopping on the street corner to look at Dan. "You wouldn't either. You wouldn't stay in a job like that."

"I did for a while. I had to play a few unworthy games myself to move up in the pecking order at the university. I didn't enjoy them, but I played them sometimes nevertheless."

"But, in the end, you left."

"I had somewhere else I wanted to go, other things I wanted to do. Maybe Brian doesn't have that option. Or doesn't think he has."

"He might be wise to look around for other options then if he wants to hang on to his self-respect."

"You're just disappointed in him right now. You know it's not as simple as you're making it sound. Different people react differently in the same situation."

Grace's gray eyes searched the fathomless green depths of his. He was right. Brian wasn't like Dan. Dan was so secure in himself, such a free spirit, that he'd never remain in a position that violated his principles for very long without bucking the system or simply walking away from it. It was strange. The very quality in him that had enabled him to leave her two years ago and cause her pain now evoked her utmost respect. She smiled with faint bemusement.

Dan grinned back and playfully tapped the end of her small, straight nose with a fingertip. "Come on," he invited, leading her along the side street where he had parked the van. "Before we go on to Knoxville National, I'll treat you to a hot dog for lunch. A gourmet meal will cheer you up."

She laughed. He had always been able to take any mood

93

of hers and transform it into something beautiful. He was still able to do that. He was a special man.

That night Little Bit awakened Grace with a series of urgent meows. Struggling to open her eyes, she found the kitten perched on the side of the bed, her wide eyes glowing faintly in the dark. Outside the rain had stopped, and Grace slipped groggily from beneath light covers. "Need to go out?" she murmured, stifling a yawn, and when the cat answered with another meow, she picked her up and carried her out of the room. In the upstairs hall she looked for Buster, thinking the dog too might need a few minutes outside, but the setter was nowhere to be seen. At bedtime a torrential rain had been lashing the house, so Buster had been allowed to stay inside, and now it appeared she had also managed to gain permission to sleep in Daniel's room. She's probably in there, Grace thought, wondering if she dared try jumping up on the foot of his bed to sleep.

If she needed to go out, she would let him know, Grace was sure. Holding the soft warm kitten, she padded down the steps, switched on the hall light, and walked through the shadows to the kitchen. She turned the light on in there too, then went to open the door to the porch, putting Little Bit down. Ever cautious, the cat peered out into the darkness for several long moments. Grace waited patiently, then gave her a little nudge with one foot.

"Go on if you're going." But the dawdling kitten hung back. Yawning again, Grace looked out the door, and her yawn broke off suddenly when she thought she saw something move in the darkness beneath the trees. The clouds had dispersed overhead; the moon shone down, and her breath caught in her throat with a sharp gasp when a distinctive shape emerged from the shadows, a man's silhouette. The moment she saw him, the unknowing kitten took the plunge, shooting out the door with a pounce. Heart hammering, Grace made a grab for her and missed, and as the kitten disappeared off the porch into the night,

94

she didn't dare go after her. The man still stood there, his very posture threatening, and she could almost feel his eyes boring into her as she stared incredulously at him. Spinning around, she threw the door shut and locked it with fumbling fingers before racing upstairs to Daniel's room. She didn't wait to knock. She opened the door and burst inside, rushing to the side of his bed where he was already stirring. Her trembling hand found his shoulder, lightly shook it.

He slowly opened his eyes. "Gracie, what—"

"A man. Outside. I saw him when I let Little Bit out."

Dan was wide awake in an instant and out of his bed, on the run down the stairs. Aware of the excitement, Buster scrambled after him, and Grace quickly followed. They rushed into the kitchen, where he opened the door again to let the dog out. Buster dashed across the porch into the yard, but oddly enough, she didn't bark, even once.

"He's gone," Dan said, raking his fingers through his tousled hair. "He probably took off as soon as he realized you'd seen him."

"But he didn't. For a long time he just stood there, looking at me while I looked at him."

"But he's gone now," Dan murmured, touching her cheek reassuringly. "He must be, or Buster would be raising hell."

That made perfect sense. Taking a deep calming breath, Grace stepped out onto the porch to call the kitten. She called and called for what seemed to be at least five minutes, but the cat didn't reappear. Finally she looked at Dan, who stood next to her. "He was still here when she ran out."

Daniel frowned.

"You don't think he might have grabbed her, do you?" Grace urgently exclaimed. "These people are really beginning to scare me. How far do you think they might go to try to intimidate us?"

95

"This thing is getting out of hand," Dan suddenly exploded, the strict control he held over his quick temper snapping at last. Fury glinted in his eyes and made a muscle work in his tensed jaw. He clenched his hands into fists. "It's gotten to the point where we have to worry about them harming a helpless kitten, and I've had enough. Tomorrow, I'm going to see Thad Compton and tell him that we're not going to put up with this kind of harassment."

"But, Dan, what good will that do? He'll just say he doesn't know what you're talking about." Grace gazed out at the rain-washed trees. "I can't believe they'd hurt an animal just to get to us."

"They didn't. I'm sure she's just fine," said Dan softly, forcing himself to simmer down a little. "Someone strange to her would never be able to catch her. She's too quick."

Grace's eyes sparkled with tears; her chin wobbled a little. "Do you really believe that, or are you just saying it to make me feel better?"

His expression gentled. He brushed back the curve of hair that had fallen forward across her right cheek. "I really believe it," he whispered. "And I'm going to get some shoes on and my robe and go out and find her right now."

She waited as he went upstairs. When he returned a couple of minutes later in his robe and shoes, she handed him the flashlight she had taken from the pantry. They walked outside together, and she stood on the porch, watching him cross the barnyard, Buster at his heels, as he called for the kitten. Grace called too but without success. The minutes passed so slowly. It seemed Dan had been gone such a long time when finally he reappeared, carrying Little Bit in one crooked arm.

Breathing a heartfelt sigh of relief, Grace welcomed him with a beaming smile. "Where did you find her?"

"Settling down for a nap in the hayloft."

"Next time I call you, come," she halfheartedly scolded

96

the kitten, taking her from him to carry her into the kitchen. There she poured Little Bit a saucer of milk and gave Buster a doggy treat. As Little Bit eagerly lapped up the milk, Grace shook her head. "Do this to me again, and I'll be tempted to take you back to the pound."

"Oh, you're scaring her to death," Dan teased. "She knows you'd never do anything like that."

"Oh, really?" Grace turned to him with a cheeky grin. "Are you insinuating I'm a softie?"

"I hope you can be sometimes," he answered huskily, stepping very close to her to tilt up her small chin with one lean finger. "If you can forgive her for wandering off for a while, maybe you can even forgive me for doing the same thing two years ago."

As he lowered his head, she shook hers, her heart leaping. "Dan, no, I . . ." His warm firm lips touched hers, and she moaned as electricity seemed to whip with sparks between them, sending bolting currents throughout her body. Muscular arms enfolded her, and she swayed against him, dizzied by his deepening kiss and his roaming hands upon her back. Desire flared up in her, searing and irrepressible. The virile contours of his long powerful body straining against her inflamed senses, she wrapped her arms around his waist, delighting in the sensations that ran riot in her as her soft curves yielded to his superior physical strength. She kissed him back, her mouth opening to invite the tasting probe of his tongue. Sparks of fire rushed through her veins, throbbing in her pulses, and when his hands curved over the rounded swell of her bottom and he widened his stance to press her against him, the evidence of his passion made her moan softly once more.

"Gracie, I want you," he murmured between kisses. "I need you so much."

And she needed him. Somehow, insanely, she had fallen in love with him all over again, and she could no longer lie to herself and try to believe she hadn't. Love raged like a fever in her, a fever she couldn't at that moment hope to cool. She touched his face, his jaw, the column of his neck, then tangled her fingers in the soft hair brushing his nape. When he lifted her up to cradle her in his arms, she never considered protesting. Every inch of her skin tingled with anticipation as he carried her out of the kitchen, up the stairs, and into her room, where he gently put her down upon her bed. He came down beside her, kicking off his shoes.

She gazed up at him. It was good to love again and to admit to herself that she did. She felt free to visually explore his face, to sweep her hands over his thick clean hair, to follow the shape of his ear with one fingertip then stroke the firm line of his jaw as she had done so often in the past. Emotion welled up in her, intensifying the physical pleasure she experienced simply by being with him.

Briefly, she closed her eyes. Her black lashes lay in feathery crescents upon her creamy smooth skin. Dan leaned down to kiss each eyelid, then her eyebrows, her temples, the end of her chin. His lips traced her high cheekbones and brushed slowly toward her mouth. She turned her head, her own lips seeking his, inviting them to taste their sweetness. Gently he did, again and again, and every gentle but warming kiss they exchanged made the current of sensual electricity leaping between them all the more powerful and binding.

Lying down on his side in the bed, he turned her to face him, bringing forward a swathe of her dark hair to curve it over her neck. His fingers played through strands which felt like fine, warm silk. He buried his face in its luxuriant softness, inhaling fresh fragrance.

"Gracie, you smell delicious," he whispered close to her ear while his hand shaped the curves of her slender, lissome body, then came to rest upon the side of one breast. His palm pressed lightly against the tantalizing fullness. "And feel good, so good."

A small sensuous smile was her silent answer as she

drew lazy circles over his broad bare chest, her fingertips stirring fine dark hair. His muscular arm went around her waist, and he eased her nearer to him. Warmed to the very marrow of her bones, she skimmed a thumbnail down the length of his spine, making a quick shudder run over him.

"I need you so much," he gruffly uttered, caressing her firmly rounded hips as his mouth captured hers again.

And she needed him. Wishing these precious moments they were sharing never had to end, she was lost in their thrilling sweetness, their engulfing magic that transcended rational thought. In her bed, in his arms, she felt she was where she always belonged, as if she had previously been a little lost and never even realized it. Beneath her wandering feathering hands, taut muscle highlighted his large frame; touching him was bliss. The clean firm lineation of his powerful body enthralled her, and when his hand cupping her buttocks pressed her tight against him, and she encountered the hard throbbing of his aroused masculinity, she moaned softly, remembering. . . .

They were drifting into a wondrous journey of rediscovery, tentatively caressing, measuring each other's responses, which became more ardent with every second that passed. Mutually their lips became more demanding, melting together in hot impassioned kisses. When he gently pushed his tongue inside her mouth, she boldly drew it deeper, trembling as its tip slowly flicked over the sensitive flesh of her inner cheek. Her arm tightened around his waist; her fingertips scampering over the small of his back.

Making a low growling sound, he rolled swiftly onto his back, pulling her over atop him, his narrowed gaze imprisoning hers as her lovely hair fell forward around her face and down to tickle his chest. Through her sheer cotton gown, her slender yet generously curved body was warmly irresistible. He lightly massaged her delicately boned shoulders and back, down to the enticing upward arch that led to her womanly hips. With slow evocative deliberation, he drew the backs of his fingers down along her thighs before reaching up again to cup her breasts in his palms, the edges of his thumbs rubbing their tips.

A mighty tremor raced over Grace. "Oh, *Daniel*," she breathed.

"Daniel," he softly repeated, a quick glint of triumph flaring in his magnificent eyes. "You never call me that except when we're . . ."

Leaning down, she kissed him, softly parted lips dancing over the firm shape of his, halting his words before he could finish. Then a soft gasp escaped her when he easily lifted her upward above him, his mouth leaving hers to seek her breasts. Weakened by longing, she could only cling to his broad shoulders while he plied rounded cushioned flesh, searing her skin through fabric too thin to be an effective barrier to his lingering kisses. He found the sensitized crests, taking first one then the other between his tenderly nipping teeth. Keen ripples of sheer delight shot through Grace, and she pressed her nails into his shoulders' corded muscles.

As swiftly as he had brought her over atop him, he impelled her back down upon the mattress, moving one long leg across both of hers while stretching her gown taut over her breasts so that their outlines were visibly distinct. He watched their rapid rise and fall for several spellbinding seconds, then raised his gaze to meet hers for an instant before lowering it again. He touched her. Almost with reverence, he stroked the soft mounds of feminine flesh, merely skimming over the surfaces at times, lightly pressing and squeezing and massaging during others. And as his hands expertly coaxed, her hands drifted softly as butterfly wings over him too. Had he not been a caring man, he would have possessed her completely then and there, but he did care and was capable of being patient and considerate enough to wait until he knew without a doubt that she wanted him as much as he wanted her. His toying fingers played over and around her nipples until they were tipped with hard little nubbles. Smiling faintly, he lowered his head to kiss and nibble at each repeatedly. Dampened cotton became practically transparent upon her peach-tinted crests. He raised up slightly to rub his fingertips back and forth over them, pleased as her hands momentarily covered his, holding them tightly against her.

"Honey, this isn't nearly enough for me. I need more, much more," he groaned a second later, starting to raise the hem of her short gown up over her shapely thighs. But his action was delightfully postponed when she wound her arms upward around his neck, lifted her head from the pillow, and began to scatter kisses over his chest, around the hard pectoral muscles until her lips commenced her own tormenting game with his own flat nipples. Propped on his elbows, he closed his eyes, succumbing to the delicate lashes of her tongue and the sensations that spread throughout him, threatening to wrench away the tight rein he held on his desire. Gracie had always been able to drive him crazy; she still was incredibly adept at doing that. To maintain control, he could only retaliate. He disentangled her arms from around his neck to sweep her nightie upward and off over her head, baring her upper body, which shimmered opalescently in the glowing lamplight. The weight of his torso pressed her down flat again as he imprisoned both her wrists in one hand and held them back above her head upon the snowy white pillow. "Shameless vixen," he teasingly accused, passionate intent readable in his carved features. With a thumb and forefinger, he spanned the space between the twin peaks of her breasts. "Now it's my turn again. The other night I touched you here . . . and here. But tonight, I have to taste."

"Daniel, I . . ."

"Gracie, I have to. Right now."

Scarcely able to take one reasonably deep breath out of every three, she lay transfixed by the green ember-glow in his eyes until she could no longer see it as he continued to lower his head until at last his warm persuasive lips

101

made the awaited contact with her skin. He inscribed erotic circles of kisses ever upward around her left breast, then the right, forsaking one only to explore the other, repeating the evocative process again and again, taking his time, making her wait for what they both knew must come next.

"Daniel!" The soft gasp spilled from her throat in a husky whisper when he finally closed his lips around one swollen throbbing crest, capturing it between his stroking tongue and the roof of his mouth, drawing deeply at the tender morsel of firmly crowned succulent flesh as if he could never get his fill. She strained against him, felt his lips form a tiny smile around her, and tangled her legs sinuously with his. When he released her wrists a moment later, her hands floated down, not to attempt resistance, but to run tremulously over his hair, along the strong sunbronzed column of his neck and past his shoulders to clasp together tightly across his broad back. It felt so good to have her arms around him, to hold him very close.

She did love him so much. Once upon a time two years ago, after he had left her, she had convinced herself she'd never actually loved him at all. She was no longer convinced. She suspected she had really loved him then and maybe had never stopped, and even if she had, she loved him again; and to try to banish that overwhelming emotion would be as foolish as trying to will her heart to cease beating, and as impossible. She felt drugged by the pleasure he was giving until the sensations he elicited became so piercingly exquisite that his mouth upon her became nearly a torment, and taking his face between her hands, she urged his lips upward to hers once more and the languid unhurried kisses they shared suppressed, for a time, the very basic subconscious doubts buried deep in her mind.

It was only then that he slid lean fingers beneath the waistband of her lace-edged panties, easing them down over her finely honed hipbones while his other hand eased between her thighs, fingers brushing upward. At that intimate caress, hungry emptiness flowered open deep within her, a hunger so frighteningly intense that she was immediately brought back to reality with a jolt. Her traitorous body still ached for completion, but her brain was screaming warnings she couldn't ignore, telling her she had allowed herself to be led down the primrose path one more time. Oh, yes, she was in love with Daniel again, but didn't want to be. As a business partner she had faith in his knowledge of what he was doing; she could trust him. But, as a person, as a lover, he was unreliable. He might decide to wander away again any old time, to go off and leave her the way he had before. Oh, he would probably stick around at least a year or two because starting the garden shop seemed truly important to him. But would his interest in the business last? Would a few years of physical gratification compensate for the loneliness she would feel when he went his merry way again sometime in the future? *No.* That was the only answer that made sense. She loved him, but surely she could handle that if only she didn't allow herself to drift into a physical intimacy that would irrevocably bind her body and soul to him and leave her utterly bereft when it ended. After his first desertion, she had emerged from the experience wiser, stronger, more self-reliant. But she was afraid her luck wouldn't hold a second time around. She was, in fact, afraid of him and of his ability to wound her, though he might never mean to.

"Honey," Daniel muttered roughly, feeling her stiffen beneath him. "Don't go all tense on me now."

Employing all the inner strength she could muster, she closed her ears to his gruff plea and pretended to lightly laugh. "Dan, this is just crazy."

"You think this is amusing?" he growled, raising up to catch her chin between a thumb and forefinger, anger replacing the desire in the depths of his emerald eyes. "Don't you know what you're doing to me?"

"It's not amusing, just crazy," she repeated, steeling

herself to the feel of his hands ranging over her body. "We're business partners. We can't jeopardize that relationship by getting involved . . . like this."

A muscle throbbed rhythmically in his clenched jaw as he looked down at her. "You want me, Gracie, as much as I want you."

Unable to speak, she shook her head.

"Little liar," he whispered. "I know you too well. You wanted us to make love."

"All right, yes, maybe I did . . . for a minute or two," she tersely admitted, determined to conceal her true feelings. "But . . . oh, Dan, I just want you to go back to your own room."

"Do you really?"

"Yes," she murmured, her heart lying, her mind forcing out its own contradictory truth. "I—I do want you to leave."

And he left. In one fluid motion he rose up to stand beside her bed, a mocking smile fleetingly appearing upon his compressed lips when compulsion caused her to hug her arms across her naked breasts. Then he turned and was gone, pulling her door shut as he stepped out into the hallway, leaving her alone and feeling as if she were cloaked in the heaviness of sheer silence.

Entering his bedroom, Dan stalked over to the window overlooking the shell of the garden shop. Plowing his fingers through his hair, he uttered a frustrated curse aloud. Gracie was as stubborn as she had always been, letting obstinate, almost excessive practicality stand in the way of uninhibited responses. Of course, that was exactly what had kept her from going away with him two years ago. Yet, coming back here, he had hoped she might have become less staid and restrained. And sometimes he glimpsed some subtle differences in her. She seemed more open at times, and what he had told her tonight had been the truth. She had wanted him. Perhaps she hadn't needed him as much as he'd needed her, but she had needed him, obviously more than she wanted to confess. Staring out at the black-velvet star-studded sky, he suddenly relaxed and smiled to himself. All right, if she thought she wanted nothing more than a platonic relationship with him, he wasn't going to press the issue. There was a hint of obstinacy running through him too. If she believed she only wanted him as a business partner, that's all he would be . . . until she realized that what they had once had together had been very special and could be even more special this time, if only she'd let herself go.

"The next move is yours, Gracie," he vowed, then strode across his room and got into bed.

CHAPTER SEVEN

The following week went smoothly. There were no more incidents at either the shop or the house and no further threats of vandalism. No more threatening strangers appeared in the middle of the night. By Thursday, the garden shop was under a roof; the electrical wires had been pulled through the inside studs; the basic plumbing had been roughed in. Grace was pleased with the progress Dan and the builders were making and was immensely relieved that no one had attempted to intimidate them in recent days. She would have felt completely at ease had it not been for the change that had occurred in her relationship with Daniel. Since that night in her bedroom he had acted pretty much at ease while she had imagined a nearly tangible pall of tension coming between them. It didn't seem to bother him one whit that she insisted their relationship remain strictly business. But then, that made perfect sense, didn't it? He'd never loved her, so she couldn't possibly upset his equilibrium. But she had loved him two years ago and had fallen in love with him all over again. She couldn't possibly be as calm and collected as he was whenever they were together. He could touch her often, always casually; that contact of skin against skin apparently meant nothing to him, while she took great pains never to touch him because her heart skipped, her breath caught, and her flesh grew hot anytime she inadvertently did.

She tried to avoid him. He didn't make that an easy accomplishment. Every day he worked out in the shop while she sat at her computer in her office. He came in frequently for ice water for the construction crew and never failed to step in to see her and tell her what he was doing. In the evenings he stayed at the farmhouse, reading while she patiently stitched up tiny doll outfits. Sometimes they listened silently to soft music on the stereo or silently watched a movie of mutual interest on television. Despite the fact that he seemed fairly at ease, the camaraderie they had shared the past few weeks suffered. Grace felt the strain of being in love and unable to express her feelings, although she knew Dan was fond of her. But fondness isn't love and it was love she needed from him and to have to hide that need naturally made her tense.

Thursday evening, soon after dinner, Grace shooed the dog and cat outside, then stood at the screen door looking out over the veranda as the two animals loped down the steps. To her astonishment Buster suddenly turned on Little Bit and started chasing her around the front yard. In a flash Grace was out the door and down the stairs yelling at the dog, who didn't pay her the least bit of attention. Drawn by the commotion, Daniel came dashing out of the house to grasp Grace's arm.

"What's wrong?"

"Buster is chasing my cat, that's what's wrong!" she exclaimed, spinning round to face him. "I won't put up with that, Dan. Little Bit's so tiny Buster could break her back with one bite. Would you please call her off?"

"Calm down," he murmured, visibly relaxing, inclining his head toward the two pets as they darted back and forth among the trees. The kitten scampered up the trunk of one, flipped around, and pounced down onto the ground again to turn the tables and chase Buster for a while.

"Oh. They're playing," Grace uttered, her weak smile

sheepish. "I've never seen them do that before, so I just thought . . ."

"Do you really believe Buster would do anything to hurt that kitten?"

Grace shrugged. "Well, she doesn't act very comfortable when Little Bit tries to love up to her."

"You can't expect miracles. She's just a dog. But standoffish as she acts, she's fond of the cat. I've seen them playing this game a couple of times," Dan explained, a barely discernible hint of impatience hardening his voice while he looked speculatively at her. "It's just that you've been a little edgy for the past few days, and that's obviously got you jumping to conclusions. Care to tell me what the problem is?"

"No problems," she hastily replied, flippantly tossing her hands up before wrinkling her nose and uttering a deliberately deceptive half-truth. "It's not a real problem, anyhow. I guess I have been sort of tense because I feel like I'm waiting for the other shoe to drop. I mean, nobody's harassed us lately, and I keep expecting something else to happen."

"Ummm, I know the feeling," Dan conceded, watching as Buster and the kitten ended their game, then went their separate ways beneath the magnolias. "I don't think our 'friends' have given up on us quite yet either."

"Wonder what they'll try next," Grace said, worrying a strand of her hair while leading him back into the house to the parlor. She sat down, picking up her sewing as Dan settled back comfortably on the sofa. "I know it's useless to try to outguess them, but I can't help thinking about all the things they could possibly do, and it's not very pleasant to lie in bed at night hoping no one's outside pulling dirty tricks on us."

Dan regarded her somberly. "What you need, what we both need, is some time away from here," he announced. "And I have the perfect excuse for us to get away. Monday, our loan goes through at the bank, and we'll transfer

108

it directly into our business account. Tuesday, we'll drive down to Atlanta to the firm that sells prefabricated greenhouses and pick out the style we want. We'll stay the night there and drive back Wednesday."

Grace swallowed hard. In her chair she shifted her position uncomfortably and plucked at a loose thread on the frilly doll's petticoat she was currently working on. "I can't go, Dan. It's near the end of the month, and I have to balance all my clients' accounts. And besides, you don't need me along anyway. You're the greenhouse expert. I don't know a thing about them, so you choose the design you think's best for us and I'll be satisfied."

"You said you wanted to be involved in every aspect of the business."

"Yes . . . but, I never meant I was going to be a fanatic about it. So you go to Atlanta and I'll stay home."

"No."

"No?" A quick frown etched her smooth brow. "What do you mean, no? I just said I'm too busy to go and—"

"And I'm saying right now that I'm not about to leave you here alone after everything that's happened," he brusquely cut in, his tone no-nonsense. "Whether you're busy or not, whether you want to or not, you're going with me to Atlanta, where we can find the largest selection of greenhouse designs on the East Coast. You'll have plenty of time to balance your accounts when we get back."

"I don't like to have to rush," she argued, breathing an exasperated sigh. "And, for heaven's sake, Dan, I'll be fine here by myself for one night. I'm not afraid of being alone. I've told you that before."

"Yes, you have, but do you really want to spend all next Tuesday night awake in bed listening for strange noises?" he questioned with uncharacteristic bluntness. "And don't try to tell me you won't, because you just said you've been tense the past several days because you're waiting for the other shoe to drop. Think how you'd feel here all alone."

She was thinking! *She was thinking!* And he was right.

Lowering her eyes, she stared at the gleaming wood floor. She certainly didn't relish the idea of staying here by herself while he went to Atlanta . . . yet, going there with him and spending the night might be more dangerous, at least emotionally, than staying behind at home. She lifted one hand in an uncertain gesture. "But, if we both leave, Compton's thugs won't have to worry about anyone calling the sheriff. They'll be able to come out here and do all the damage they want."

"We'll leave Buster outside to guard the place. I'm sure one of your neighbors will be glad to come over to give her and the kitten water and food. And if anyone comes around, she'll raise quite a commotion with her barking. You know how ferocious she can sound. She's scared these people away before, and I have no doubt she'll do it again. Now, are you satisfied? You have no good excuse to stay here, so you will go to Atlanta with me."

"All right, I'll . . . go." She reluctantly agreed, lifting her head to meet his relentless gaze again. "But I don't see why we have to spend the night there. Why can't we leave early Tuesday morning, pick the greenhouse we want, then drive back home the same day?"

"Because I see no reason for us to wear ourselves out by doing that," he said flatly. But a trace of a smile appeared on his lips, and his voice softened as he added, "What's the matter, Gracie? Afraid to spend a night in the same hotel with me?"

"Why should I be?" she pertly retorted. "We spend every night together here."

"Ah, but you might discover you're less inhibited away from home."

"I'm not inhibited, just practical-minded. And since I do have my accounts to balance, I think we should drive back here Tuesday evening."

"And miss the Willie Nelson concert at the Omni?" he inquired with a quick grin on his lips. "I managed to get

110

tickets, and I'd hate to see them go to waste after all the trouble I went to."

"Willie Nelson? Really?" Grace softly exclaimed, gray eyes brightening even as she surveyed Daniel suspiciously. "You know how much I like him. Are you trying to bribe me?"

Comically, he cocked one eyebrow. "Me? Would I ever try to offer you a bribe?"

"In a minute if you thought it might work."

"And did it? Want to stay in Atlanta Tuesday night or come home and miss the concert? It's your choice. Take it or leave it."

"I'll take it," she answered without further hesitation. Daniel smiled.

Tuesday night after the concert, which had been terrific, Grace slipped out of her dress in her hotel room. Softly humming "On the Road Again," she tapped one stockinged toe while putting on her robe. She started toward the bath just as Daniel knocked on one of the double doors that adjoined his room to hers.

"Good, I didn't get you out of bed," he said when she opened it. He took a step forward, crossing the threshold. "You wouldn't happen to have some aspirin handy, would you?"

"I think so," she said, a concerned frown appearing on her brow as she reached toward the dresser for her purse. "What's wrong?"

"Headache," he explained stoically, then produced a small grin. "Guess you gave it to me by doing all that screaming at the concert."

Grinning back, she cut her eyes sideways at him. "I've never screamed during a concert in my life, and you know it. After all, you're the one who's always accusing me of being a stick-in-the-mud, so I'd never be a screamer even while seeing one of my favorite singers live and in person. The girls sitting behind us must have given you your

111

headache. Don't blame me for it or I might decide not to let you have any of these aspirin." Taking a small tin out of a zippered compartment of her purse, she held it for a few seconds before finally handing it to him. "And maybe you should order yourself a drink to help you get right to sleep."

"I considered that. But I hate to drink alone," said Daniel, looking down at the tin from which he removed two tablets. "Care to join me?"

"Why not?" she readily replied, moving away from him toward the bedside phone to call room service. "It *is* a festive occasion. We'll toast Willie's fantastic performance."

After placing their order while Daniel went into the bath to wash down the aspirin with a swallow of water, Grace perched herself on the edge of the king-size bed and watched him walk over to pull out the desk chair and sit down also. He had shed his sport coat, and the top three buttons of his shirt were undone, exposing a sunbronzed vee of hair-roughened skin. As he stretched his long legs out, crossing his ankles, he rubbed his temple once more, and she frowned again.

"Hurts bad, huh?"

He shrugged. "Just a nagging ache. I'll survive. I'm tough."

She smiled at his lighthearted tone. "During your two years of wandering, didn't you find someone to teach you to will pain away by going into a trance or something?"

"No, but I didn't travel over the country looking for mystics," he answered curtly, sparks of irritation flashing in his eyes as he glared at her. "Maybe if you'd try to be a little less narrow-minded, you could understand that I didn't do what I did because I was searching for my identity. I've known exactly who I am for years, but I thought it was time to see how some people outside the academic community live. But if you don't want to believe that, I—"

"Whoa, hold it," she cut in, eyes widening as she raised her hands, her gesture silently requesting a truce. "Jeez, I didn't realize a headache could make you so touchy. I was only kidding about the trances."

"According to Freud, people don't usually say anything they don't actually feel, at least subconsciously."

"Since when did you become an expert in psychiatry?" she shot back, a thin veneer of coolness creeping into her voice. "I thought philosophy was your field."

As Daniel opened his mouth to answer, a quick rap on Grace's door prevented him from uttering a rather scathing retort. It was just as well. His head did hurt, and because of that he lacked the patience to deal with her straitlaced attitude. When the waiter put the tray bearing their drinks on the desk then left with his tip, Daniel took a small sip of his gin and tonic, silently observing her while she bobbed a piece of ice up and down in her glass with the tip of her little finger.

After a while, as they very slowly nursed their drinks, they started talking again but took great pains to stick to impersonal topics and mainly discussed the greenhouse design they had chosen that afternoon. When even the ice in Daniel's drink had melted and he had swallowed the last possible sip, he had no excuse to remain any longer in Grace's room. He got up to leave.

"How's your head now?" she asked, walking with him across the room. "Feeling any better?"

"Some, but it's still there. Maybe I'm catching a cold."

She reached up to touch his forehead. "You don't feel feverish."

"I'll probably be just fine in the morning," he murmured, catching her small fingers in his to lower her hand.

For a breathtaking instant something in the expression on his face made her expect him to haul her into his arms and passionately kiss her. Instead, he released her fingers and stepped into his own room, saying, "We should start back about seven in the morning. Okay with you?"

"Fine. 'Night," she whispered, and after he replied, she stood motionless, watching as he closed his connecting door with a knob only on his side to ensure privacy. Then, with a deep inward sigh, she shut her door too.

Wednesday afternoon, after Grace and Dan had returned from Atlanta, Jim O'Donnell drove out to the farmhouse to check on their progress. They had coffee in the cozy kitchen while he looked over the plans of the greenhouse Dan and the construction workers would start to build as soon as the prefab materials arrived.

"Looks real good," Jim assessed after several minutes, nodding his approval. "Lots of room."

"We decided to build it larger than we actually need right now," Dan explained. "In case we need more space later."

"Oh, you're going to. I can just about guarantee it," said Jim, beaming a confident smile. "I've mentioned your plans to several people, and reactions have been positive. Most of them have asked when the shop will be open for business. I tell them you should be opening in three or four weeks. Isn't that about right?"

Dan nodded. "We're pouring the slab floor for the greenhouse Friday, so we'll be able to start building as soon as the materials are delivered from Atlanta Monday morning."

"And I've reserved ad space in the Knoxville papers," Grace said, then shrugged lightly. "Just as Compton's man warned—threatened—I was told there was no ad space available in the Alpine Springs *Gazette*. But their circulation isn't that high anyhow, and we can certainly use the money we save there to help pay for the TV spots Dan's going to tape next week."

"Well, no offense to you, Dan, but why aren't you going to be in the TV ads too, Gracie?" Jim asked her. "A lovely woman like you inviting customers to the shop would certainly help bring a lot of men in."

114

"I've tried to tell her that, but she's stubborn," Daniel said wryly. "She refuses to appear in the spots with me."

"Because he's the charismatic half of this partnership." She good-naturedly defended her decision. "I'm content to stay in the background."

Dan smiled knowingly at her. "What she really means is that she's terribly camera-shy."

"Oh, but you shouldn't be," Jim persisted. "If you'll just make yourself forget the cameras are there, you'll do fine. Really, I'm sure of it."

Laughing, Grace shook her head. "You're wasting your time, Jim. Dan's already tried telling me I wouldn't be that nervous, that I'd do just fine, but he didn't get anywhere with his arguments, and neither will you. I'm not going to change my mind."

Jim looked at Dan. "She is stubborn, isn't she?"

"That may be the understatement of the year" was Dan's teasing reply, and he simply grinned when she wrinkled her nose at him.

Later, after Jim left, Dan went back outside, and Grace returned to the computer in her office. She worked for about ten minutes when someone knocking at the front door interrupted, and she went to answer it, gasping when she found Jim on the veranda leaning against the front of the house, his face fiery red and streaming perspiration, his breathing shallow and quick.

"Oh, my God, what's wrong?" she exclaimed, taking hold of his arm to help him inside. She felt him tremble and began trembling herself, scared he was suffering a heart attack. After guiding him to the nearest chair in the parlor, she bent down to make certain his collar was as loose as possible. "Jim, are you having chest pains?"

"N-no." He gulped for air. "The heat got me. The sun's so hot today. I . . . guess I shouldn't have tried to walk back here after conking my head against the steering wheel."

"You had an accident in the car!"

115

"It's in a ditch about three quarters of a mile down the road."

"Thank God, you were able to walk away from it, though you're probably right. Maybe you should have waited until someone drove by instead of walking all that way back here." Worry shadowed her face as she watched him gingerly probe his scalp an inch or so back into his receding hairline. "Any head injury can be serious. Will you be all right by yourself while I run out and get Dan so we can get you to a hospital?"

Jim weakly waved one hand in a dismissive gesture. "Oh, I don't think I need to go to the—"

"And I think it's better to be safe than sorry," she murmured, nipping his attempted protest in the bud before running outside to the site of the garden shop.

After she had told Dan what had happened, he beat her back to the house, outpacing her easily. By the time she rather breathlessly dashed into the parlor again, he was already next to the chair, gently examining the raised lump on the older man's head. Grim-faced, he straightened to turn toward Gracie. "I'll get the van."

"Do you think I could have some water before we make this frantic drive to the emergency room?" Jim inquired, some of his old spunk returning now that his breathing was less labored. "This bump on my head isn't bothering me nearly as much as my dry throat. That sun made me wish for a cool glass of water, and I'd sure rather have that before I have to go let some doctor poke at me."

"I'll get you some." Grace hurried away, heading toward the kitchen.

"What happened?" she heard Dan ask Jim as she stepped out into the hallway. "Did you lose control of the car?"

"Nope, I'm a careful driver. Got forced off the road by some damn-fool idiot! He started to pass me—at least that's what I thought he was doing. Then he swerved and sideswiped my car so fast that I ended up in the ditch before I knew what was happening. And he wasn't even meeting another car. He was free to pass."

"It was a man who ran you off then? Can you remember what he looked like? Have you ever seen him before?"

"Couldn't say. He was wearing a cowboy hat pulled down low. That's about all I had time to notice."

"You must have noticed the make of the car."

"It was a rusty old Chevy pickup."

"Did you see the license plate?"

"My head was smacking against the steering wheel at the same time he gunned that old heap and disappeared around the next curve."

In the hall listening to the men's voices, Grace discovered she had come to a dead halt, her heart racing as the implications raised by the overheard conversation bombarded her mind. A little niggling fear tried to take root in her; she fought it, shook her head to reassemble her thoughts, then proceeded on into the kitchen to get the requested glassful of cool, clear well water. Yet, when she returned to the parlor to hand the lead crystal glass to Jim, she was in no mood to play charades. She fixed a perceptive gaze on Dan's finely hewn face and forthrightly announced, "I heard what you two were saying a minute ago. You think maybe one of Compton's people ran Jim off the road, don't you, Dan?"

Although Jim, who was sipping his water, hastily looked away, Daniel surveyed her impassively, his expression neither affirming nor denying. "We can talk about this later" was all he would say, inclining his head toward the older man. "Right now, let's just get Jim to the hospital. Okay?"

"But for goodness sake, when you call Dottie to tell her what happened, don't act like you suspect somebody might have run me off the road on purpose," Jim swiftly spoke up, fondly shaking his head. "Besides coddling me, Dottie's one of the world's worst worriers. No use getting

117

her all worked up about something that might be nothing."

Might be nothing. Grace wished she could believe that, but she couldn't. Intuition told her what had happened to Jim had special and frightening significance. She sank the edge of her teeth into her lower lip. Yet she didn't press the issue. Dan was right—talk could wait; getting Jim to the hospital was their priority right now.

"I'm going to pull the van right up to the veranda steps," Dan said, stone-faced as he walked by her toward the opened double doors. "While I do that, why don't you call the sheriff's department and ask them to have a deputy meet us at Memorial Hospital. That's out of this jurisdiction, but the . . . accident happened in this county, and they'll have to talk to Jim before they start an investigation."

Nearly an hour later Grace and Dan sat in molded plastic chairs in the waiting room of emergency in the large university hospital. Nervously picking clear polish off her fingernails, she inhaled the antiseptic medicinal smell of the hospital. She glanced at the swinging doors through which Jim had disappeared, then sideways at Dan, who was sitting back beside her, seemingly relaxed, long fingers linked across his flat midriff. Only the working muscle in his jaw betrayed the fact that tension was beginning to mount in him too. After a few more minutes passed, young Deputy Watson returned from the examining rooms, where he had been allowed to go to question Jim. Shaking his head, he walked over to them.

"Sorry, folks, but there's not much to go on here," he apologized. "No telling how many rusty old Chevys there are just in our county. And Mr. O'Donnell can't remember anything else to add to that description, so I doubt we'll ever find this particular truck. Of course, we'll take paint samples from the side of Mr. O'Donnell's car and see if that leads us anywhere. But . . ." Watson's shrug was almost defeatist. "Well, I reckon there's a chance that the whole thing *was* just an accident, pure and simple."

"I think that's highly unlikely," Daniel said softly but firmly, already on his feet as he looked steadily at the young, uniformed man. "Don't you?"

"Probably so," the deputy conceded, glancing down at his feet before stiffening his shoulders, obviously rebuilding his self-confidence. "But I promise I'll do everything I can to find out who ran Mr. O'Donnell into that ditch."

Daniel's expression became less stern. "That's all we ask: that you do your best."

"Better get out to the site of the accident . . . er, incident, then."

"After you examine Mr. O'Donnell's car, have it towed to Lassiter's Garage off Chapman's Highway," Dan politely requested. "Have them bill me for all the repairs."

Deputy Watson nodded, smiled faintly at Grace, then turned to leave, striding out the exit doors of emergency's waiting room at the same moment a tallish woman in her fifties with neat salt-and-pepper hair hurried through the entrance, clutching the straps of her black leather purse at chest level. Her eyes darted around.

"That's Jim's wife, I bet," Grace quietly said, rising to her feet beside Daniel, and when he nodded agreement, they walked over to introduce themselves and reassure the woman as much as they could that Jim's injury had seemed quite superficial.

"I just don't understand how it happened," Dottie O'-Donnell muttered thoughtfully, less tense at last but still confused. "I mean, how could Jim just run off into a ditch?"

Daniel led her over to a chair. "I suppose anyone can lose control of a car, Mrs. O'Donnell."

"Just about everyone could *except* Jim," the woman said, beginning to twist her purse straps once again. "He's slow as a turtle when he drives. Sometimes, I get on to him, but he always says he likes to take his time and look at the scenery. So I don't see how he could have lost control of the car." She eyed Grace and Dan with some suspicion. "And I get this feeling there's something the two of you aren't telling me. I've been around a long time and raised three children, so I can usually tell when somebody's trying to keep something from me."

Grace had never been a liar and never would be, not a convincing one anyhow. Her honest gray eyes sought Dan's, and she could find no opposition to her need to tell Jim's wife the truth as they knew it. "So, Jim seems to think the driver of the pickup forced him off the road deliberately," she concluded after divulging the details of Jim's misadventure. "I'm sorry to have to tell you that, believe me."

"Oh dear, I was afraid . . . I mean, I just had this feeling," Mrs. O'Donnell muttered, as if to herself, before looking at Grace, then at Daniel, then at Grace again. Dragging a folded tissue from the depths of her purse, she dabbed it at her eyes. "We went through this once before, you know, when we owned our first bakery in Ohio. I was terrified then, and I never imagined we'd get involved in something like that again, after we moved here. Now, I'm scared again. Oh, I hope the two of you will have all the luck in starting your business, but I . . . I don't want to be harassed and threatened again. I just couldn't stand it if something bad happened to my Jim. I'm sorry, but I don't want him to be involved in any of this."

"We understand how you must feel, Mrs. O'Donnell," Dan began, but cut his words short when Jim stepped through the double doors into the waiting room, his step fairly jaunty, his smile broadening when Dottie rushed over to embrace him, asking him if he was all right, if he was supposed to be out of bed. He patted her back, grinning at Grace and Dan over her left shoulder.

"I've been released, sweetheart," he told his wife comfortingly. "No concussion or anything else serious wrong

120

with me. I just may have a headache for a couple of days, that's all. Stop fretting."

Dottie sniffled, raised a tissue to her nose, and quietly blew. Her voice was hoarse with emotion when she pulled back to look at her husband and confessed, "I told Grace and Dan that I . . . don't want you involved in . . . all this."

"You're trying to coddle me again, Dottie," Jim lovingly accused, squeezing her shoulders. "But you know me. When someone starts trying to push me around, I push back. You knew I was like that when you married me. You can't expect me to change after all these years."

"But I don't want you to get hurt, Jimmy."

"I'm not going to."

"But—"

"Jim, Dottie, we're going now." Dan gently intruded on the affectionate argument that undoubtedly would never end in an uncontested victor. "Jim, take it easy and get some rest. Let us hear from you when you're feeling better."

"That'll be in a day or two," the older man promised, robust as ever once again. "Just remember, we're not going to let somebody like Thad Compton make us back down. Right?" When Grace nodded and leaned over to kiss him on the cheek, he kissed hers too, whispering, "And don't you worry about Dottie. She worries a lot, but she'd be shocked if I didn't stand up for what I believe in. It won't take much for me to convince her I'm doing what I have to do. All right?"

A smile tugged at the corners of Grace's mouth. "You're a regular con man, aren't you?"

"Nah, just a charming old gentleman," he retorted merrily, then reached over to lightly slap Dan's left shoulder.

Good-byes said, Grace and Dan left the hospital and took the interstate toward home, speaking very seldom until they reached the farmhouse and they entered the kitchen. Fidgety, she tugged at a tendril of her hair while glancing around the cheery room. "Well, it's my night to make dinner," she murmured at last, for lack of anything more scintillating to say. "Broiled flounder all right with you?"

"Sounds delicious. Buster and Little Bit will be quite pleased with the menu too," Dan answered lightly. "And while you get started on that, I'll go out and see how much farther along the guys got after we left."

"She's scared. Jim's wife, I mean," Grace called when he started to turn away toward the door to the side porch. Her troubled eyes fixed on his as he looked back at her again. She stood tense and erect in the center of the room. "And I think she has every reason to be afraid. If Compton's willing to harass and threaten a senior citizen just because he's giving us advice . . . what else might he be willing to do? Dottie's scared. And I . . . think I am too after what happened this afternoon."

With one long stride Daniel was close in front of her, tilting up her small chin with one long finger. "There's no reason for you to be scared, Gracie," he whispered, his low-timbred voice appealingly rough-edged. "Believe me."

Oh, she wanted to. But most of all, she wanted him to hold her close and allow her to hold him closely too so she could be sure he was safe and out of harm's way. Instead, his hands curved around her upper arms and he held her away from him as he reiterated, "You have no reason to be afraid. I'm here; Buster's here; you're perfectly safe."

"But . . ." she began, then her voice choked, and she lapsed into silence when he started out the porch door. She couldn't explain what she was feeling without revealing too much. *But he simply didn't understand the awesome power of the emotions that gripped her.* Like Dottie O'Donnell, she wasn't really afraid for herself. It was the well-being of the man she loved that she cared most about.

CHAPTER EIGHT

The following Monday was Daniel's birthday. Throughout the morning and afternoon Grace acted as if she didn't realize it was a special date, wondering if he would start dropping little hints. He never hinted even once, and she was able to maintain the element of surprise after they finished the more-elaborate-than-usual dinner she had prepared and she carried a freshly baked rum cake into the dining room. The one flickering candle in the center illuminated his astonished expression when she placed the cake in front of him.

"Surprise! Happy birthday, Dan."

"I . . . Gracie, you—"

"Wait, there's more," she gaily interrupted, taking three party hats from the antique mahogany sideboard behind his chair. She plopped a silly one on her head, then placed another on his, and swiftly took his picture with the Instamatic camera she had at the ready. Then she put the remaining hat on Buster's head and also took the dog's picture as the setter looked up at her with patient but rather confused brown eyes. "I didn't get a hat for Little Bit because cats aren't as willing to put up with a little nonsense as dogs are, and she does have needle-sharp claws. Now, you'd better make a wish and blow out the candle before there's wax all over the cake."

A pleased smile tugged up the corners of Dan's mouth

and reached his forest-green eyes in a warm glow of amusement while he paused an instant, then gently blew out the blue and orange flame.

Her gaze met his when he looked back up at her. "Make your wish?"

"Yes."

"What did you wish for?"

"Ah, you know I can't tell you that. It won't come true if I tell."

"I think that's an old wives' tale."

"Maybe you do, but I happen to be too superstitious to take any chances."

Softly laughing, she carelessly threw her hands up. "Be that way then. It's your right, I guess. After all, it *is* your birthday."

"How did you know that? I haven't mentioned it was coming up. Did Mom call today while I was out at the shop and tell you it was my birthday?"

"She didn't call. You did receive a package from her in the mail. But no one had to remind me of your birthday. I remembered."

"I wonder why, Gracie," he said, his tone deepening as he seemed to try to search out secrets in the depths of her gray eyes. "Does it mean something special that you remembered the date?"

Her heart skipped a beat or two. He was asking a question she didn't dare answer truthfully, fearing she would reveal too clearly her love for him. And to allow him to know how she felt would place her in a far too vulnerable position. "Well, I don't mean to disappoint you, but I always remember everybody's birthday," she replied evasively instead. "I have a terrific memory for dates."

"Do you?" he challenged, dark brows lifting. "Then tell me Allison's birthday."

"Uh . . . July twenty-sixth."

"Eric's?"

Grace only hesitated half a second. "November twen-

124

tieth." She shrugged. "There, you see, I'm just good at remembering dates. How about you? I bet you don't know when my birthday is."

"You lose your bet then. January twelfth. And I even remember what we did on your birthday two and a half years ago," he said, his voice nearly a whisper. "We went out to dinner and went dancing, then . . . you spent the night at my place. Do you remember that night, Gracie?"

Oh, she remembered all right, every heavenly moment she had shared with him, wildly in love, too naïve to be afraid to give freely. *Back in the old days before he had left her and she had learned to erect self-protection defenses against him.* And, for a frightening moment, she could feel those defenses slipping. With sheer will power she gathered them up again and turned away to take the dessert plates off the sideboard.

"I thought about inviting Allison and Eric over to help us celebrate, but they're always so negative about the shop, and I didn't want them to put a damper on your birthday," Grace murmured, ignoring his question as if he hadn't asked it. "Besides, we've both been working very hard the past few weeks, so I decided it would be better to have a quiet, relaxing evening."

Dan didn't reply. He simply watched the intriguing fluid movements of her slender hands while she placed the plates on the table and plucked the single white candle from the center of the glazed cake. Finally, he asked, "Why only one candle?"

She gave him a cheeky grin. "Heavens, Dan, it's not that big a cake. I couldn't possibly put a candle for every year on it. I'd have started a bonfire."

"A cruel thing to say," he muttered, pretending to be greatly hurt. "I see no reason for you to make remarks about my advancing age."

Still grinning, she served him a generous slice of rum cake. "Oh, try not to be depressed. After all, you're as young as you feel."

At that moment, as he looked at her lovely face, he felt about eighteen and as sexually impulsive as a boy that age. Desire stirred powerfully in him, and he wanted to pull her into his arms, ravish her with kisses, then carry her upstairs to stay the whole sweet night in his bed. But he was old enough, wise enough, to hold passion in check. He knew Gracie well. She was stubborn, and he realized he would ruin everything if he tried to rush her into intimacy before she was ready to resume that intense a relationship.

"How about that package from home?" he asked several minutes later as they slowly sipped the coffee she had served with the cake. "I think it's time to open it."

She shook her head. "You'll get your presents later, after we go to a movie in Knoxville that's getting great reviews. My treat. And since you're the birthday boy, I'll even let you get out of washing dishes. I'll do them. You just relax."

"No. You wash. I'll dry," he insisted, lithely rising to his feet when she pushed back her chair to get up too. Expertly, he gathered up coffee cups, saucers, and dessert plates, and with a nod of his head indicated she should precede him into the kitchen. He gave her one of his most winning smiles when she glanced back at him with some concern. Shaking his head, he chuckled. "Don't worry. Gran's china is perfectly safe with me. Remember? I told you I worked as a waiter to pay my way through under-graduate school, so I'm an old pro at this."

"Yes, a man of many talents," she said with a slow smile, proceeding to the sink, which she filled with hot, soapy water.

Three hours later, at almost eleven thirty, Grace and Dan returned home from Knoxville. "The critics certainly are right about that movie—it was hilarious," Daniel said, unlocking the front door. "I'm glad we didn't miss it."

"I thought we needed something comical right about now," she commented as they stepped together into the entrance hall. "I was getting tired of constantly wondering

126

what Compton and his thugs might try next, and it was nice to spend a couple of hours watching a crazy comedian's antics."

"Gracie, are you that worried?" he asked rather huskily, touching her left shoulder.

Faking a fairly convincing smile, she gave his hand a brief squeeze, then stepped back beyond his reach. "Let's forget about Compton. It's your birthday, and now it's time for you to open your presents. They're in my office; I'll get them. Be right back."

A couple of minutes later she returned to find Daniel in the parlor, relaxing on the sofa, hands clasped behind his head. She walked across the room to give him the package wrapped in brown paper, then perched herself on the edge of the opposite chair as he opened it and extracted two gifts, one wrapped in white, the other in blue. In the blue one he found a box of stationery, which he showed to Grace with a wry grin. "From my sister. Obviously Beth is hinting for me to write more often."

Grace watched as he unwrapped the gift wrapped in white, and when he lifted out a green crew-neck cashmere sweater that perfectly matched the color of his eyes, her eyes lighted with approval. "That's beautiful; it really is."

Dan nodded. "Mom loves to knit."

"She does lovely work," Grace said, taking the sweater he handed her and recognizing the perfection of the rows of loops and purls. Her fingertips caressed the fine cashmere. "I wish I could make something like this, but I'm afraid I've never been very good at knitting."

"You can't be good at everything," he said softly, smiling at her. "Your specialty's obviously dolls' clothes."

"I did try something different . . . for you . . . for your birthday," she said, handing him a gold foil box adorned with a green bow. She sat very still while he opened it.

Tiny indentations appeared in Daniel's cheeks as he smiled and lifted a green denim chef's-style apron. Emblazoned across the front in gold embroidered block letters was NATURE'S GARDEN CENTER, and beneath the wide left shoulder strap in script, Gracie had embroidered "Dan."

"Fantastic. Just the right touch," he murmured, looking over at her. "I like it very much. Thank you, Gracie."

"Better try it on," she advised, made suddenly uncertain by the mysterious unreadable light that appeared in his eyes. "I . . . it might not be a perfect fit. I had to guess at the measurements."

"I can't imagine why. If you don't know my measurements, who in the world would?" he countered mischievously as he got up to put the apron on. When Gracie stood before him, shaking her head with a frown, he playfully tweaked a strand of her hair. "Okay, Miss Perfection, what's wrong?"

"I made the shoulder straps too short, but I can let them out an inch or two."

"No problem, then. Did you make an apron for yourself?"

"Not yet. I wanted to get yours done first, since you'll be spending more time in the shop than I will. I thought I'd make a couple more for you if you really like it."

"As I said, I like it very much," he said, deep voice lowering as he bestowed a light kiss on her cheek. "What I'd like to know is how you managed to work on it without my seeing it."

"That's my secret. I might need to be sneaky again sometime." With a rather naughty, pleased-with-herself smile, she briefly touched his arm. "Now wait right here. There's one more surprise."

Awaiting her return after she strolled from the parlor, Dan took off the apron and folded it neatly, a faint smile lingering as he wondered what she was up to. He didn't have to wait long to find out. Only a couple of minutes later, Gracie carried in an unopened bottle of chilled champagne and two slender stemmed glasses.

"Would you open it?" she asked, handing over the bottle, then putting the glasses on the coffee table. "I'll go get you a piece of cake to go with the champagne if you like."

"After all the buttered popcorn I had at the movie, I think I'd better wait to have more cake until tomorrow," he said, chuckling. "I'd like to still be able to get that apron around me when we open the shop."

Grace sat down next to him on the sofa, watching while he removed the foil from around the neck of the bottle, then eased out the cork. Accompanying the muted pop, frothy bubbles rose up, spilled over a little, then subsided. He poured a generous amount of the sparkling effervescent wine into both glasses, handed one to Grace, and immediately took a sip from the other. Smiling, he nodded his approval.

"Delicious."

She smiled back. "Of course. Would I give you inferior champagne on your birthday? It's a special occasion."

"You've made it a very nice celebration."

"And a quiet one. But I thought you might enjoy something simple more than you would a party with a lot of guests."

"You thought right. I've enjoyed it being just the two of us," said Dan, his dark eyes holding hers. "There is just one more thing you could give me to make the evening perfect though."

"Oh? What?"

"A dance. We haven't danced for a long time," he quietly reminded her. Getting up, he walked over to put a long-playing record on the stereo, then came back to reach for her hands with a trace of a smile. "Dance with me, Gracie. You can't refuse. It's my birthday."

She never even considered whether or not her response was foolish. Setting her glass aside, she simply reacted to the warm, comfortable mood of the moment. She placed her hands in his, rose gracefully to her feet and glided into his arms just as the first soft strains of the music began. Through the side windows a gentle breeze wafted into the room, moving the lacy old-fashioned curtains and caressing Grace's bare arms. For several moments she unwittingly kept some distance between herself and Dan but felt so incredibly relaxed that she offered no objections when he drew her closer until their bodies were lightly touching.

"Now, I'm happy," he murmured very near her right ear. "Everybody should have a chance to dance on his or her birthday."

"Hmmm, and it's a lovely night for dancing, isn't it? Not too warm or too cool, just a perfect evening."

"And no animals to get under our feet with the dog and cat outside," Dan added wryly. "Who could ask for more?"

Who indeed. Grace certainly felt content, alone with him in the lamplit parlor. Outside the house were the faint natural noises of a country night. Inside, there was only the quiet ticking of the grandfather clock and the flow of the low music. Everything was peaceful. She could forget about Thad Compton and his threatening errand boys and allow herself to enjoy Dan's warmth. His tautly muscled thighs created a tingling friction brushing against the slender length of hers. The first musical arrangement on the record faded into another, one with a softer, more lazily romantic tempo. When Dan moved nearer, slipping his arms securely round her waist to cross his wrists over the small of her back, her own hands drifted up to rest upon his broad shoulders as they moved in perfect unison in time to the slow, sensuously throbbing beat. The heat of his large hands permeated her sheer georgette dress as her hands curved with feather-lightness around his smooth sunbronzed neck. She closed her eyes, caught up in the experience. He was right; it had been a long time, and she had missed dancing with him. He was superb, moving with an easy natural rhythm. Even when he swept her hair to one side and bent down to kiss the creamy skin near her nape, she had no desire to resist and merely leaned back slightly in his embrace, exposing the ivory column of her

130

neck to a continuing interwoven chain of that same kind of pleasurable little kisses. Her eyes flickered open again. She looked up into his face, saw his tender gaze. Was it calculated, a deliberate ploy to try to coax and charm her? She didn't think so and felt like losing herself in the forest-green depths of his mysterious eyes, unaware that hers were softly issuing a certain invitation. It seemed the most natural thing in the world to stretch up higher on tiptoe to touch her lips to his, to explore their firm sensual shape and texture and to seek a swift possessive response.

"Gracie," was all he was able to utter, sampling her honeyed taste for an instant before burying his face in her silken hair. His arms tightened around her. Her feminine warmth and the pliant contours of her slim yet deliciously curvaceous form moving sinuously against him inflamed his senses, but he exercised restraint as he held her fast, and they continued to dance.

Frequently, they exchanged kisses, each one deeper and longer-lingering. In love, Grace cherished his caressing hands moving over her back and hips and even the sides of her thighs sometimes. Intensifying heat spread throughout her, weakening her limbs, filling her soul with an abundance of warmth she needed to give to him. The clean male scent of him, the hardness of his long, lean body, and his very gentleness transcended all her uncertainties for a time. Her basic wariness of him had magically vanished. Although she didn't dare express it in words, she could only feel abiding love.

In the soft glow of the lamp, in the shadowy areas beyond its immediate reach, they moved in slow synchronization to the sultry music. Even after the record ended and the stereo turned off automatically, they stood enfolded in each other's arms, swaying together until at last Dan drew back slightly to look down at her. She looked back at him, her face appealingly small in its frame of shining dusky hair.

"Honey?" he whispered, his voice rough, his tone ques-

131

tioning. And as her lack of an answer seemed an answer in itself, he was enthralled by the very freshness of her skin and the inviting curving softness of her lips. Deep down inside, he felt he should call a halt, suspecting she wasn't truly ready to follow this path to its logical end. Yet the slight smile she gave him was his undoing. Suspicion burned to ashes in an explosion of inner fire, and with a muffled endearment he lowered her down upon the thick plush area rug in front of the cold stone fireplace. From the sofa he plucked a round throw pillow to place beneath her head. He knelt beside her. His narrowed gaze wandered over her, from her hair all the way down to her toes and up again, before his hands retraced that same route, resting here and there upon irresistibly feminine rounded flesh. He heard her breathing quicken and could almost imagine he felt sensations singing just beneath the surface of her skin. With the utmost care he raised her up just enough to allow him to lower the back zipper of her dress.

Cool air touched her bared skin but did nothing to diminish the wildfires raging in her. As he lowered her bodice down to drape around her trim waist then eased off her pale blue camisole also, she trembled with desire when his work-roughened fingertips grazed her midriff. Lost, hopelessly lost in love, she lifted her hands to run her fingers through his hair, then link them together over the nape of his neck. Slowly, provocatively, she pulled him toward her.

"Daniel," she breathed as he lightly probed the flesh rising just above the lacy cups of her bra. He touched and caressed, then sought the roseate circles darkening the summits of translucent fabric. Toying, he gently squeezed and rubbed, arousing firm-tipped buds. Swiftly unbuttoning his shirt, she slipped her hands inside and allowed them to roam freely over his lean flanks, broad back, and chest. Her parted lips found his. *"Daniel,* kiss me."

He did, many times, his tongue tangling with hers as she gave him back kiss for kiss. Sexual tension, coiled tightly in him, made him ache for release as their mutual desire increased in a crescendo of nearly intolerable sensation that tempted him to take her without any further torturing delay and caused a discernible tremor to flutter over her. He felt it and needed her even more than before.

In a dizzying instant he deftly unfastened the back hook of her bra, and that sheer garment joined her camisole on the area rug. Then he removed the tiny gold earrings she wore and the dainty gold chain around her neck, murmuring, "I don't want anything to get in my way."

She didn't want anything to get in his way either as he blazed a trail of hot nipping kisses across her shoulders and along the length of her neck, warm lips pausing on the hammering pulsebeat in her throat and the scented hollow just beneath. His warm breath tickled her inner ear as he turned her head from side to side to nibble at the lobes, and in response she played her fingers over and around his nipples.

He groaned. Then his mouth was closing around the peaks of her breasts, each in its turn, drawing deeply at ultrasensitive flesh, driving her crazy with his lips, his teeth, his tongue as his hands beneath her back arched her upward.

Grace wrapped her arms around his waist, but when he slid a hand beneath the elastic band of both her half-slip and panties, long fingers ranging down, ever downward across her abdomen, she tensed involuntarily. *What are you doing?* common sense shrieked, but she paid no heed. Primitive physical need and raw emotion superseded realistic logic. There was an aching hollowness in her, evoking a hunger only Dan could assuage. As much as he seemed to need her, she needed him, and she had gone too far to deny either of them the satisfaction they sought at this late moment. Loving him, wanting him with her whole heart, she tried to relax again. But the mind is not always easily conquered.

Dan sensed her tension and groaned inwardly, frustration building swiftly in him. As he had suspected, she wasn't yet ready for this. Perhaps she didn't consciously realize that herself, but he did, and much as he needed her, he wanted her to be able to give and take freely, eagerly, and without the possibility of subsequent regrets. When the right time came, he wanted it to be perfect for them. This wasn't the right time, and he forced himself to accept that fact. He pulled away from her.

"Get dressed," he commanded gruffly. "I should never have let this happen tonight."

Her eyes flew open, darkly bewildered as they met his. "But, Daniel, I want—"

"That's just the point. You don't know what you want, Gracie. I can tell."

"But—"

"You don't," he reiterated stonily without looking at her as he quickly buttoned up his shirt. And he caught her fingers in a viselike grip when she started to touch his face. He glanced at the clock, saw it was twelve fifteen, and smiled humorlessly. "And you don't have to be especially nice to me now. It's after midnight. My birthday's over."

"But, Daniel, that's not—"

"I wouldn't want you to wake up sorry in the morning," he continued as if she hadn't spoken, still not looking at her. "You might decide Buster and I should find another place to live. And we're beginning to feel at home here." He rose to his feet. "Speaking of Buster, I'd better go outside and see that she and the kitten have enough water for the rest of the night."

Stunned to silence, Grace watch him stride out of the parlor, out of her sight. Feeling numb, she slipped her arms back into her dress, suddenly embarrassed by her naked breasts and eager to cover them. Scooping up her bra, camisole, necklace, and earrings, she rushed out into the hall and up the stairs toward her room, biting her lower lip so hard that it hurt. The pressure of tears that needed to be shed gathered hotly behind her eyes as she

134

opened her door. She had offered everything of herself to Dan, and he had rejected her. She was a fool to love him. Of course, where he was concerned, that was nothing unusual—she had been a fool before. But she had survived her foolishness then. She would again this time.

Five minutes later Dan returned to the parlor. It was empty. Gracie had left, apparently to go to bed. Wishing like the devil he was in her bed with her, he walked over to refill his glass with champagne. He drank it slowly, hoping to relax and ease some of the frustration still roiling in him. When he went up to bed, he wanted to have some chance of falling asleep. He didn't relish the idea of lying awake half the night thinking of Gracie only a few doors down the hall from him.

About seven the next evening Dan left the small studio in downtown Knoxville where he had finished the three different commercials for Nature's Garden Shop that would be aired on local television. He had had a late appointment, during which twilight had enclosed the city. Overhead the sky was overcast. Only the lights in several nearby towering office buildings and a distant streetlamp seeped into the shadows of the sidewalk as he walked, hands in his trouser pockets, toward the adjoining parking lot, where his van and three cars were the only remaining vehicles. Less than ten feet from the van he suddenly stopped short, certain he had heard a noise behind him. He glanced back, saw nothing in the shadows, and continued on. Then he heard something move in front of him, and without further warning hands from behind him tried to catch hold of his wrists to wrench back his arms. He was too quick, too agile to be so easily caught. He spun around, resisting, his closed right fist glancing off a man who was nothing more than a vague silhouette. He struck out again, but fighting soon proved futile. There were two attackers at first, then three. Alone, Dan was no match for them. They pounced quickly, aiming their fists at him. He was able to ward off some of the blows but not all, and as they came at him from three sides, he was punched twice in the stomach and once in the face, just below his left eye. Then as suddenly as the assault had begun, it ended. Muttering unintelligibly, one of the assailants took off across the dark parking lot and his cohorts dashed madly after him. All of them quickly disappeared.

Leaning heavily against the side of the van, Daniel uttered an angry curse even as he tried to catch his breath. His expression grim, his thoughts grimmer, he spotted a pay phone and walked over to call the police, deciding he'd better report the incident, although he didn't expect his attackers to be caught. Everything had happened so fast, and it had been too dark for him to see the faces of the three men.

It was nearly eight thirty when Grace heard Dan drive in and park next to the farmhouse. Leaving her checkbook and the bills she was paying on the kitchen worktable, she went over to the stove to lift the cover off the simmering stew, and she was standing there stirring it when the screen door to the side porch opened and he stepped into the room.

"I didn't think the taping would take this long," she commented, then gasped as she turned around and saw Dan's torn shirt and the bruise high up on his left cheek. She rushed toward him, exclaiming, "What happened to you? You weren't forced off the road too? Are you all right?"

"It's nothing serious, Gracie," he assured her, laying his hands on her shoulders while she touched his chin to turn the left side of his face toward the light to see it better. "I didn't get run off the road. Just attacked in the parking lot next to the studio."

"Attacked? You mean mugged and robbed?"

"Not robbed. The men who jumped me didn't take anything. Just bounced me around a little. Another warning, I guess, an even less subtle one this time."

Some of the color had faded from Grace's cheeks, and disbelief mingled with worry in her eyes. "You think it *was* Compton's people, then? Oh, Dan, how far are they willing to go with this madness? I was appalled when someone deliberately forced Jim off the road. I even hoped whoever was responsible had nothing to do with Compton, that maybe it was just some fool looking for kicks. But now . . ." She shook her head. "They actually sent men to rough you up! Did you recognize them?"

"It was too dark and over so fast that I didn't get a glimpse of their faces."

"But you did call the police, didn't you?"

"Yes, and I went to the station where an officer made out a complete report. That's why I'm late."

"And?"

"And there's almost nothing the police can do in a situation like this. I certainly can't prove Compton or some of his people were issuing another little warning tonight. I can't even describe the three thugs who jumped me, except to say that two of them were about my size and the other was short and skinny. That didn't give the police much to go on."

"Three against one; how brave of them," she muttered, contempt briefly twisting her lips until she cautiously touched her fingertips to his bruised skin. Then she breathed a sigh of relief. "We're just lucky the three of them didn't hurt you worse than they did."

Dan's answering smile was contemptuous too. "They didn't act like they had much experience at working someone over. Mostly, they just piled on and threw punches then ran away."

"Not fast enough. That's a nasty bruise, and your skin's scraped. I'll get some antiseptic from the medicine cabinet."

"It can wait."

"But it must hurt."

"A little," he admitted, fingers tightening over her

137

shoulders when she started to turn away. "But right now, I'm more interested in food. It's been a long time since lunch, and I'm starving."

"That's a good sign then," she said, relaxing enough to give him a grin. "You can't be in too bad a shape if you can complain about having dinner late."

He grinned back. "That's stew I smell simmering. You think I'm going to let a bruise and a scrape keep me from that?"

They ate in the kitchen, talking now and then. After Daniel's second helping of his favorite stew, he folded his napkin and sat back in his chair with a nod. "Exactly what I needed. Gran made the best stew in the world, and yours tastes just like hers did."

"I certainly hope so. She had me memorize the precise ingredients," Grace wryly said, then looked past him out into space. "I wonder what she would have thought about this whole silly mess. Knowing her, she probably would've marched over to see Thad Compton and told him just what she thought of him. Sometimes, I'm very tempted to do that myself."

"So am I, but we both know he'd only deny everything, and the harassment wouldn't stop." Dan leaned forward again, elbows on the table, steepled fingers supporting his chin. He looked long and hard at her, somberness etching his features. "Gracie, after what happened to Jim the other day and me tonight, I have to offer you the chance to get out of this entire situation. With the shop nearly finished and the greenhouse already going up, I thought about getting a loan to buy out your half of the business but—"

"You're kidding!" Grace's widening gray eyes pinioned his. She shook her head. "No way. I'm not about to chicken out and sell my half of—"

"Whoa, wait a minute. I *thought* of offering to buy you out, but that wouldn't solve the problem. The shop would still be on your property—you'd still be involved. So maybe we should seriously consider dropping the whole thing and stop building right now."

His suggestion stunned her to utter silence for an instant, reawakening that old dread with a vengeance. Was he looking for a reasonable excuse to take off again? She'd known all along he might go eventually but not this *soon*. Just when she was becoming deeply involved with him again, he had to pull this on her. Resentment born of pain flared hot in her.

"I can't believe you," she declared. "I thought you'd at least wait until the shop was finished and we'd opened it before you decided to hit the road again. You're—"

"*You're* jumping to conclusions," he cut in impatiently, his words as clipped as hers had been. "Did I say anything about leaving?"

"You seem eager enough to give up all our plans. If you don't want to leave, how can you even think of giving up, just because some troublemakers are causing us a few problems? I think you just must be bored with the whole business and ready to go on to something else."

"You think wrong, then, because boredom has nothing to do with it. Good God, Gracie, I'm worried about . . . safety. Look at my face. I didn't get these scrapes and bruises by accident. And who knows what might happen next. To you . . . or me."

She felt a sudden pang of intense guilt. She hadn't been attacked tonight. He had and could have been severely injured. The very thought terrified her and made her realize he had justification for suggesting what he had. Still, after going this far with the shop, she couldn't quit now. The only thing she could do was offer him a way out.

"I'm sure getting beat up wasn't any fun. I wish it hadn't happened. But I can't give up on the shop. I'll get a loan and buy out your half."

"Dammit," he muttered, scowling, "you've missed the point. I'm worried about your safety. You'd better think this over carefully. You're in danger too."

139

"Me? But nobody's threatened me personally, so why should you think someone might?"

"Because these people obviously have few scruples, and to them, you're fair game."

"But—"

"And you're a woman. Maybe you can be tough as nails sometimes, but they probably don't realize that," Dan continued relentlessly. "The point is you *look* fragile and very vulnerable, which might make them think you'd be a perfect victim of harassment."

Grace's chin jutted up and out a fraction of an inch. Determination flashed in her eyes. "I'm not going to be anybody's victim, and I'm not going to give up the shop."

A muscle worked rhythmically in Dan's tight jaw. "Then we're going to have to be more careful. I'm laying down a few laws. You can't be here in the house alone at night, and you can't go out alone either. You might be willing to court danger, but I'm not willing to let you. Is that perfectly clear?"

"Dan, this is a little ridiculous. I won't be a prisoner in my own—"

"Will you be quiet for a minute and stop trying to act so damned independent," he growled, his words more a command than a request. "You can't fool me, Gracie. Your eyes have always betrayed you, and even if you deny it a million times, I can see you're at least a little scared. Maybe you'd better think this over a few days."

"I don't need to. My mind's made up. But if you want to sell your half—"

"Forget it. We're in this together."

Relief surged over her. He was going to stay, a while longer anyway. "We won't let them defeat us, Dan," she said softly. "In the end we're going to beat them. I know we can."

"I think so too. And if you understand how serious the situation is, I'm willing to keep going."

"Good thing, I have to go through with this now," she

140

confessed after a long moment of silence. Hoping to inject some humor in the somber discussion, she comically grimaced. "I . . . Just this afternoon, two of my clients who own businesses in Alpine Springs called to say they no longer need my services as an accountant. Now, we *have* to make a go of the business."

The oath Dan uttered beneath his breath was blistering and explicit. "Do you think you'll lose the rest of your clients too?"

"No, I don't think so, because the two who called today both have mortgages with First American Bank, which explains everything. They were pressured to drop me. But my other client in town has been in business over thirty years and paid off his mortgage long ago. He owns everything free and clear. And I don't think my dairy farmers would drop me just on Compton's say-so. They're very independent and they knew Gran. I'm not too worried about them."

Dan shook his head. "I'm sorry I got you into this mess."

"You didn't get me into anything. I decided I wanted in, and I don't plan to ever back out. But . . . are you really sure you don't want to?"

"I'm sure." His darkening gaze traveled slowly over her face. "It's beginning to seem like you and me against the world—at least against almost everybody in Alpine Springs. Doesn't it?"

"Yes, I guess it does," she whispered, laying her hand over his closed fist upon the tabletop. In a way, she felt closer to him than she ever had.

CHAPTER NINE

Later, after tossing and turning in her bed for nearly an hour, unable to get to sleep, Grace flung back the light covers. She got up, thrusting her feet into heelless slippers and stalked, frustrated and disturbed, out of her room. At the head of the stairs she paused, seeing the light seeping out from beneath Dan's door. Either he was awake too or had fallen asleep reading, and after a moment's hesitation she decided not to risk disturbing him if he was indeed sleeping. She padded down the steps, heading for the kitchen to make a cup of hot cocoa.

Twenty minutes later she went back upstairs again, feeling a bit more relaxed than she had been. Dan's light was still on, and she found herself fretting about him. Before he had retired to his room at about ten thirty, she had noticed him stroking his temples as if his head hurt. She turned down the hall toward her room, stopped abruptly, and spun around to glide noiselessly back to his. It wouldn't hurt for her to peek in on him, and if she discovered he was asleep, she would feel reassured. Quietly as a mouse, she opened Daniel's door.

"Something wrong, Gracie?" he asked, smiling as she jumped at the unexpected sound of his voice. Propped up against pillows at the head of the carved maple bed, he closed the book he held in his lap on one finger to keep his place. He looked at her steadily. "You didn't hear any strange noises outside, did you? I haven't heard any."

"Me . . . either. I just . . ."

"Can't you sleep? Try reading. That usually helps."

"I know, but it didn't work for me tonight." Stepping farther into his room, she wrapped the lightweight white duster that matched her gown more securely around her. "But I expected you to be asleep by now. What's the matter? Have a headache?"

"No, I'm fine."

"I never did put anything on that scrape of yours. Did you?" When he shook his head, she left him to go to the hall bathroom, returning quickly with a bottle of ethyl alcohol and a sterile cotton ball. She walked over to sit down on the edge of his bed next to him, trying to ignore his bare tanned torso and wandering gaze as she unscrewed the bottle and soaked the cotton in the chilly fluid. She winced for him as his quickly indrawn breath whistled between his teeth when she swabbed his cheek. Then she tossed the cotton ball into the nearby wastepaper basket. "There you go; you should be just fine now."

"I imagine I'll have quite a shiner by morning."

"I know," she whispered, very gently touching the darkening skin beneath his left eye. "My poor honey."

"You haven't called me honey for a long time," he murmured, catching her fingers in his, drawing them down to his lips to kiss each tip. "I think it's worth a black eye to hear you say it again."

Smiling, she lightly rubbed the tiny scar close to the corner of his mouth. "You know, you never did tell me how you got this."

"No, I didn't." He glanced away. "And I'd rather not discuss it now either."

"Why?" she asked, studying the strongly drawn contours of his face. "Does it upset you to think about it?"

"Let's just say it brings back painful memories."

"Maybe you should tell me, then. Sometimes it helps to talk."

"It might, I guess," he conceded, looking back at her, his expression a mystery. "All right, I'll tell you the whole sad story. It was a painful accident. I turned my tricycle over and landed on our cement driveway when I was three."

"You devil, that's not true and I know it," she admonished, seeing the laughter leap up in his eyes and having to fight back a responsive smile. "You probably don't even remember being three years old. So what really happened?"

"Would you believe I walked too close to the high school cheerleaders once while they were doing high kicks and was permanently scarred by the toe of a black and white oxford shoe?"

Grace had to laugh. "No, I don't believe a word of that either. Why don't you try telling the truth?"

"Because I like teasing you," he replied with an unabashed grin. "And being a man of mystery is sort of exciting."

"Then you're never going to tell me?"

"Oh, I might . . . someday if you're very persuasive."

"What can I do to persuade you later if I can't persuade you now? Never mind. Forget I asked," she said, wryly shaking her head as he slowly looked her over from head to toe with theatrically wicked intent. When he chuckled, she smiled indulgently at him. "For a man who's just been attacked, you're in a great mood."

He gave her a wink. "Why shouldn't I be, with a nurse like you? You have a terrific bedside manner."

"And you're a very frisky patient, obviously feeling well enough to take care of yourself," she answered with exaggerated primness, starting to stand. "So I'm going off duty now and back to bed."

"But will you sleep?" he questioned, one arm gliding across her midriff to hold her still. "You wouldn't be up

144

right now if you were able to fall asleep, but you never told me why you couldn't."

"No particular reason." Her shoulders rose and fell in a slight shrug. "Too much on my mind, I guess: all the vandalism and veiled threats, what happened to Jim and . . . you."

Lean fingers moved soothingly over her ribcage, warm through the thin layers of her duster and gown. His slow smile was reassuring. "At least I was able to tape our commercials before getting a black eye."

"Oh, that's right, the commercials! After seeing that bruise and your torn shirt, I forgot all about asking you how the tapings went."

"Smoothly. But I still agree with Jim—you should have done them with me."

"Easy for you to say. Things like that don't make you nervous. They do me, and I wouldn't have been very effective on television with a quavery voice and terror showing in my eyes."

"It wouldn't have been that bad. I would have been there with you. Wouldn't that have helped a little?"

"Not unless you could hypnotize me." Covering the large hand curved round her waist with her own, she eased it away. "Well, good night, Dan. I'd better get to bed."

"Not yet," he whispered, capturing her in encircling arms. "Stay awhile longer."

"But . . ." Her voice faltered. Suddenly, teasing amusement had vanished from his eyes to be replaced by a fiery yearning that made her pulses race. "But we both need to get some sleep."

"Needing sleep and being able to get it are two different things," he said softly, his compelling gaze never wavering. "And we're both too wound up to go to sleep yet, so we might as well be awake together. We can talk."

"Talk . . . about what?"

"Anything. Everything. About how beautiful your hair is, falling down around your shoulders." Touching a wayward tendril, he pulled her toward him. "About how lovely you are."

"Dan, I—"

"Hush. Come here."

And when his fingertips brushing over the side of her neck scorched the surface of her skin, she went, unable to stem the tide of love surging up from the depths of her soul. Her hands grazed over his chest; she felt hard muscle ripple and tilted back her head to accept his first tenderly coaxing kiss. Her lips parted to the slowly graduating pressure of his, then nudged and caressed and toyed with them until a low groan rose from his throat. Excitement flew in sharp-tipped arrows through her, and she audibly caught her breath as his tongue pushed possessively into her mouth, touching, tasting, tantalizing the receptive nerve endings of her own. And the tip of her tongue fluttered against the undersurface of his, inviting him to tighten his embrace. She felt the awesome power of his arms' flexing muscles pressing against her back and found sweet delight in his physical strength as she laced her fingers over the nape of his neck and her breasts yielded to the hard plane of his chest.

Her cushioned flesh straining against him fuelled the fires of passion he had been trying to bank for too long. And she merely fanned the flames when the tip of her tongue scampered over his lips, playing around each corner of his mouth over and over and over until he could stand it no longer and retaliated, his even teeth nipping at her soft lips, his own exploring their bow shape. He wanted to drain every drop of sweet essence from her lovely mouth.

He didn't have to take anything from her. She was more than willing to give. Caught up in waves of erotic pleasure made real and pure by the sheer force of her love, she breathed a soft sound as his hands ranged over her arching back to the rounded curve of her bottom. Eyes closed, she danced fingertips over his finely carved face, tracing his eyebrows, feathering the ends of his thick lashes, stroking the bridge of his nose and his cheekbones and the sensuous shape of his firm mouth. He caught the end of her index finger between his teeth and gently bit it. Trembling, she moved her hand to curve it around the powerful column of his neck and kissed him again.

His lips hardened, ravishing the soft texture of hers as a hot aching built deep inside him, threatening to erupt in a lava flow of passion neither of them would be able to halt. Cradled in his arms, lying across his lap, she had become all femininely acquiescent, and he longed to take what she seemed to be offering him. For an agonizing instant, he hesitated, then feathered the palm of one hand over her tight uprising breasts.

"Gracie, I can't keep my hands off you," he groaned. "You're warm, so warm."

"You . . . are too," she whispered back, thrilled and even more aroused by his impassioned tone. Snuggling closer to him, she rubbed the heel of one hand slowly across his broad chest, then gently rubbed the hard nub of his left nipple between her thumb and forefinger, feeling the violent shudder that rambled over him and then his sudden tension.

"God, do you know what you're doing to me?" he uttered, stiffening to push her away from him. "Gracie, you'd better know what you're doing, because if this goes on any longer, I might not be able to let you go, whether you want us to make love or not. I think you should go back to your room if you're not sure what you want yet."

Her eyes opened slowly. She saw the enticing ember-glow glinting in his. For a long moment she lay in his arms looking at him. Then she rose up, lowered her feet to the floor, and stood up next to the bed, her gaze still fixed on him as she asked, "You're sure your head doesn't hurt?"

"How the devil should I know?" he snapped, raking a burning gaze over her. "And right now, who cares?"

"I do. It doesn't still hurt?"

147

"*No*, dammit."

"Well then . . ." A faint sensuous smile flitting over her lips, she shrugged the cotton duster off her shoulders, then removed it slowly,. her movements deliberately provocative, her eyes searching his. Without any doubts whatsoever, she knew she didn't want to go back to her lonely bed. She wanted to stay with Dan; she knew she was where she belonged when she was with him. Her robe fell to the floor around her feet silently. Boldly, she stepped closer to the bed. "I . . . don't want to go to my room. I'd rather spend the night in here . . . with you."

His answering smile promised heaven. Flipping back the corner of the light covers, he reached for her right hand, then drew her down upon the mattress next to him, leaning over her as he pulled the top sheet up over both of them. He touched her cheek. "You're sure about this, Gracie?"

"Yes."

"But you said—"

"I changed my mind."

"Why?"

"Ummm, because you're too sexy to resist."

"You only want my body?"

"I want you, your strength, your . . ." She might have said "love," for that was what she truly wanted. Maybe he would never be able to give it, but if by some wondrous chance he could someday, she wanted him to give it freely, without any prompting from her. And in that moment it wasn't necessary for him to adore her; she knew he cared, and she felt so close to him that it was enough for her to give her love. "I want your tenderness. And all your passion."

Searching her face, he stroked back her hair. "And in the morning?"

She made her smile sultry. "Oh, I'll probably want you again then too."

"Or will you be sorry this happened?"

148

"I doubt it. You never disappointed me in the past."

"You can be such a delightfully brassy vixen," he whispered, brushing the ball of his thumb back and forth across her lips. "And sweet and warm and a little vulnerable. No wonder I can't leave you alone. Gracie, I need you so much."

"Show me," she challenged, curving one hand over the back of his head to bring his lips down upon the waiting fullness of hers.

He dropped down beside her. His arms went around her waist. Swiftly, he pulled her over above him, his mouth capturing hers. He turned again, and the evocative weight of his body pressed her down in the center of the soft bed. Her long shapely legs parted slightly to the pressure of his knee, and he released her lips to trace the dainty shape of her ear with the tip of his tongue, murmuring, "Remember the night we . . ."

His deep voice rumbling intimate words thrilled her, heightened anticipation, and brought a smile to her lips. She felt so right with him. Two years ago they had shared all the pleasures of intimacy; their knowledge of each other had been complete; then they had drifted apart for a while. Now, it was time to know each other again. It was meant to be. He was so special to her and made her feel that she was nearly as special to him. During the past few weeks he had once more become such a vital part of her life that she could no longer pretend she didn't want to resume a sexual relationship with him. She did. She was a normal, healthy young woman in love and he . . . He was Dan, and no other man had ever come close to making her feel as alive as he did.

Turning her head aside on the pillow, she silently invited the tingling touch of his lips upon her neck. As he encircled the throbbing pulse in her throat with kisses, her arms wound around him, her fingertips inscribing arousing scrolls on the smooth taut skin of his naked back.

"Gracie," he uttered roughly. "You're not just feeling

149

sorry for me, are you, because I got pushed around a little tonight?"

Grabbing a fistful of his hair, she playfully tugged at it. "What do you think?"

"I think that was the dumbest question I've ever asked," he admitted, raising his head to gaze down at her somewhat sheepishly. "I know you better than that. And besides, even if this was just an offer of sympathy sex, I think it's too late to stop now."

"I *know* it is."

A lazy smile exuding sensuality touched his firmly shaped mouth. Warm green eyes roamed over her face. "I may not let you get much sleep tonight."

"Promise?"

He softly laughed, then cupped her jaw in one hand as his mouth descended to take possession of hers again. The lush ripeness of her slender responsive body negated all the frustrations he had experienced since moving into her house. Brushing the straps of her gown aside, he nuzzled the contours and hollows of her shoulders. "You don't know how many nights I've been tempted to break into your room and ravish you."

"But you have more finesse than that. You're no macho marauder. Good thing too, because I would have fought you tooth and nail."

"You're not fighting now."

"This is different. You're seducing me, and I like it. Seduce me some more."

"I'm not sure who's seducing whom," he said gruffly and meant it, for her small hands floated up and down along his sides, making muscles tense and ripple and generating an electriclike current that pulsed powerfully through him, stimulating every nerve and shaking him to the very core. She was such a mesmerizing intriguer. Every time he thought he really knew her, she revealed yet another mystery he couldn't quite solve, as if she always kept at least one secret. Two years ago he had believed she was too straitlaced and cautious to go away with him. But, by going into business with him, she had proved she was willing to take risks. And tonight, after weeks of holding him at arm's length, she had become a temptress, eager and more than willing to recapture the ecstasy they had once found with each other. Would he ever figure her out completely? He had his doubts. But she was the most unforgettable woman he had ever known, and he needed her more than he'd ever needed anyone else in his whole life.

Transfixed by his strange unreadable gaze, she touched his chin. "Wh-why are you looking at me like that?"

A slow smile was his only answer. He could keep a secret or two of his own. Wordlessly, he plied the corners of her mouth with too-brief, teasing kisses, repeating the process until she breathed his name and her lips opened with the fresh softness of a flower to his.

In soft golden light, they began to come together as one again. Kisses lingered. Caresses aroused sensual tension to a fever pitch. She threaded her legs between his, feeling his forcefully potent response, glorying in it. His hand over the curve of her hips arched her closer against him.

"Honey," she whispered.

"Say that again," he commanded huskily, then implored, "please."

"Daniel . . . *honey*."

His hands glided upward along her thighs, raising the hem of her gown, finally baring her midriff and breasts and pulling the garment off over her head. He tossed it aside. Then he slipped his thumbs beneath the waistband of her panties and removed those next. Her satiny skin shimmered pearlescently, and his wandering gaze explored every inch. He touched her warm firm breasts and bent down to kiss a luscious peach-tinted tip and its mate: then the shallow hollow of her navel. "Lovely," he uttered against her fluttering flesh. "Do you know how many times I've dreamed of you like this?"

151

"You have me at a disadvantage, sir," she said, her voice unsteady. Reaching out, she untied the waist of his pajama bottoms, pushing them down and smiling when he obligingly stood to shed the pants completely. His skin was like burnished copper in the lamplight. Her own gaze roamed everywhere, taking in the breadth of his chest, his tapered waist and lean hips, and his long legs, subtly muscled and strong. She lifted her arms toward him, inviting him back into bed.

Flinging the covers out of the way toward the foot of the bed, he rejoined her, clasping her to him with one arm while claiming her lips, tasting the honeyed moistness of her mouth. He whisked her away in a whirlwind of quickening sensations and swirled, himself, in soaring desire. With his hands, fingertips, and lips, he worshiped her, touching her with the lightness of whispers everywhere they traced and caressed. With his tongue he etched patterns of fire on her creamy skin. With his teeth he nibbled and charted the hills and plains of her spellbinding body.

She was as daring, exploring him with an eagerness that delighted them both. Her lips dallied with his. Her tongue teased and aroused. Fascinated by his face, his arms, his legs, the very line of his strong back, she wanted to continue holding him forever.

"Gracie, yes," he groaned as her hands grazed down over the flat of his abdomen, her touch becoming more intimate. He parted her thighs, fingers brushing upward, caressing.

As he touched her there and continued the touching, she pressed the tips of her nails against the muscles of his shoulders, lost in pleasure. Her other hand moved over him, and she felt smooth rigidity surge against her stroking palm. She made a soft sound, moving ecstatically while he explored her physical femininity, then sought her ultimate inner warmth and released a torrent of longing centrally within her. Her legs parted wider.

Their eyes met. He kissed her, excited by her fervent

response and the sweet clinging of her tenderly shaped lips to his. He possessed her mouth insistently but not roughly because he wanted to be gentle, though the promise conveyed by her hands made restraint more difficult with each passing second. At last his strict self-control snapped. He swept her directly beneath him, supported himself on his elbows above her, and ran his fingers through the hair fanned out upon the pillow, capturing her lambent gaze. "I can't wait any longer, Gracie."

"No, don't wait," she whispered, breath catching. "Love me now."

His thighs pressed down, urging hers to open more. She drew her knees up, but as he throbbed potently against her, she tensed a little, and he understood that tension. Two years is a long time. Tonight was like a brand-new beginning. Poised above her, he smiled indulgently and trailed kisses across her cheeks toward her lips.

"Relax," he coaxed, his deep voice a soothing caress. He felt the tightness begin to ease out of her body again. "Try to relax."

She curved her hands over his buttocks urging him closer until the pressure of him against her increased. "Daniel, I want you to . . ." Her words ended in a joyous gasp as, with a tenderly swift penetrative thrust, he entered, filling her warmth that flowered open to receive him. That wondrous feeling of flesh meeting flesh made her tremble then tingle all over as his hard body merged completely with her own, filling the very emptiness he had induced in her.

Watching her face, he was still, his breath nearly taken away by the sensuousness that glowed in her features and in the darkest depths of her gray eyes. "Honey, you feel so wonderful," he murmured, skipping a fingertip across her lips. "It's good to be back with you like this again."

And it was good to have him back. Somehow, tonight, she had felt it would be. For some reason all her uncertainties had subsided; loving him and the proper giving of her love had seemed all that mattered. She laid her fingers against his lean cheeks then wound her arms and legs around him. "Daniel," she whispered, kissing him slowly once, then again and again until he began to move inside her, deeply, and she met each of his unhurried rousing strokes.

Together they created a misty exclusive world only a caring man and woman can share. Unaware of individual movements, they soared up from level to higher level of exquisite sensation, their hunger for each other too all-prevailing to allow either of them to slow the mounting urgency of their reunion. Soon, Grace cried out softly, suspended on the finely honed pinnacle of sheerest bliss before tumbling down into incredible fulfillment, feeling his release within her, holding him close, having to bite back the words of love that rose emotionally in her throat.

Dan arched her nearer, groaning her name as completion overtook him in a tumultuous rush more intense than he had ever experienced. The sheer force of it momentarily drained much of his strength, and he was so relaxed in Gracie's embrace he feared his weight was crushing her. He turned onto his back, drawing her to his side.

For several long moments they lay silently together, legs still entwined as their hearts began beating more normally once more and their breathing slowed. Gracie's head rested on his shoulder, and his long fingers played with her tousled hair. He shifted slightly so he could look down at her face. Heightened rose color flushed her cheeks, and her parted lips were curved into a faint smile. He tapped the end of her nose.

"Aren't you going to say 'welcome home'?"

She laughed up at him. "I think that's what I just did, don't you?"

"I guess you did," he conceded, chuckling. "And a very nice welcome it was, too."

There was a sudden near-painful catch in the center of her chest. With all her heart, she wanted to tell him how

154

much in love she was again. Yet, pride held her honesty back. He had left her once, hurt her, and if she ever spoke words of love again, he would have to speak them first. She didn't regret tonight. Nothing would ever make her regret what they had shared, yet she was still not free to reveal the depth of her emotions to him. Someday, perhaps . . .

"Well, are you going to throw me out of your bed now?" she asked as lightly as she possibly could. "Force me to go back to my own room?"

"Don't even try to leave," he warned. "You're not going anywhere."

"Ummm, good. I'm too lazy to move anyhow," she softly said, but as she reached back to turn off the lamp on the table next to her side of the bed, her wrist was quickly imprisoned in his fingers.

"Not so fast, lady," he teasingly growled, skimming his other hand over her breasts. "It's been two years, and that's a very long time. We have a lot of making up to do, and I told you I wasn't going to let you get much sleep tonight. I haven't changed my mind about that."

"Sex maniac," she accused, almost giggling as he briefly tickled her ribs.

"*Yes,*" he admitted with an unabashed grin. "With you, I am." He raised her knees, moved between them, and proceeded to fringe nibbling kisses over the sensitized skin of her inner thighs. He heard the quick pleasured intake of her breath, felt her fingers tangle tightly in his hair, and triumphantly smiled.

The next morning Grace awakened to discover a strange heaviness lying around her waist, yet it felt strange only for an instant. Before she could fully drag herself up out of sleep and open her eyes, she knew it was Dan's arm around her. She turned beneath its weight to snuggle against him. Memories of the night sent a thrill through her, and she lifted a hand to cup Dan's jaw. A day's growth of beard roughened his skin, but she enjoyed rubbing her fingertips over the light stubble.

Daniel's eyes slowly opened. He blinked once or twice, then lazily smiled, his arm around her waist gently squeezing as he grazed his lips across her forehead.

"Morning," he murmured, his low-timbred voice still husky with sleep. "I thought you wouldn't wake up until very late after—"

"You didn't close your shades. The light woke me, I guess." She carefully touched his left cheekbone. "That black eye makes you look a little rakish. Hurt much?"

He faked a terrible groan. "Excruciating. You're going to have to do something to help take my mind off the pain. What time is it?"

"I'm not sure; early, I think." She turned her head to look at the clock on the bedside table. "Good heavens, it's not even six o'clock yet."

"Ummm, then we have plenty of time."

"Oh, no!" she resisted, laughing when he started to kiss her. "Daniel Logan, control yourself. We have work to do today."

"Ah, but we're self-employed. We can take the day off if we want to. And I do. I plan to keep you in this bed for the next several hours."

"But, Dan," she started to say before his lips descended on hers, and her words of protest were silenced and soon forgotten.

A light thump on the foot of the bed and an accompanying plaintive meow immediately drew their attention. The calico kitten had nudged open the door, which had been left open a couple of inches, and she loped over the sheet Dan had drawn up to cover them in the early morning hours. Purring, she started to curl up in the small space left between them.

"No way, cat," Daniel declared, scooping the kitten up in one gentle hand. "We just don't have time for you now."

"But she's been in all night; she might need to go out," Grace reminded him. "And she could be hungry too."

Daniel sighed. Getting out of the bed, he slipped into a short terry cloth bathrobe, picked up Little Bit, and strode to the door. He looked back at Gracie. "I'll take care of her and Buster. You just make sure you stay right here."

Less then ten minutes later, when he returned to his room, Gracie had vanished. He walked down the hall, but the bathroom was empty and her door was open. She wasn't there either. But he knew. A smile tugged at the corners of his mouth. It was a game they had played before, in his old apartment, never in this house. She was hiding somewhere, waiting for him to find her, but there were so many rooms here, it might take him some time. But find her he would. And when he did . . .

Downstairs, Grace tiptoed across the dining room, clutching her sheer cotton duster around her. She loved this game, always had. *The thrill of the chase.* She would run and hide; he would pursue and eventually discover her hiding place. But she had never made it easy for him and didn't ever intend to. She stopped, stood quite still, listening, though she knew he could move quietly as a tiger. He could very well be right behind her. She spun around. He wasn't there. Excitement accelerated her heartbeat. She opened the door to the kitchen, found it empty, and silently sped through the room to the other door, which opened to the long hall. Her back to the wall, she eased her way to the parlor, looked in. He wasn't there either, and she darted inside. She knew every nook and cranny of this house. He didn't. Would it really be fair to take advantage? Yes, she decided. *All's fair.* She dashed over to squeeze herself into the narrow space between the grandfather clock and the east wall.

A minute or so later she heard the creak of a wooden floorboard as Daniel stepped into the room. Holding her breath, she perked up her ears, listening carefully, hearing him move toward the windows that looked out over the veranda and front lawn. She made her move. Easing out of her hiding place, she darted toward the double doors, gasping when he reacted with swift precision to grasp the back of her robe. Stopped short, she spun around to face him, wrenched her robe free, and backed away. Her heart skipped several beats as she met his supposedly relentless gaze, although she knew it was only a game.

"So," he muttered, one long stride bringing him close to her. "You thought you could escape?"

She bowed her head, curtsied, and fought to suppress a smile. "Oh, m'lord, have mercy. I'm just an innocent country girl."

"A country girl, perhaps. Hardly innocent after last night," he intoned villainously, reaching out to strip off her robe and bare her naked body to his theatrically raking gaze. His hands moved toward her. "And I shall have you again. Come here, my lovely wench."

She turned and ran. Before she reached the second step of the stairs, he caught her, one arm darting round her waist to pull her back, curving her body to the length of his. Sweeping her up, he cradled her against him and kissed her when he reached the landing. Their lips met and their irrepressible laughter intermingled. He carried her back to his bed, put her down, and came down beside her.

"You're mine," he declared imperiously. "Mine and mine only. You understand?"

"M'lord," she pretended to gasp, playing the game. Yet she understood better than he did that his word, spoken in jest, had been in actuality the truth. She was his, irrevocably, because she chose to be.

158

CHAPTER TEN

Saturday morning Daniel returned from the shop and strode into the kitchen, where Grace was still sipping her coffee. "That was fast. You just went out," she commented. "Forget something?"

"No. Had to come back to call the sheriff," he told her, tight-lipped as he went over to the wall phone. "All our paint and wood stain was stolen out of the shed last night."

"Dammit," she uttered hoarsely, replacing her cup in its saucer with an angry clatter. Watching him swiftly dial a number, she heaved a sigh of frustration, lifting a hand to her neck. Her throat was scratchy; her head ached a little, and she was certainly in no mood for this sort of aggravation. She was sick of the harassment. If only there was some way to make it stop . . .

Finishing his call, Dan joined her at the table and poured himself another cup of coffee. He took a hearty swallow. "A deputy's on his way."

Grace nodded, her expression both angry and bewildered. "The shed was locked, so they had to break in and must have made some noise, but why didn't Buster bark?"

"Sometimes she takes off after a rabbit. Maybe she wasn't around when it happened," Dan said, then added with dark humor, "or maybe these people have made friends with her. They're out here often enough for her to be used to them by now."

Grace sighed again. "Aren't these idiots ever going to leave us alone?"

"Maybe after we open the shop they'll realize we're very serious about our business and give up. If they don't, we may have to consider taking legal action against them, which won't be easy unless we can find some way to prove exactly who they are."

"If we do find proof, I'd hate to get involved in a court-room battle right when we're trying to build up the business."

"What other choice would we have, Gracie? We would have hired a lawyer already if we could prove who's responsible for harassing us," Dan declared, unyielding determination overlying his features. "Neither of us is willing to let outsiders interfere in our lives, are we?"

There was only one answer to that question. A resounding no.

A few minutes later a deputy arrived to inspect the jimmied lock on the door of the shed. After calling in on his car radio for a man to come out to dust for fingerprints, he talked to Grace and Dan a few moments while jotting down notes.

"There's really very little to tell you, Deputy Gaines," Dan finished. "Neither of us saw or heard anything unusual last night. All we know is that the cans of paint and wood stain we bought for the interior of the shop were in here last evening. This morning, they're gone."

Bobbing his head up and down, the deputy started to walk around to the far side of the shed. "Wish I could tell you folks we'll be able to recover your property, but . . . Well, we might, I guess, if we hear about somebody trying to sell the stuff cheap."

Grace and Dan looked at each other.

"More likely, they'll find everything spilled along a roadside somewhere," Dan murmured, and when she nodded agreement, he lifted a hand to touch her hair, his green eyes solemn. "I think it's time for us to pay a little visit to Thad Compton, don't you?"

"Maybe that's not such a bad idea."

"Could help. Can't hurt—we're not making any progress like this. We'll go see if he's in his office today as soon as Deputy Gaines goes."

Forty minutes later they passed through Alpine Springs, and about a quarter mile into the southern outskirts, Dan turned the van off the road onto a large paved parking lot. Compton's Garden Center and Landscaping occupied nearly four acres of rolling land upon which stood a vast inventory of trees and shrubs, their roots balled in burlap. To the left was a building housing earthmoving equipment, and in the center was the main shop, a low-slung white brick edifice with marble front pillars. Recently built to replace the original shop, it was modern in design, and its exterior seemed to scream "outrageously expensive." Dan parked. Next to him in the passenger seat, Grace shook her head and laughed softly.

"It's really ridiculous, you know," she said, flipping her palms up in a confused gesture. "Look at this place. It's grand. And it's not just a garden shop. Thad Compton has the resources to bid for state projects, like roads. He has no reason to worry about competition from us. It just doesn't make any sense to me."

"Why don't we go in to talk to him and see if he can make some sense of it?" suggested Daniel, getting out of the van to walk around and open her door.

Inside the garden center a few customers browsed around, checking out displays of seeds or examining potted house plants. At the counter Dan asked the clerk if Mr. Compton was in and received a quick nod in answer.

"Good. We'd like to see him, please."

The young man glanced up from the cash register tape he was removing to replace a new roll. He shrugged. "I'll go ask if he's busy." Ambling toward the back, he disap-

161

peared, then returned less than a minute later. "His secretary will help you. Come this way."

Following his lead, they passed a storeroom on their right and the entrance to the greenhouse left of them. The clerk opened a solid wooden door, and stepping over the threshold was like entering an entirely different world. The rich earthy fragrance of the shop vanished. Here the air was lightly deodorized, and deep springy carpeting was beneath their feet. Halfway down a short corridor a thin thirtyish woman with closely cropped streaked hair leaned out from a doorway and beckoned somewhat imperiously to them. She was back behind her desk, though still standing, when they entered a very nicely appointed office.

"May I be of assistance?" she asked, her voice stilted. "I'm Mrs. Simons."

"Gracie Mitchell and Dan Logan," he politely said. "We'd like to see Mr. Compton."

"Well, maybe I can be of some help if you'll just tell—"

"We need to talk to Mr. Compton personally," Dan insisted, his tone quiet but recognizably adamant too.

The secretary sniffed. "Very well. Wait here, please. Have a seat."

Grace and Dan remained where they were. When Mrs. Simons opened the double doors behind her desk, slipped between them, then closed them firmly behind her, Grace had to grin at him.

"Think we'll ever have to hire a secretary for our business?"

He cocked an eyebrow. "We might need a part-time secretary someday, but right now I just want enough customers to justify hiring a clerk."

"We'll have the customers but won't need to hire anybody. Since I've lost two of my clients, I'll have time to work in the shop."

"You wouldn't mind doing that?"

"Why should I? I told you I wanted to be completely involved."

162

"Little did you know you'd have to share harassment like—" Daniel began, but didn't finish when Mrs. Simons opened the double doors again and stepped out without smiling.

"Mr. Compton will see you now," she intoned as regally as if the queen of England had granted them an audience.

They stepped into an overly opulent office decorated in muted red, blue, and gold with exorbitantly expensive furnishings that would have looked more appropriate in the executive suite of a big-city bank. Thad Compton, a fairly well preserved man in his late sixties or early seventies, clad in designer slacks and a designer shirt, rose from behind his massive desk and moved forward to meet them with a practiced smile and affable greeting. He inclined his head at Grace, then shook Dan's hand. He wasn't overly friendly but not at all hostile either, and he motioned them into chairs while he sat on the edge of his desk, his hand-tooled cowboy boots planted firmly in front of him.

"Well, now, I've heard of you two," he announced boomingly. "What can I do for you?"

"It's very simple," was Dan's calm answer. "We don't want to be harassed anymore. We'd like for you to tell your people to stay away from our shop."

"My people? Your shop," Compton blustered, ruddy cheeks darkening slightly. "I don't have an idea in this world what you're talking about."

"Harassment. Intimidation. Veiled threats," Dan sternly replied. "And I assure you that some of your employees would know exactly what I mean."

"I think you'd better explain to me then."

Daniel did just that, describing every nasty incident that had happened, never raising his voice, although his face was a stony mask. He looked over at Gracie. "Miss Mitchell and I intend to finish building our shop and to open it for business in a couple of weeks; we're not going to back out now. And I don't want any more rocks thrown through the windows of her house; I don't want her to be

163

accosted on the street by thugs, and I don't want to be attacked again myself. I don't see how I can make myself any clearer than that."

"I'm afraid nothing is clear to me," Compton responded, his smile still affable but beginning to fray a bit around the edges. "Are you insinuating some of my employees are responsible for these . . . uh . . . acts?"

"I'm not insinuating anything. I'm stating the facts as we know them. And no one else has any reason whatsoever to give us any trouble, but it's obvious that someone involved with your garden centers doesn't want any competition. That message has come across to us loud and clear."

"Nonsense, nonsense," the older man boomed, touching his mane of black, silver-shot hair. "Nowadays, property is destroyed and people attacked for no good reason. These teenagers—they're a menace. They'll do anything, *anything*, mind you."

"People have been saying that about teenagers for centuries," Grace put in, sitting straight in her chair, her expression as adamant as Dan's. "One of these incidents *could* have been a prank, but there've been too many of them. Someone's planning them, trying to scare us into giving up the idea of the shop. One of your own managers, Pete Royce, came out to my house and made several not-too-subtle threats."

"Pete! Oh, don't mind him." Compton's chuckle was dismissive. "He isn't always good with people, sticks his foot in his mouth sometimes. But he's a good, decent man. Don't worry your pretty little head about him. He's harmless."

"You may think he is. We don't," Daniel tersely interjected. "And if you didn't know until today what he's been up to during the past few weeks, you know now, and it's time to have a talk with him."

Compton actually hissed, and it was as if a dark thundercloud settled on his face. For a moment Grace thought

164

he might pitch a real temper tantrum, but he closed his hands into fists and smote the desktop with one instead. "You're making mountains out of molehills, and I won't talk to Pete about this nonsense," he snapped, all his previous "charm" vanishing in a twinkling. "He's not only an employee; he's a good friend. I have complete faith in him. He's a fine manager and a good man."

Grace turned her "pretty little head" to look at Daniel, her darkening gaze posing disturbing questions: Was Compton merely acting, trying to play the part of an innocent who had no idea what had truly been happening? Or was he just a sap, a dim-witted fool of a man, easily flimflammed by his so-called friends? Either way, he was dangerous as long as his associates believed they could do anything they pleased to achieve their goals, knowing they were protected whether he was involved or not. If he wasn't, he'd still gullibly defend them, and his wealth and clout in the community would be their protection. And if they made points with him in the meantime by squashing competition, all the better for them. She knew it was useless to talk to him. She could see he wasn't willing to listen. A thoroughly narrow-minded man. She disliked him immensely. In Daniel's narrowed green eyes, she read agreement. They were simply wasting their time here. She rose to her feet.

Dan stood too. "I advise you to talk to Mr. Royce," he said succinctly. "Miss Mitchell and I will file suit against him . . . and you, if we have to."

Disrespectfully, Compton looked them over, then glanced around his opulent office, as if to say: "I'm wealthy. You're not. Do you really think you could win a case in court, *against me*?" Snorting in his inimitable narrow-minded way, he turned his back.

They left. In the van a minute or so later, Grace stared out her window as Dan gunned the engine, backed up, drove out of the parking lot, turning left onto the highway.

"I don't like that man," she said at last, chewing her lower lip. "Something about him makes my flesh crawl. I thought Pete Royce was a snake, but Compton . . ."

"I didn't exactly fall in love with him either," Dan said, a faint frown nicking his brow. "He's either a fake or an idiot. Maybe he's involved in all this; maybe he isn't. Even if he's not, he's obviously not willing to listen to anything he doesn't want to hear, which means he won't talk to Royce and get him off our backs."

"In other words, we can expect more harassment?"

"What do you think?"

"I think you're probably right," she uttered rather miserably, pulling a tissue from her purse, sneezing into it, then breathing a long sigh.

By Monday Grace had a dilly of a cold. In the morning Daniel ordered her to bed, and she gladly went to doze most of the day away. In the evening he knocked on her bedroom door, and when she called him in, he entered, carrying a tray.

"Chicken soup," he announced with a flourish and a bow from the waist after depositing the tray on the bedside table. "For what ails you."

She cut her eyes up at him. "From a can, I imagine?"

"No. Homemade. I'm not a stranger to a kitchen, you know. Besides, I found Gran's file of recipes, and this one was in it. And it smells so good, I thought I'd join you. You do feel like eating something, don't you?"

"How could I say no after you went to all this trouble?" she countered, smiling, love for him surging through her veins. He could be so considerate, so incredibly gentle, and as he placed one bowl of soup on the table then transferred the tray to her lap, she inhaled the peppery aroma that brought back many memories of childhood and Gran. With each bite of succulent tender chicken and each spoonful of broth, her nose felt less stuffy. Her throat still ached, but the warmth of the soup eased the hurt a little. She finished the whole bowlful and the cup of hot tea with lemon that accompanied it. Touching the corners of her mouth with a white antique linen napkin, she sank back into the softness of two pillows propped against the headboard of her bed.

"Delicious," she proclaimed, smiling at Daniel. "Thanks."

"You're welcome," he murmured, taking the tray from her, replacing his own empty bowl upon it, and putting it back down on the table. His eyes captured hers. "Feeling any better, Gracie?"

"A little, I guess," she lied, then comically grimaced. "I'm really tired of sneezing and having to blow my nose, though. And I shouldn't have spent all day lying around up here. I have too much work to do."

"You should stay in bed tomorrow too. Better two days than a couple of weeks," he said, his tone severe. "I remember that cold you had two and a half years ago that turned into pneumonia."

"Well, yes, but nothing like that's happened since," she assured him. "Besides, I don't feel as dragged out as I did then. Mostly, I just feel a little tired."

"Ready for another nap? I can go if—"

"No, I think I'm all slept out for a while," she told him, wanting him to stay, needing him to be near. Tucking the covers up beneath her chin, she wriggled her hips, making herself more comfortable upon the mattress. "What have you been doing today, besides making chicken soup?"

"Staining the counter in the shop and doing a little painting. Luckily, I was able to replace everything stolen Friday night."

"And nothing else has happened?" she questioned. "No more threats or . . . anything like that?"

"Nothing."

"You're sure?"

"I wouldn't lie to you," he insisted, but with an indulgent smile. "We're equal partners, Gracie. The problems are ours to share."

Believing he meant what he said, she looked hopefully at him. "Do you think this means Thad Compton might have had a talk with Royce after all and maybe we don't have anything else to worry about?"

Regret tugged down one corner of Daniel's mouth. "I think that this is probably just another lull between incidents. I'm sorry, Gracie, but that's the way I feel."

She shrugged off his apology. At least he was honest, and she couldn't fault him for that, though it would have been nice to believe Compton had experienced a change of heart. *Fat chance of that happening, however.* She had a strong feeling that if he'd ever had a heart, it had been squeezed into nonexistence by his very narrow-mindedness. If she could have been convinced he wasn't actually involved in the scheme to harass Dan and her and was merely Royce's pawn and excuse to act like a hoodlum, she might have felt sorry for him. But she wasn't at all convinced he was innocent. Deep in her heart she didn't trust Thad Compton; that charming act of his simply didn't ring true. Merely thinking about him made her uneasy, and as she touched a tissue to her nose yet again, she felt too weary to fret.

"I want to forget about Compton and all that mess," she said. "Let's talk about something else."

"What would you like to talk about?"

"Something pleasant."

"Okay. I've been thinking about Maine a lot lately, and that's always pleasant," he began, smiling reminiscently. "It's a beautiful state. You've never been there, have you?"

"No, but it sounds like an intriguing place. You must have thought so. During your . . . travels, you stayed there several months, didn't you?"

"Nearly all that first autumn."

"Exploring the magnificent coastline—your postcard said."

"The scenery's incredible. So many little towns and villages overlooking harbors and bays. You would've loved it, Gracie. You'll have to let me take you there someday. I've heard it's beautiful in any season. I'd like to be there in winter."

"Sounds like a nice little trip," she murmured, smiling slightly, hoping he was merely referring to a vacation and wasn't beginning to miss moving from place to place. If he left her now after she had committed herself completely again, she was afraid the loneliness would be devastating. And if he decided to leave and asked her to go with him, would she say yes this time? In her heart, she'd want to; in her mind, she'd have grave doubts. She just wasn't the wandering type. She needed a home base. Twisting the tissue around one finger, she surveyed Dan's face as he gazed out her bedroom window for several silent seconds. What was he thinking? Maybe it was better for her not to know, and she tried to push all her niggling fears into the farthest corner of her mind.

At last, Dan turned his head and gave her a wink. "Enough of the travelogue. You look tired. I'll go and let you get some rest."

When he stood, then bent down to lightly kiss her, she laid a hand against his right cheek. "You might catch my cold."

"Umm, that's a chance I'm willing to take."

"Stay a few minutes longer, then," she said, the hoarseness in her voice not due entirely to the cold she had. "I don't feeling like sleeping, and I don't want to read. Would you stay and just hold me, Dan?"

"Honey," he whispered, sitting down against the head of the bed to cradle her against him. As his lips moved over her hair, his warm breath stirred wispy tendrils. His long strong fingers lightly massaged her back. "Try not to worry too much about Compton's thugs. Everything's going to work out all right."

Nuzzling her cheek into his shoulder, she drew in a deep breath. He didn't understand that the thought of further harassment didn't upset her nearly as much as the possibility of losing him again.

CHAPTER ELEVEN

Grace's cold wasn't entirely gone by the weekend, but it was mercifully much improved. As she sat sewing in her chair Friday evening, Daniel looked up from the notebook he was scribbling in and allowed his gaze to wander speculatively over her. Her eyes no longer looked weak, and she seemed to have regained all her old energy. She was herself again . . . almost, anyhow. He sensed a vague difference he couldn't pinpoint and define, but it made him suspect she was far more worried about Compton and his cronies than she was telling him. Thoughtfully, he tapped the side of his ball-point pen against his jaw.

"Gracie," he said, softly interrupting the silence in the room. "What are you thinking about?"

"Nothing very earth-shattering," she answered good-naturedly. "I was just trying to decide whether or not to put tiny pearl buttons on this christening dress. See, not very exciting. But why do you ask?"

"You're sure you weren't fretting about what Compton's people might try next?"

"I try to keep my mind off that as much as possible."

"But you do think about it?"

His solemn tone made her raise her head and meet his questioning eyes. "Sure I think about it occasionally, but that's only natural, after everything that's already happened."

"But I don't want you to worry excessively."

"I don't."

"As long as we're careful, we won't be caught off guard, and I plan to go into town with you tomorrow when you go grocery shopping."

A quick frown knitted her porcelain-smooth brow. "Oh, come on, surely that's going a bit far, isn't it? After all, town's only a couple of miles away, and I'll be going in the middle of the day."

A flicker of confusion crossed over his face as he leaned toward her. "I don't want to take any chances, and I thought it might make you feel better to know I don't plan to take any, especially now. Nothing's happened for a while, and I have a feeling that's going to change in the next couple of days."

Smiling ruefully, she threw up her hands. "Heavens, if you're trying to make me feel better, it isn't working out that way. I'm more worried now than I was."

"I'm sorry. I thought . . ." He shrugged, his gaze fixed on hers. "Look, Gracie, you can still get out of this situation. We can close down . . ."

"I've told you before I'm not going to let a few creeps scare me away."

Daniel shook his head, still bewildered. "Obviously you're not as worried about this as I imagined. So what else is bothering you, Gracie?"

"Bothering me?" she asked, hastily looking down at the dress in her lap. She slipped a snippet of lace beneath the edge of a narrow tuck and proceeded to stitch it down. "I don't know what you mean."

"Something's troubling you. I can tell," he persisted. "You get too quiet sometimes, like you're drifting away from me. I want to know what's wrong."

Without looking back up at him, she turned up one palm. "Nothing's wrong. I don't know why you think something is. Maybe I act a little bit draggy because I'm still getting over this cold but—"

172

"That's not it."

"Must be. It's nothing else," she lied with considerable aplomb.

"Gracie, there's something you're not telling me."

Pretending to concentrate on needle and thread, she sighed inwardly. Damn his perceptiveness. He knew her too well, but that didn't mean she had to justify his suspicions. For days his comments about Maine and going back there someday had nagged at her, but at last she had accepted the fact that she wanted to give her love to him as long as he stayed with her. It was a high-stakes gamble, but she was a grown woman, and she had the right to take a few chances. If he decided to stay with her, she would be gloriously happy and glad she had risked so much. If he left again, she would handle that too; it would be painful, but she was a survivor. In the meantime, however, she didn't intend to pressure him in any way by telling him how she truly felt. If he decided to stay and make some kind of permanent commitment, she wanted that decision to be made of his own free will. It wouldn't mean much any other way.

"I'm afraid you've lost me, Dan," she said finally. "I don't know why you think there's something I'm not telling you, because there isn't."

"I wish you'd tell me the truth, because I'm going to be very honest with you," he murmured, reaching over to tilt her chin up with one curved finger to make her face him. "When we make love, you give everything without holding back, and that's fantastic, the way I want it to be. But the rest of the time, especially during this last week, I've felt like you're keeping some kind of secret."

"Secret? Me?" She lightly laughed. "I'm an open book, always have been. And I didn't know you had such a vivid imagination."

Regarding her intently, Dan sat back, willing to drop the subject for the moment but fully intending to bring it

173

up again soon. She was keeping something from him. He knew it.

Grace began to relax as his silence continued. After a couple of minutes she looked over at him, noticing again the notebook on his lap and the pen in his hand. "What are you doing?"

"I've decided to write a book," he answered. "On organic gardening."

A smile lit up her face. "Really? That's a great idea. How much have you done?"

"Rough draft of the first chapter. Outlines of the next two."

"I imagine you're going to work in a little philosophy?"

He quirked one eyebrow. "I hadn't thought of that, but a few pertinent quotes placed here and there probably would make the subject matter a little less dry. I think I'll give it a try."

"Need a proofreader?"

"You volunteering?"

"Sure. If you can find the time to write, I can certainly find the time to proofread what you've written. And I won't even charge for my services."

"Hmm, yes, I know how generous and giving you can be," he whispered, tossing the notebook aside to reach out once more and take the doll's dress from her. Then his fingers closed around her wrists, and he drew her to him.

Willingly, she went. Perhaps if she had been wise, she would have resisted, but in that moment she didn't even want to be wise. She loved and needed Daniel too much to be influenced by mere misgivings.

When he pulled her onto his lap and her slender arms wound upward around his neck, he pressed her close against him, seeking the slim column of her neck with his lips. He still believed she was keeping something from him, and he fully intended to discover what her secret was. But as her tender mouth found his, he decided that could wait until later . . . much later. . . .

174

Buster broke her right hind leg. They never knew exactly how she did it, but since she came back limping from the meadow, they suspected she had stepped into a rabbit hole during a high-speed chase. Luckily, the break was a clean one, and after putting the leg in a cast, the vet allowed Dan and Grace to take her home, where they made a comfortable pad for her in one corner of the kitchen. She practically inhaled a few morsels of leftover chicken, proving her appetite hadn't been adversely affected by her accident, then settled down on her right side, her soft brown eyes watching rather balefully as the kitten loped over to pay a visit, purring as she rubbed against the setter's chest. Buster sighed but made no effort to escape the cat by switching positions.

"She's a fraud," Dan commented. "She tries to pretend she doesn't like that kitten, but I think she's very fond of her."

"Good thing," Grace replied wryly. "With that cast on, she's only going to be able to hobble around, so Little Bit will be able to keep up with her wherever she goes."

"I don't think she'll mind. Look," he said, inclining his head toward the animals, both of whom were drifting off to sleep, lying side by side.

That evening Allison and Eric Kingston came to the farmhouse for dinner. Coffee and the strawberry cheesecake Grace had made was served in the parlor, and the two couples talked about a variety of topics. Eric ignored his wife's suggestive glance at his waistline and accepted a second helping of dessert.

"I hate to bring up an unpleasant subject," Allison said after Grace returned with second helpings for Daniel as well as Eric, then poured fresh coffee for everybody. "But what are you two going to do now that Buster's in no shape to be a guard dog?"

"I'm sure she'll still raise quite a ruckus if she hears strange noises, and she has a very growly intimidating bark," Grace explained. "If I was doing something sneaky and heard her, I certainly wouldn't stick around long."

"Well, I guess she might still be a little help," Allison conceded, though doubtingly. "But she isn't going to be able to chase anyone away. And how alert can she be here in the house? So what are you going to do? The two of you can't take turns standing guard around the clock."

"No, we don't plan to do that," Dan assured her. "It's not necessary for us to turn this place into a fort."

"But it is beginning to sound like you're under siege," Eric remarked, strumming the tips of his fingers together, frowning. "We're having dinner here tonight because when Allison called to ask you to our house, Grace told her you both felt you shouldn't go anywhere. And when it reaches the point where you're afraid to leave the house and shop untended, you're in a very serious situation, in my opinion."

"Oh, but that's not why we felt we should stay here," Grace said, exchanging an amused glance with Dan. "Allison, I didn't mean to give you that impression. Buster's the reason we didn't think we should leave; she's still a little groggy from the pain medication the vet gave her, and we didn't want to take a chance on her stumbling around the house. The last thing in the world she needs is another broken leg."

"Thank heavens," Allison exclaimed. "It's a relief to know that."

"It certainly is," her husband quickly agreed. "It sounded like you were in real trouble here. Driving over, I was wondering if we were entering a battle zone."

"We're not surrounded by the enemy. If we were, it would be simple for the sheriff to make arrests. But these people are too cagey to attack us openly," said Dan, anger hardening the line of his jaw. "They hit and run, and so far they've left no clues behind. But sooner or later I think somebody's going to slip up, and since it's obvious they're

176

being paid to harass us, if even one of them is caught and talks, we'll know exactly who's responsible."

"And if that doesn't happen, maybe they'll just leave us alone once we actually open the shop," Grace hopefully suggested. "It's all so silly anyhow. Why are they so afraid of a little competition?"

"Because some people want to have it all," Eric stated matter-of-factly, then turned to Dan. "Grace mentioned you went to see Thad Compton. What came of that?"

While Daniel started to answer, Grace quietly gathered the empty dessert plates, coffee cups, and saucers, nodding agreement to Allison's offer to help. It seemed a good time to retreat to the kitchen; she didn't want a discussion of Compton to interfere with her enjoyment of the evening. The more she thought about the man, the more convinced she became that he was a rather worthless individual, all smiles and glitter in the personality department, which masked an inner hollowness and emptiness. Judging by some of the offhanded jocular comments he had made during the meeting with Dan and her, she had reason to believe he was one of those pitiful human beings who knew the cost of everything but the worth of nothing. All that truly mattered was the final total in the profit column, and she had the feeling amorality was a way of life for him. He didn't even have to be directly involved in the dirty tricks his employees engaged in; he was their boss, and with his very silence he was condoning whatever they did. He could stop them if he chose. The fact that he didn't said nothing good about his character.

Resolutely, she pushed all thoughts about him aside temporarily and, in the kitchen, ran hot water over liquid detergent in the dishpan. "I'd rather cook than wash dishes," she said, handing Allison a clean plate to dry. "But it was Dan's turn to make dinner, so it's my turn to do them."

"You made the cheesecake."

"Because I wanted to."

"What you need is an automatic dishwasher."

"Hmm, maybe," Grace murmured, glancing around the large cheery room equipped with most modern conveniences while retaining its old-fashioned appeal. "I might think about buying one after Dan and I make our first million."

"You're lovers again, aren't you?" Allison abruptly asked, then grinned somewhat sheepishly. "I'm not trying to be nosy, but it's just that you act like more than business partners now. Something's changed between you since the last time Eric and I were here. And to tell the truth, I'd be surprised if you two hadn't gotten back together by now, living here in the same house. It was inevitable."

Grace merely nodded, a faint smile touching her lips.

"But you told me you'd decided you'd never really been in love with him two years ago," Allison continued, wiping another plate busily. "Obviously you've changed your mind."

"I don't know, I'm not sure. Maybe I only thought I loved him then. Or maybe I did and never really stopped. That doesn't matter though. All I know for certain is I love him now."

"And what if he decides to leave again?"

Grace looked at her friend. Allison could be terribly blunt sometimes, but the direct approach was simply her way of dealing with things and she meant no offense. And although Grace wasn't offended, she couldn't answer the question she had asked herself countless times. Finally, her shoulders rose and fell in a slight shrug. "If he does leave again, it won't be until we open the shop and we've made the business a success, however long that takes."

"But you think he might go eventually. And you're willing to accept that? You've always been such a cautious person."

"I've turned over a new leaf," Grace blithely declared. "I've decided to live for today, let tomorrow take care of itself, and hope everything works out."

"Be careful, for God's sake; I don't want to see you hurt by Dan. He's a terrific friend and I love him, but . . . well, it was crazy enough for him to give up tenure at the university, but we were shocked when he told us he wanted to open a garden shop. That seems so irresponsible. He's such an excellent teacher; teaching is what he should be doing."

"Obviously, he doesn't agree," Grace reminded her tersely, leaping compulsively to his defense. "What's right for Eric and you isn't necessarily right for him. And, after all, it's his life, isn't it? He has every right to decide what to do with it."

"Well, that's all the proof I need," Allison murmured, the corners of her mouth tugging upward. "Only a woman madly in love would react that emotionally. But you're right. Dan's life is his own; he doesn't need Eric and me meddling in it; we just care about him and you. Accept my apology?"

"Of course," Grace said, returning her friend's winning and genuinely fond smile while handing her the crystal goblet she had just washed. "Our grand opening's next Friday. Think you'll be able to make it out here?"

"With bells on," Allison quipped. "How much do you think I should spend to encourage your other customers to buy too?"

Grace laughed. "I hope we won't be needing a shill, but thanks for the offer."

"Anytime," Allison drawled, laughing too. "After all, what are friends for?"

Later, about eleven o'clock, the Kingstons started to leave. Grace and Dan were following them out of the parlor when there came three loud resounding thumps against the side of the house, and in the kitchen on that same side, Buster began to bark hysterically.

As the men rushed out the front screen door, the women hurried into the kitchen, nearly tripped up by the cat, who came careening down the hall, then up the stairs, wanting to put as much distance between the commotion and herself as possible. Buster had made her way to the door opening onto the porch and was wobbling slightly even as she practically howled. Uttering soothing words and gently patting, Grace urged her back to her pad, but even when she sank down upon it, woofing sounds came up from her throat, low and tense. Hearing the muted shouts coming from outside, Grace and Allison looked at each other nervously, Allison's face visibly paling. Then, in the distance, two car doors slammed shut, an engine roared, and tires squealed on asphalt. When quiet settled again, Buster calmed down, and her broad tail beat a steady rhythm on the floor when Grace called her a good girl.

The moment the front door opened, the women rushed back down the hall, breathing simultaneous sighs of relief when they saw Dan and Eric.

"What's going on?" Allison exclaimed. "What was that noise?"

Grace stepped toward Dan, asking, "What now?"

"I'm not sure. We'll have to see," he muttered grimly. "Let's go through the kitchen and pick up the flashlight on the way out."

The four of them trooped outside, where Dan played the beam of light over the side of the house. Allison gasped while Grace merely closed her eyes for an instant then forced them open again. Upon the pristine white clapboard, red paint ran and dripped from three great blotches.

"I'll be damned," Eric uttered disbelievingly. "They must've known somebody was in the house, but they did this anyway."

"They weren't taking that much of a chance," Dan said, his tone ice-edged. "It doesn't take long to throw three paint-filled balloons. They knew they could get away."

Grace turned toward him. "Did you even see what they looked like?"

180

He shook his head. "They were halfway across the front yard before Eric and I got out the door. And there was a car waiting for them."

Moving close to her husband, Allison wrapped her arms around his waist. "I don't see how you can stand this, knowing something could happen at any time. You must be feeling like prisoners in your own house by now," she said, then forced a shaky smile, aiming it in Dan's direction. "Are you s-sure you don't want to try to get back on the faculty?"

One corner of his mouth turned up. "I'm sure."

"But—"

"We should be getting home now, darling," Eric said, his troubled gaze focused on Grace and Dan. "We enjoyed dinner, the entire evening. Sorry it had to end like this."

"Just another episode in the continuing saga," Dan joked. "We're sorry you had to be involved in this one."

Soon good nights were said and the Kingstons left. In total silence Grace and Dan went back to inspect the damage to the house. Suddenly her temper flared. "Damn them all to hell," she uttered furiously, small hands balled into fists at her sides. "How many coats of paint is it going to take to cover up this red mess?"

"Several. I'll go buy the paint tomorrow and get right on it."

"But you're going to have to paint the entire side of the house over and over or it won't look right. And you have too much work to do already! Hell, I'm so tired of these—these horrible people trying to screw up our life!" Spinning around on her heels, she marched up the steps, across the porch, and into the kitchen, where she tried to ease the nervous energy that seemed close to exploding inside her. Busying herself with filling Buster's bowl with dog chow and Little Bit's with kitten food, then filling the water bowl they both shared, she began to settle down. Her anger subsided a few degrees as she took long deep breaths and told herself she couldn't let someone as worthless as

Compton or any of his lackeys upset her equilibrium. They simply weren't worth the worry. On her pad Buster was once again dozing. Even the kitten returned to the kitchen to curl up in a cozy ball near the dog's nose. She heard the clinking of glasses in which Daniel had served brandy, and she knew he was in the parlor apparently gathering them up. More relaxed, she suddenly remembered she had left the bag of sundry items she had purchased at the drugstore in the trunk of her car. Digging her keys from the bottom of her purse upon the counter, she flipped on the side porch light and went out, but before she had gone three paces along the path, her heart lurched as her left upper arm was enclosed in a rough viselike grip. She nearly screamed until Daniel hauled her around to face him, and she knew no stranger had attacked her. But the bad scare he had given her added to her anxiety, and trembling, she lost control of her temper.

"Don't jerk me around like that!" she snapped. "What do you think you're doing?"

"That's my question: what the hell do you think *you're* doing?" he snapped right back, his fingers pressing into her flesh down to delicate bones. "What in God's name made you come out here in the dark?"

"I happened to leave something in the car, and I wanted to get it."

"I hope it's a bar of gold or something equally valuable."

"Don't be silly," she retorted, stung by his sarcasm. "I forgot to bring in the things I bought at the drugstore, and since I'm out of hand lotion . . ."

"Hand lotion! You risked coming out here alone just for that?" he exclaimed, his tone harsh, his expression harsher. "Didn't it occur to you that some of our 'friends' could be lurking around out here and would be happy to grab you and teach you a little lesson if they had half a chance?"

"They've already done their dirty work for tonight. They won't be back."

"Are you really so sure of that? If you are, maybe I should just go back inside while you go explore the shadows. How about it, Gracie? Want to try that?"

The whispering breeze rustled the magnolia leaves, and scuttering clouds snaking in front of the half-moon overhead made the ground shadows form ominous patterns. As Grace hesitated in answering his question, he turned her back toward the porch, impelled her up the stairs and back into the house, where they stood glaring at each other in the brightly lit kitchen.

"Think next time before pulling a damn fool stunt like that," he growled, eyes glinting. "You can't begin to predict what people like this are going to do next, and they could very well be out there again right now. Understand?"

"*Yes.* You made your point," she ground out, yanking her arm free of his tight grip to rub the skin where his fingers had been. "And I understand something else. Allison's right. We are becoming prisoners in this house. If I can't even walk out to my car at night . . . It's utterly ridiculous, and I don't like it one bit."

"Think I'm thrilled with the situation? I'm not. But since we can't prove who's responsible for harassing us, we can't do anything except wait them out and hope they'll give up eventually."

"I'm tired of waiting!"

"What do you propose we do then?"

"I don't know. Just something. Anything. I don't want to just sit here and take it anymore. It's driving me batty."

Daniel's jaw clenched. "I've offered you a way out."

"I don't want out. How many times do I have to tell you that? Giving up would mean they won, and I'm not going to let them win. But I'm tired of having to always wonder when they're going to do something else."

"And there's something else bothering you, Gracie.

183

Don't deny it. I can tell there is," he murmured, his features gentling as he moved a hand toward her. "It's not only this."

"Isn't this enough?" she softly exclaimed, stepping back beyond his reach. Suddenly, she felt very weary. She still hadn't gotten over her cold completely, and physically she wasn't up to par yet. Emotionally, she was beginning to feel like a wreck, harassed by degenerates and plagued by all her uncertainties about her relationship with Dan. Tears of sheer frustration sprang to her eyes, and she turned away before he could see them. Needing time alone to try to sort everything out, she hurried out into the hall with nothing more than, "I'm tired. Good night, Dan."

He didn't follow. After closing and locking the front and kitchen doors, he sat down at the worktable with a mug of beer and opened his notebook to look over the outline of his third chapter. Only a couple minutes later, he slapped the notebook shut again, unable to concentrate. He was tired too, and after one last swallow of beer he rinsed the glass, then went upstairs—but not to Gracie's room. He went to his own, where he hadn't slept for many nights, not since the first one they had spent together. With his foot he closed the door; it shut with a little bang, and he uttered an oath beneath his breath. She was capable of bedeviling a saint at times, and he had too volatile a temper on occasion to ever be considered saintly. At that moment he was tempted to stalk into her room and force her to tell him the truth. He needed to know what, besides the obvious, was troubling her, but she was too stubborn or inhibited or both to confide in him. And he was getting tired of receiving no answer to that question. Rubbing his jaw, he decided it was time to change tactics. He wouldn't ask her anymore; let her wonder why he didn't. Maybe if he didn't press her, she would feel more at ease and allow that crazy barrier she had recently erected between them to start breaking down again. It was worth a try anyhow. And since, with her terse good night, she had clearly reinstated the old separate bedrooms policy, she would have to be the one to show a desire to resume their intimate relationship. In the past he had always been the initiator; this time she would have to be. He could be extremely stubborn too, perhaps more stubborn than she was when he thought obstinacy might help him gain precisely what he wanted. And he wanted her to come to him freely, without any lingering inhibitions, able to share every thought, every need, every fear, with him.

CHAPTER TWELVE

The grand opening was a huge success. Daniel proved as charismatic on the television screen as he was in person, and the commercials brought the customers in. As Jim had advised, they had free coffee and donuts and balloons for the children. As expected, many people already interested in organic gardening wanted organically grown seedlings, shrubs, and house plants, which only this shop could offer. A steady stream of customers kept Grace and Dan busy all day, which delighted them both. Even the weather was kind, mild and sunny, befitting the festive occasion. Luckily, the majority of people made a purchase after browsing around, and all who did seemed quite pleased to be taking home plants that hadn't been nurtured chemically.

"You know I hear such dreadful things about so many chemicals lately that I'd rather not mess with any of them," an elderly woman told Dan while he totaled up the price of twenty-five running juniper shrubs plus the cost of four amaryllis. "I used to use all those fertilizers and insect sprays and powders but not anymore. My vegetable garden is organic, and I think everything tastes better grown that way, don't you?"

Daniel smiled. "Especially the tomatoes."

"Oh, my, yes. I can't wait for mine to get ripe," the woman declared with much enthusiasm, probing the soil of one potted juniper with a finger. "Now, I've never had any experience tending organically grown evergreens. What'll be good for these?"

"A mulch of oak leaves and grass cuttings," he told her, then added, "Of course, manure's the answer."

"If that's the answer, I'm certainly glad I missed the question," Grace murmured so only he could hear her as she stepped behind the counter next to him after having helped a customer in the greenhouse. When he turned his head to look at her, she grinned up at him, then showed no visible reaction as he retaliated by playfully swatting her fanny, his action so discreet that his white-haired customer didn't witness it.

It was that way between them. On the surface, especially around other people, they interacted easily and were able to enjoy each other's company. Yet, underneath that surface camaraderie was a barrier of tension that became uncomfortable and intrusive when they were alone. They hadn't really talked since that night she had gone to her room alone; they merely conversed, and neither of them mentioned the possibility of sharing a bed again. Grace wanted to sometimes but couldn't bring herself to do it. He wanted to all the time but wouldn't. It was a stalemate.

When Grace smiled at the woman across the counter, Dan turned his attention back to her too, telling her the total price of her purchases. After she paid, he carried the flowers and shrubs outside to load them into the back of her station wagon.

Grace waited on a young man clad in a jogging suit adorned with a collegiate crest who was trying to decide between an African violet with white blossoms or wax begonias as a gift for his girl friend. After asking Grace's advice and twenty minutes of consideration, he chose the begonias, and Grace tied a jaunty white ribbon around the pot. He left happy.

It was about ten minutes later when Grace looked up from the cash register and saw Pete Royce amble toward the back of the shop, where he stopped to rub a frond of a fluffy ruffle fern between a thumb and forefinger, all the while glancing rather furtively around. Her heart seemed to take a little dip down toward her stomach before sheer resentment heightened the color in her cheeks. Seeing Dan assisting a man over by the selection of garden implements, she went to him, waiting until he had finished with his customer before gaining his attention by laying a hand over his arm. When he turned to her, she nodded in Royce's direction, her features strained.

"Old Pete's come to see us," she muttered. "Wonder what the devil he's up to."

"No good, I'm sure," answered Dan, lightly cupping her right elbow to escort her across the shop. "Let's find out."

Royce produced one of his outrageously fake wide smiles as they joined him. "Nice-looking ferns," he said, disrespectfully and ungently flipping up one frond with an index finger. He shook his head. "But they're delicate, temperamental plants; these probably won't survive long without a chemical fertilizer."

"Wild ferns flourish without any outside help," Dan reminded him flatly. "And since these have grown from spores without the aid of chemicals and are very hardy, I don't think you need worry about them."

Royce had no answer for that but was undaunted nevertheless. There was something obnoxiously cocky in the way he looked the shop over while stroking his hair. He gave them another patently false smile. "You have a fair number of customers. Been this way all day?"

"Heavens no, it's nearly four o'clock, and things have slowed down a lot," Grace just had to say, because it was true and also because she couldn't help rubbing it in a little. "There was a crowd in here when we first opened, and it didn't thin out much before one or two. And since then, we've been very busy."

Supremely confident, Royce smiled on. "Openings always draw a lot of people. The problem is to keep them coming back. That's not easy. Next week might be mighty slow for you folks. Know what I mean?"

"We'll have to wait and see what happens," Dan replied, his expression neither friendly nor antagonistic. And his tone was bland as he added, "We talked to your employer about you."

"Thad?" A scowl carved deeply into Royce's brow.

"Yes, Thad. We told him we wanted the harassment to stop and that we know you're responsible for what's been happening. Did he mention our visit to you?"

"Harassment? I don't know what you're talking about. And Thad hasn't said a word to me; I guess he didn't think what you had to tell him was very important."

"More likely, he chose to ignore it," Dan said. "Or he's involved himself, which I think is very possible, and he had no reason to talk to you about our complaints."

"Involved? In what? I—"

"Oh, come on," Grace broke in, thoroughly disgusted with him and his dreadful lack of acting ability. "We know what you've been doing, and I, for one, think you're a complete idiot. Surely you don't believe we can put Compton's Garden Centers out of business. Oh sure, there are many people interested in organic gardening. But there are more who aren't, so what are you worried about?"

"Exactly," Daniel concurred. "Think of us as a specialty shop. We aren't going to appeal to everybody, so Compton's monopoly will remain pretty much intact."

Royce's scowl deepened. He viewed them both with scarcely veiled animosity before he retreated. Yet, even as he left, there was a swagger in his walk when he tossed back over his shoulder, "Just remember: the retail business can be very tricky. Amateurs don't have half a chance."

Grace's lips thinned. "What a son of a—"

"Forget him," Daniel advised.

And when a customer found her a moment later to ask for assistance, she did.

Later, after closing the shop, Grace and Dan joined Jim and Dottie O'Donnell for dinner in a quietly elegant Knoxville restaurant to celebrate the opening. It was great fun. Dottie was as warm and likeable as her husband, and she never once mentioned how scared she had been the afternoon he had been taken to the hospital after being run off the road. It was too victorious an evening to bring up unpleasantries, and Grace lifted her glass of white wine when Jim offered a toast to the continued success of Nature's Garden Shop.

"I've been thinking," she announced after finishing delectable stuffed shrimp and declining dessert. "We should keep the coffee maker in the shop, available to any customer who wants some. That would make the place cozier. And I'd like to get a little table, chairs, and some toys for the children to keep them occupied. Then their parents will have all the time they want to browse around."

"A wonderful idea," Jim said. "I like it."

"Me too," his wife agreed. "It's so difficult to try to shop with young children."

"My partner," Dan said, his warm smile in Grace's direction softening his eyes. "A natural-born entrepreneur."

"You agree with my ideas, then?" she asked. "No objections?"

"None whatsoever," he replied. "Who am I to question a practical woman's intuition, especially one who's had such a keen sense of business?"

Was there an underlying message in his words? She couldn't tell and finally decided there must not have been since his slight smile seemed to envelope her in warmth.

After the celebration ended an hour or so later and the O'Donnells headed home in their own car, Grace and Dan returned to the farmhouse, where Buster greeted them in the kitchen from her pad with an enthusiastic thumping of her tail on the floor and the kitten rubbed against their ankles, meowing her own hello.

Grace patted the dog's head and scratched the cat's chin. "They both probably need to go out."

Dan nodded. "I want to check out the shop anyhow."

With some anxiety she awaited his return. When he came back into the kitchen about ten minutes later, both animals close at his heels, she released her lower lip from between her teeth to ask, "Everything okay?"

"Fine. No problems."

She sighed with relief. "Thank goodness. I was afraid Royce might have sent somebody over here while we were gone. And it's been such a nice day that I'd hate to see it spoiled in any way."

"We did have a very successful opening," Dan murmured, green eyes holding hers for an instant before he leaned down to just touch her lips with his.

Grace's heartbeat quickened. It seemed like forever since he had kissed her, and she wanted more. Yet as she started to move closer, he pulled back, ending the subtly sensuous moment before it had a chance to begin.

"And it has been a nice day. But if you're as tired as I am, I suggest we get some sleep," he added. "We have to open again in the morning."

He turned away from her, and when he did, raw emotion squeezed her throat. Tonight they had been so comfortable with each other, seemingly so attuned that she had secretly hoped he would give her some indication that he wanted to share her bed again. Had he done so, she would have welcomed him. But it was obvious he wasn't interested, and a knot of disappointment gathered in the very center of her chest.

"You're right. We need plenty of rest," she said, maintaining a steady voice. "'Night, Dan." She left him and went upstairs. If it didn't matter to him whether or not they spent their nights together, it wouldn't matter to her either. At least, that's what she tried to tell herself.

191

* * *

The next Tuesday morning Daniel was looking at the newspaper when Grace came down to the kitchen. He looked up to watch her move about, then waited until she poured a cup of coffee and sat down across from him at the table before sliding a folded section of the morning's edition of the Knoxville *News* over in front of her.

"Take a look at page ten," he advised. "And don't be too surprised."

Curious, she turned the pages, and suddenly the yawn she was hiding behind one hand broke off with a tiny gasp. Her eyes widened as she glanced over the full-page ad for Compton's Garden Centers.

"My Lord, these prices!" she softly exclaimed. "They're slashed to the bone! They can't possibly make a profit selling rose bushes this cheap. Or these big-bulb azaleas. Or any of these items they're advertising."

"Apparently they're willing to give up profits for a while just to draw the customers in . . . and away from us." Dan shrugged nonchalantly. "At least they're reacting to competition legally this time, by lowering their prices— for a few days anyway."

"Which means we'll have to lower ours, but it won't seem like such a drastic reduction we're giving because our prices haven't been high from the beginning. Oh, I hope this doesn't turn into an all-out price war. I guess we can get by without making a profit for a little while, but we can't afford to run the shop at a loss. We just don't have the resources."

"Compton does have the advantage there," Dan agreed. "But we still have something to offer he doesn't—plants that are chemical-free."

"I hope the customers remember that."

"We'll have to remind them if they don't."

Grace looked down at the newspaper ad, then back up again, some uncertainty shadowing her eyes. "What happens if Compton decides to start selling organically grown plants too?"

"I wouldn't doubt he's already considered the idea, but if he's looked into it carefully, he's probably decided it isn't worth the trouble. His people wouldn't be able to rely on chemical fertilizers and sprays to make them flourish. And I doubt he has one employee with any experience in organic gardening."

"But still, he could probably hire someone who is experienced."

"If he wanted to, yes, but I don't think he does. In fact, he gave me the impression that he thinks all the interest in organics is a foolish fad that won't last long. He doesn't think the use of chemicals should scare anyone, since it doesn't scare him."

"Well, it does scare lots of people whether he thinks it should or not."

"Exactly, but I think he's a little too simplistic to realize his opinion isn't shared by the entire population, so he's not apt to get into selling everything we offer."

That theory made sense; Compton did appear to be an unperceptive old goat who assumed that people who disagreed with him were absolutely wrong and would soon come to see the errors of their ways. Organic gardening was such an alien and progressive idea to him that he probably wouldn't bother to cater to customers who might be interested. She understood that but still felt concerned. She tapped the newspaper with one finger. "But he does want his monopoly back, and I wonder how long he'll fight us with these kinds of low prices."

Daniel's shoulders rose and fell in a shrug once more. "I don't know, but we'll lower our prices as much as we possibly can until he gives up. But you're right. We can't afford to operate at a loss. Let's see how the next few days go. And don't worry, Gracie. In the end, it'll all be fine."

She believed that. She had to. But even that belief didn't

lessen her resentment of Thad Compton and his attempts to make their lives difficult.

The remainder of the week dragged by slowly. The shop wasn't emptied of customers, but their ranks had noticeably thinned, and Dan was easily able to serve them all. Grace's assistance wasn't warranted. She spent her time with her computer, keeping up with her dairy farm accounts and wondering too often if it might be wise for her to try to find new clients to pick up the slack left by the ones who had dropped her as accountant because of Compton's influence over them. Every time the idea popped into her head she tried to dismiss it, but it always came back. She didn't want to feel negative about the shop, but after all, she had always been practical-minded. And it never hurt to be prepared for any eventualities, especially ones that could be extremely disappointing.

Friday night after dinner she curled up in one corner of the sofa, picked up her sewing, then put it back down, a little too edgy to deal with delicate stitchery. She looked across the parlor at Dan, who sat at the antique secretary in front of the portable electric typewriter he had placed there. His back was to her as he worked busily on his manuscript, and she noticed the rippling of muscle beneath his shirt when he leaned forward to proofread the page he had just completed. He removed it from the machine and started to insert a clean sheet.

"Dan, excuse me for interrupting, but I'd like to talk to you," Grace quietly announced. "It's . . . well, to be perfectly honest, I'm getting nervous. Business is really getting slow, and I think we'd better try to do something about it. I have an idea."

Turning sideways in his straight-back chair, resting one arm upon the top, he gave her his full attention. "All ideas are welcome. What do you have in mind?"

"I think it might help for you to tape a new commercial for local TV. You know, to remind people that low prices aren't everything and that we have something to offer no one else in the area has. In other words, you get what you pay for, and our prices are reasonable for chemical-free plants."

A slow smile moved his firmly shaped lips. "We must be on the same wavelength because I've been thinking a new commercial might be in order too. I planned to talk to you about it. And, as a matter of fact, I called the studio this afternoon and got an appointment to tape it Monday morning," he said, rising to walk over and join her on the sofa. "And, Gracie, there's something else I think we should try. Compton's centers offer very few exotic plants, and they appeal to many people. We need to take advantage of that. Phillips' Organic Nursery stocks a wide variety of exotics, and we can get a good price if we order a large selection."

"That does sound interesting," she murmured, but the reservation in her voice was clearly evident. "How much would it cost us, though?"

"Nearly two thousand dollars."

She almost winced. "That much? Oh, I don't know, then. That would dip deeply into the cash reserve we agreed to keep for possible emergencies."

"This may very well be an emergency. Compton can probably go on underselling us indefinitely. The more specialties we have to offer, the better our chances of keeping our business afloat."

"But two thousand dollars! I don't think we can afford it. It's so risky, and what if it doesn't help bring more customers in? I don't think I can go along with this, Dan."

A discernible spark of impatience flared in his eyes. "Have you forgotten that sometimes you have to spend money to make money?"

"No, I haven't forgotten that. Have *you* forgotten there are limits?" she retorted, her own patience wearing thin, her spine tensing. Sometimes, more often with every day that passed, she regretted the fact that they had decided against building him living quarters behind the shop because the additional construction costs were too high. But that decision had been made when his remaining in the house with her seemingly posed no problems. That had been before a pall of tension had descended like a miasmic cloud around them, a tension that seemed to threaten to smother her now. Nerves tautly strung, she shook her head emphatically. "I don't want to gamble two thousand dollars."

"It's not a gamble. It's a good investment."

"You said this shop would be a wise investment too," she blurted out, prompted by anger and worry and resentment toward him for not loving her. "I'm beginning to have some doubts."

"Cheap shot, Gracie," he growled, frowning darkly. "And unworthy of you. You went into this partnership with your eyes open, and it's foolish of you to start panicking already, for no good reason."

"Don't tell me I'm being foolish!"

"Don't act that way and I won't tell you. And you might as well accept it, Gracie; I'm going to order a selection of exotics because that will add to the appeal of the shop."

"And take away from the sum total of our bank account," she argued, flags of angry color flying in her cheeks. "I think it's a lousy idea."

"Too bad, because I'm going through with it anyhow."

"For God's sake, Dan," she shot back, all the old resentments flaring up again and loosening her tongue. "When are you ever going to start acting like a responsible human being?"

His icy gaze raked over her. "When are you going to stop being afraid of taking chances?"

She jumped to her feet, furious with him. She had been upset and worried enough anyway. A scene like this was just what she hadn't needed. "I've had enough." She started to turn. "I'm going to bed."

"I wouldn't advise you to walk away," he warned ominously. "We haven't finished this discussion yet, and until we do, you're staying."

"Don't give me the caveman act. It's not your style. You can't stop me from leaving."

He could and he did, his right hand shooting out to clamp around her left wrist.

Her heart hammered, and she imagined she could feel her blood pressure rapidly rising as she glared down at the long tanned fingers holding her prisoner. "Take your hands off me," she commanded as haughtily as she could, then called him an uncomplimentary and explicit name when he didn't release her.

CHAPTER THIRTEEN

"Let me go," she repeated. "Now, Dan. You're hurting me."

Then he lessened his hold on her, but he didn't let her go completely. Instead, he pulled her down onto his lap, effortlessly stilling her twisting attempts to free herself and silencing all verbal protest by pressing roughened fingertips to her lips. "I'm sorry if I hurt you. I never meant to," he murmured, holding her fast. "Gracie, this is insane. It shouldn't be like this between us."

In no mood to allow herself to be cajoled, she struggled again, pressing her shoulder hard against his chest, all to no avail. His arms were like steel bands wrapped around her, yet somehow no rougher than velvet. Still, she valiantly tried to resist him.

"Honey, be quiet," he coaxed, drawing her arms up around his neck while his emerald eyes held hers captive. "Don't you see what's happening? Compton is going to win if we keep fighting each other so much we have no time left to fight him."

The wisdom of that statement struck her with the force of a lightning bolt, and as her breath softly caught, she relaxed against Dan, turning her face into the hollow of his shoulder as she mumbled, "Damn, I don't want him to win."

"Neither do I. And I don't want us feuding with each

other anymore either," he whispered, bending his head down. His lips covered hers, and as they parted for him, all remnants of anger vaporized in the fiery passion that exploded between them. Need gathered in him and was tempered only by an equal need to be tender. But Gracie's response as his tongue pushed into her sweet mouth and hers tangled erotically with it made tenderness more difficult to achieve. Her slender arms tightened around his neck. Her warm cushioned breasts strained against his chest. His firm lips plundered the softness of hers, and he held her nearer and nearer but could never get her close enough.

Piercing daggers of delight shot through her as she returned his possessive kisses, thrilled by his strength and dizzying virility and the deep abiding love she felt for him. His fingers were in her thick hair, skimming her scalp, evoking shivers of awareness that ran up and down her spine. Cupping the back of his neck in one hand, she trembled against him when his mouth sought the scented hollow at the base of her throat, spilling tiny nibbling kisses upon her skin.

"Gracie," he whispered unevenly, "I've needed to hold you and touch you . . . so much."

"Wh-what stopped you then?"

"I wanted you to come to me this time."

"I'm here."

"Yes. Thank God," he uttered, his lips descending on hers with swift compelling pressure before feathering over the slight hollows of her cheeks, her eyelids, and the racing pulses in her temples. "Honey, we're both under a lot of pressure. We're going to have disagreements, but let's not turn them into battles."

Leaning back in his supportive arms, she softly smiled. "In other words, make love not war."

"You're reading my mind."

"I still don't know if we should put so much money into exotic plants though, Dan. It's—"

His lips returning to hers halted her words. "Later. We can talk about it much later. That's business and this is pleasure."

And it was. As Grace's tongue parried the rousing invasion of his, keen sensations plunged through her, igniting a central shaft of fire that spread outward from the very core of her being, soon to consume her totally in flames. Pressing closer to him, tucking her thighs tight against his side, she moved her hands across his shoulders, then down over his chest inside his shirt, fingertips gliding over contouring muscle and firm male flesh. Toying with one hard nipple then the other and hearing the tenor of his breathing increase, she stroked and caressed him, enamored as always by the warmth and texture of his skin. She unfastened the buttons all the way down to his waist, the heel of her hand drawing random curlicues over his midriff.

"My sweet temptress," he gruffly called her, his fiery hands coursing over her, exploring the shape of her long slender legs, the rounded curve of her bottom, and insweeping waist. With one palm he rubbed slow circles around the peaks of her breasts. His fingers gently squeezed and caressed taut, resilient flesh.

Though the day had been hot, the magnolia-scented night air had cooled. Yet, in Dan's embrace, Grace was enveloped in such warmth that her clothes felt confining and she wanted to be rid of them. When Dan pushed one strap of her denim sundress off her shoulder and his lips followed it as it fell down around her upper arm, tickling the surface of her skin, nerve endings felt seared as if by a fire storm. It was wonderful, an exquisite heightening of all the senses, and together they shared the pure magic of it. Unhurried, knowing each other, they drifted along a path of delight, giving pleasure by touching, finding pleasure in being touched. Her opening lips danced teasingly over his until their mouths merged together in a breathtaking kiss, then another and another, each successive one lengthening and becoming more irreversibly binding. She touched his hair, his ears, his neck, enthralled with everything about him and lost in her love. Her nails swirled through the dark hair on his chest, catching here and there. Arching closer, she captured the sensuous curve of his lower lip between her teeth, lightly nibbling and nipping.

He groaned. He crushed her to him, then lowered her other strap. The bodice of her sundress dropped an inch, revealing ivory uprising flesh, never exposed to the rays of the sun. The tanned skin above was lightly sprinkled with faint freckles, and he seemed to touch them one by one before his fingertips roamed down to the shadowed valley beginning just above the vee of her bra.

"Clothes," he muttered, saying the word as a curse. "They just get in the way."

"Then take them off," she invited, rising up enough to allow him to lower the dress's back zipper, which he did without any delay whatsoever. Even as he removed that offending garment completely and gave it a toss, she stripped him of his shirt. Her gaze wandered over his broad sunbronzed chest before lifting to meet his, and her breath caught with excitement. His eyes were smouldering jade coals burning into hers, passion unmasked and clearly readable. The deep plummeting thrills quickened in her. "Daniel, take them all off."

Deftly, he unsnapped her bra and with deliberate slowness peeled it away from her body, eased the straps down her arms, and dropped the scrap of lace upon the floor. He slid a hand across her abdomen, feeling the enticing heat of her flesh through her sheer panties. "Help me," he gently commanded, and when she raised her hips slightly without hesitation, he removed the last barrier of her clothing. She unbuckled his belt, then opened the snap of his jeans, and he moved from beneath her to stand and shed them and his undershorts completely. He knelt down beside her on the plush area rug in front of the sofa and stretched her out upon the cushions. She was lovely. Enchanting though not perfect. She was a little too short-waisted. Her hips would someday probably be a little too broad. There was a tiny nick on her right shin from shaving her legs, but these little flaws were part of what made her real, and he found them endearing. When she held her arms out to him, he bent down and kissed her, feeling the sweet roundness of her breasts brush against his chest as she started to turn toward him.

"Gracie," he rasped, pressing her back down, taking her lips with his, tantalizing each corner of her mouth with the tip of his tongue before hungrily tasting the sweetness within. Her right hand drifting down his back over his hips and thighs evoked a strong tremor while her left lazily stroked up and down and around his neck. She grew bolder, intensifying his urgent need as her fingertips scampered across his abdomen.

"Be careful," he warned, his deep voice husky. "Two can play this game."

"Oh, I hope so," she breathed, exploring the shallow bowl of his navel. "It wouldn't be any fun if we both didn't play. Kiss me again, Daniel."

He did, repeatedly, his heart thundering violently as she gave him back kiss for kiss. He pulled away only to look down at her, his ranging gaze devouring. He lowered one hand to trace the dividing line made by the legs of her swimsuit, sun-kissed thighs beneath the border, porcelain-pale skin above.

"*Daniel,*" she whispered, quivering at his delicate, evocative touch. Taking his face between her hands, she guided his lips to her breasts, moaning as he kissed the slopes of one then the other again and again. His warm mouth closed around one throbbing peak, exerting a swift pressure that quickly drove her crazy, and as the roughened surface of his tongue braised the aroused nubble of flesh, then his teeth tenderly nibbled at it, she felt as if her limbs were robbed of all strength. He lowered her right foot to the floor, parting her legs, and she allowed him to do so without any thought of resisting. She loved and wanted him too much to deny him or herself anything. It was too late for that.

As her arm tightened across his broad back, he touched her everywhere, and his mouth soon followed the precise trail his hands had blazed, compelled by the tender smoothness of her skin and a taste like heavenly ambrosia.

The tender lashing of his tongue, the searing touch of his lips, and his whispered endearments made her nearly wild with longing. His every caress was an exquisite torment.

"Love me," she murmured in ardent appeal, hands roving feverishly over his back. "Love me."

"Not here," he whispered, pulling away to sit her up, kneeling between her knees. His hands lightly clasped her hips, his thumbs stroking downward. Passion glinted in his eyes as they held hers. "I want much more than just a quick tussle on the sofa, Gracie. I want all night in my bed with you."

That was where he took her. Up through the darkness shading the stairs, down the hall to his room, he carried her, then threw back the quilted coverlet and put her down, leaning over her to switch on the lamp upon the beside table. In the sudden flash of light, she blinked, and he bent down to kiss her chin. "I want to see you; I have to."

She couldn't possibly object, because she wanted to see him too, to look into his eyes. She touched his beloved face, unsteady fingers outlining the shape of his lips until he captured the tip of one between his teeth, gently biting it. She smiled up at him.

"You're seducing me again."

"Umm, that's the general idea."

"And you're very good at it. You make me need you too much."

"Never too much," he corrected, touching his lips to

hers, his warm breath feathering. "Considering how much I need you."

His hands moved to cup her breasts, and she linked her fingers across the small of his back, urging him nearer. Nibbling the lobe of his right ear, she made him tremble a little. His control over her was no greater than hers over him, although that was difficult to believe when his thumbs, then his tongue, explored her nipples, making bold forays on aroused and arousing nubbles of flesh. Her entire body throbbed.

"Tell me what you'd really like most," she whispered, lightly drawing her nails over his back. "I want to please you."

"Honey, you are pleasing me. Come here," he said, turning onto his side, holding her close, molding her body to his as their lips met.

Time lost all meaning, and nothing and no one mattered except the two of them. Womanly and warm, tempting and enticing, she responded with utter abandon, and he prolonged their lovemaking, finding so much gratification in all the ways they delighted each other that he didn't want to rush completion. There were no limitations; for them, everything they wanted was right. Adrift in a sensual world, they were bound together by tenderness, unrelenting need, and mutual respect. Loving him, Grace felt no inhibitions and gloried in the taking and the giving. When they could no longer wait for fulfillment, they found it together, the soft sounds they made mingling as pulsating sensations mounted to the ultimate peak, and they floated down into contentment in each other's arms.

Later, Grace felt Dan's heartbeat slow to a normal pace beneath her hand on his chest. Stirring lazily in the circle of his arms, she tilted her head back and looked up at him. "More?" she asked in a sultry voice.

"Yes," he murmured, starting to turn toward her. "I won't refuse that invitation even though I may collapse from exhaustion afterward."

"Whoa, tiger, I was only joking," she said, laughing as she pushed him back down. "You're not getting any younger, you know, and you need your rest, you insatiable man."

"I'm insatiable?" he countered, amusement lighting his eyes. He playfully tugged a strand of her hair. "You started this. I didn't. Remember?" As she nodded, her eyes started to slowly flutter shut, and with an indulgent smile he brushed a kiss across her forehead, then reached over to switch off the lamp.

Grace awakened alone in Dan's bed the next morning. She sat up and stretched her arms high above her head, yawning. Squinting at the bright morning light spilling through the windows, she looked at the bedside table. The clock said two minutes to seven. Not bad. It was only thirteen minutes past the time she usually got up, and besides, last night hadn't been exactly typical. Smiling at the memory, she slipped naked from beneath the sheet and took Dan's terry cloth robe off the arm of the easy chair where he had left it for her. She put it on, rolled up the sleeves, then padded out into the hall toward the bathroom. Before she got there, she heard water running in the shower but found the door half-open.

"I'm going to brush my teeth and comb my hair," she called, walking in. "So if you hear any strange noises, it's me, not the dog or the cat or a mouse." When he acknowledged her presence, she brushed the tangles out of her tousled hair, brushed her teeth, then left to go downstairs. In the kitchen she measured ground coffee into the basket of the percolator and plugged it in.

When she went back upstairs, Daniel was still in the shower, and she went on to her room to lay out the clothes she planned to wear. Then, simply to pass time, she meticulously straightened several pairs of her shoes on the closet floor. Over ten minutes ticked by, and still she hadn't heard Dan leave the bathroom. But surely he had.

She went back down the hall, surprised that the water was still running. She walked in and peeked in around the end of the shower curtain, grinning.

"Hey, stay in there much longer and your skin's going to get all wrinkled."

Water ran in rivulets over his lean tanned body as he gave her a mysterious smile. "I thought you weren't ever going to get curious enough to come."

"What—" she began, then gasped when his hands clamped her waist and he lifted her over the rim of the bathtub and put her down right beneath the spray.

"Dan, you nut! My hair!" she squealed, laughing even as she tried to wriggle out of his grasp. "Now I'll have to dry it. And your robe's getting soaked."

"I've been waiting for you," he murmured, slowly loosening the wet tie belt.

Nearly giggling, she tried to still his hands, to no avail. "What are you doing?"

"You can't take a proper bath with clothes on. I'm just helping you out of this thing." He pushed the terry cloth off her shoulders, freed her arms from the sleeves, and allowed the robe to fall to the bottom of the tub behind her. "You planned to take a shower, didn't you?"

"Yes but—"

"I wanted us to take one together."

A flutter of excitement rushed over her. Her gaze played over him. *So tempting.* But she resolutely shook her head. "This is a crazy—"

His quick kiss silenced her. "A crazy what?"

"Idea. You know if we shower together, we'll—"

He kissed her again. "We'll what, Gracie?"

"You know exactly what," she uttered, heartbeat accelerating slightly. "We'll be distracted."

His lips swooped down to cover hers, grazing back and forth over their fullness before he pulled back again to look down at her. "Distracted? By what?"

"Oh, Dan," she whispered, her voice catching. "You're —"

"Distracted by this?" he questioned, quieting her with another kiss, one that lingered longer before he ended it. "And this?"

She quivered as his mouth took swift sure possession of her own. "Oh, you are a devil," she accused, her breathing growing ragged as she realized how easy it was for him to make her long to surrender. She loved him so much she was powerless against him. "A real devil," she repeated, but went into his arms, feeling her wet skin would surely sizzle as it made contact with his. The water sluicing over them did nothing to cool her response. Her arms wound upward around his neck, and the rounded curves of her body yielded to the harder planes of his.

Her mouth opened invitingly beneath the onslaught of his, but his tongue didn't enter and instead flicked lazily over her lush, shapely lips. Then, with herculean effort, he put her from him and reached behind her for a bar of soap. Seeing that she trembled, he almost swept her back into his arms but, mustering every last remnant of will power, managed to control that burning urge. He worked the soap to a rich lather between his palms, then spread it over her bare shoulders and down her arms.

"First things first," he told her. "You wanted a shower. I've already had mine, so it's your turn."

She tensed, expecting an erotic exploration of her body as he proceeded to cover every inch of her with fragrant bubbly foam, even rubbing it between her toes. But his touch seemed merely methodical until he finished and moved her more directly beneath the spray where she could rinse off. Methodical as his touch had been, he had kindled a fire in her, and she lifted her face to the lightly peppering jets of water, hoping to dampen the flames. But when he turned her toward him and, with a fingertip, followed a crystalline droplet down over the swell of her left breast then another and another as they cascaded down, those flames erupted into a blazing inferno that left no part of her unsinged.

Slipping one arm around her waist, he lifted her up on tiptoe, arching her against him and lowering his head to lick away the droplets that continued to trickle down.

"*Daniel,*" she gasped, weakness claiming her legs. "Y-you're driving me crazy."

"Now you know how I always feel," said Dan, his voice rough-edged, his tone impassioned as he closed his mouth around one delectable nipple, drawing deeply at it before hungrily possessing its twin.

Grace felt faint as he stepped out of the tub onto the bath mat, then helped her out to pat her face dry with a hand towel, which he also used to rub over her thick wet hair. He tossed it aside, pulled another, much larger one from the shelf, and wrapped it sarong-style around her. When he started to dry himself off, she reached out to help him, feeling the upsurging power of male response as she rubbed the towel over his upper thighs.

Her soft gray eyes met his. "Hurry," she whispered.

"Yes," he whispered back, picking her up to carry her back to his bed, crooning her name as he lowered his body to hers and undraped the towel around her.

Her legs parted easily to the gentle outward pressure of his slipping between them. Her lips found his and parted with a sigh of delight as his hands glided beneath her hips, arching her upward, and his hard body merged with hers, deeply thrusting yet incredibly gentle.

Considerably later Daniel lifted a curve of damp hair back from her forehead, which he lightly kissed.

Grace moved languidly against him, one hand curled against his neck. "You really are a devil," she reiterated, though not very seriously. "And a bad influence on me. It's a workday, and here I am, still lounging around in bed."

He kissed her forehead again. "You know the old saying though: 'All work and no play . . .'"

"I know it; I know it," she assured him, lightly poking him in the ribs with one elbow. "Everybody knows that one."

"Maybe so, but that doesn't make it any less true."

"I guess not, but I have work to do. I'd better get up," she said, moving to do so. "I have to dry my hair, and that's your fault, I hope you know."

Tightening his arm around her waist, he held her down upon the mattress and pulled up to rest upon one elbow, holding her gaze as he asked somberly, "Why are you trying to run away?"

"I'm not trying—"

"It's not only Compton and Royce you're worried about. I still think something else is bothering you. Gracie, what is it?"

"Nothing," she lied. "Why are you starting this interrogation again?"

"Because I have to know the truth."

"Okay. The truth is I'm sick of worrying about what might happen to us next."

"I can understand that," he murmured, stroking her back. "The whole situation is becoming very tiresome, isn't it?"

"Yes," she sighed, wondering bleakly if he might soon be so tired of the hassle that he was willing to give up the business and go on his merry way again, leaving her behind as he had two years ago.

CHAPTER FOURTEEN

Grace awoke in the middle of the night for no apparent reason. She wasn't thirsty, didn't need to go to the bathroom, and Dan was sleeping like a log beside her, so he hadn't disturbed her. But something had, and as she sat up in bed, she heard what it must have been—a muffled noise coming from . . . Where? She couldn't pinpoint the location. Wondering if Buster was wandering around downstairs needing to go out, she got up, pulled her robe on over her gown, and went to find out.

The moment she walked into the kitchen and heard the dog growling, she knew something was wrong, and it was easy to guess where. Hurrying to the window that looked out over the side porch, she peered outside. In the faint moonlight, shadows were moving near the shop. Her heart started to pound. Spinning around, she dashed back upstairs, but before she could reach Dan, Buster erupted in a frenzy of barking.

Dan was already out of bed when Grace ran into her room, nearly colliding with him on his way out. His hands shot out to grip her shoulders. "What's wrong?"

"I think there might be somebody breaking into the shop," she quickly answered, then followed when he swept around her. Although he took the steps two at a time, she managed to stay close behind him and entered the kitchen only a few seconds after he did. Buster was poised at the door, her sleek body tensed, the hair on her back raised, her barking becoming more and more strident. Grace clasped her shaking hands tightly together. "Something must be happening for her to act like this."

"Call the sheriff," Dan commanded, moving in two long strides from the window he'd been looking out to the door. "I'll see what's going on."

"No! Dan, you can't go out there," Grace protested, grabbing his arm. "It might be dangerous."

"Or it might be nothing. I'm going to find out which," he said, reaching for the doorknob while taking hold of Buster's collar and holding her back. "Stay here, girl."

"At least take her with you," Grace insisted, afraid to let him go alone. "Please."

"Her leg's in a cast, Gracie. What help can she be?"

"She can bark. Scare whoever's out there away. And if you won't take her, I'm going with you."

"Okay, I'll take her; we're wasting time arguing about it," he muttered, flipping on the porch light, opening the door, and striding out while Grace headed for the telephone.

Daniel followed the setter as her barking became higher pitched. More accustomed to the cast on her leg, she could move fairly fast, although her gait was rather stiff. Loping across the barnyard behind her, he too saw shadows moving at the back of the shop near the greenhouse. Two distinct shapes quickly emerged, men silhouetted in moonlight, then both darted away, heading toward the road. Giving chase, passing Buster by, Daniel cursed the slippers on his feet, kicked them off, and loped on across the grass with the steady speed of a long-distance runner. Ahead of him one of the men stumbled and fell, and Dan's adrenaline surged, driving him on. If he could just get his hands on one of these people and hand him over to a deputy sheriff, he might be convinced to give the names of everyone involved in this asinine little conspiracy. Sprinting, he gained on the fallen intruder.

In the house Grace stood at the screen door, twisting her hands as she watched what was happening, fear squeezing her throat. Dan must be crazy, chasing these men. God only knew what they might do to avoid being caught. Unable to just stand still and watch a moment longer, she sped out the door, across the porch and barnyard, and past the shop. Seeing the fallen man scramble to his feet and make it to the highway before Dan could catch him, she breathed a sigh of relief and stopped short, hearing the slamming of a door followed by the thunderous revving of an engine and the sharp splatter of gravel against an undercarriage as a pickup careened off the shoulder onto asphalt, then raced out of sight around the curve, tires shrieking. Trembling all over, she watched Daniel walk back to her.

"You should have stayed in the house," he muttered, some impatience tinging his voice as he shook his head. "Damn, I almost caught one of them."

"Why did you even try to catch him? How could you do something so foolish?" she exclaimed, unable to shake the sheer terror she had felt watching him pursue that man. "Why didn't you just let them go? Didn't it occur to you that one or both of them might be carrying a gun?"

"No. I guess it didn't. Maybe you're right. I should have thought of that," he conceded, his tone gentling as he slipped an arm over her shoulders and hugged her briefly to his side, then let her go. "Did you call the sheriff?"

"A deputy should be here any minute."

Nodding, Dan stroked Buster's head, calming her down until at last her guttural growls and low abbreviated woofs ceased completely. Then lightly touching his fingers to the small of Gracie's back, he directed her toward the back of the shop.

"They came out of the greenhouse," he told her. "While we're waiting for the deputy to get here, we might as well see if they had time to do any damage."

They'd had time all right, plenty of it, obviously, judging by the chaos Grace and Dan found when they walked in the door and he turned on the lights. "Oh, no!" she gasped, barely able to believe what she was seeing, hoping it would all prove to be a nightmare she would soon awaken from. But as she heard Dan utter a virulent oath, that meager hope died a quick death. What she was seeing was real. Littering the concrete floor were the remains of what had once been healthy exotic plants which had been ripped from their pots. Clods of dark humus soil were scattered everywhere, and dirt had been ground into the cement during the binge of destruction. She took a shallow quavery breath. "This is insane."

"Yes. But obviously our new TV commercial has been effective, too effective to suit some people. We've been getting more customers since we reminded them we can offer something no one else can," said Dan, a muscle jumping in his clenched jaw. "And apparently, either Compton or his underlings don't want us to be able to offer even more. See? Most of our ordinary plants haven't been touched. It was the exotics they wanted to destroy, and they did a very thorough job of it."

"But the shipment only came in two days ago. How did they know we even had plants like this?"

"Gracie, the greenhouse is open to all our customers. One of them during the past two days was a spy, and these plants were right out in the open for anybody to see."

Rubbing fingertips hard over her forehead, she bent down. At her feet lay a mangled bird-of-paradise plant, the vibrant orange and blue petals of its fragile avian flower torn and bruised. She picked up the trampled bloom, cradling it in both hands. She sucked in a breath. "How could they do this?" she murmured. "If they're Compton's people, they must work with plants. They should love them."

"Gracie, the men who did this love only one thing—the money they were paid to do it. And I suspect money's the great love of Compton's life too."

She suspected the same and looked around once again at the mindless destruction greed had apparently wrought. She sighed. "What are we going to do now?"

"There's only one thing we can do. We'll have to . . ." Dan's voice trailed off to silence when he heard the crunch of gravel beneath tires and looked out the glass walls of the greenhouse as the awaited patrol car pulled up along the driveway, blue light flashing. He went outside to meet the deputy.

It was Glenn Watson who had answered the call. Following Dan into the greenhouse, he came to an abrupt halt, removed his cap, and raked his fingers through his hair, exclaiming, "Holy cow!" He stepped farther inside, looking around in disbelief before focusing his gaze on Grace and Dan. "Guess you better tell me what happened."

They told him, Grace beginning because she had awakened first and suspected something was wrong. Dan finished the story because he had chased the vandals out to the road.

"They got away in a truck?" Watson asked when he had finished. "Make and model?"

"Couldn't tell. It was too dark. All I know is that it was a pickup."

The deputy stroked his chin. "Umm, I met an old wreck of a pickup on my way here. Think that might have been it?"

"Yes," Grace spoke up, looking at Dan. "It was somebody driving an old rusty truck who forced Jim off the road. Don't you think it might have been the same one?"

He nodded. "I think it's very likely."

"Then that gives us a little to go on. I didn't get the license number," said the young deputy. "But at least I have a partial description, and I can ask the sheriff to order the patrols to watch for the vehicle. It's a long shot, though, I have to tell you. Vandalism is a tough crime to solve because the perpetrators go in, tear things up, and get out fast, and most of the time there's no motive. You understand?"

"No," Dan replied flatly. "I'm sure you're right; there probably is no motive for most acts of vandalism, but this one's different. There are people who have plenty of motives."

"And I'm sure you remember," Grace added, lifting her chin, "we've told you exactly who they are."

Snapping shut his notebook and returning it to a back pocket of his uniform trousers, Glenn Watson moved nearer to them. "Listen," he spoke earnestly. "I'm on your side. Too much has happened out here. I'm suspicious, and to tell the truth, I'm ambitious enough to want to solve this case. And I can guarantee Sheriff Holmes will back me up even if I find out Thad Compton and that hotshot dude Pete Royce are involved. They've got a lot of influence, but they don't own the whole county yet."

Grace and Dan looked at each other, exchanging silent messages.

Believing Watson, Dan extended his hand to the young man. "Nice to have you as an ally."

Believing too, Grace smiled at the deputy, inclining her head. "Yes, very nice. Thank you, Glenn."

"My pleasure, ma'am," he replied, very nearly blushing as he smoothed back his hair and replaced his cap. "Well now, I'll call in and get the print man out here, but I'd bet a month's salary he won't find anything that'll help us. And in the morning, when it's light, we'll come back out and check the area between the shop and the road, in case one of the perps might have dropped something. Not likely, but we have to check it out. Procedure."

"It can't hurt to look," Dan said. "But all you'll probably find are my bedroom slippers."

The deputy grinned. "At least you gave them a run for their money."

And could have gotten himself badly hurt or even killed

215

in the process, Grace thought, feeling as if her heart had dropped down to the pit of her stomach.

"You folks don't have to wait," Glenn Watson told them. "You can go on back to the house, if you want, and after the print man finishes out here, I'll come and tell you we're leaving and you can get back to bed."

As they left the shambles in the greenhouse, Buster followed and, in the kitchen, noisily crunched a doggy treat while Grace started warming milk for hot chocolate.

Several minutes later she sat down across the table from Dan, folding her hands around her mug of steaming cocoa as she asked, "Well, what now?"

"We have to replace what we lost," he said matter-of-factly. "Luckily, our insurance policy covers acts of vandalism, so we'll be able to afford it."

"Maybe we should put the insurance money back into our cash reserve," she suggested. She had never been all that enthusiastic about the exotics in the first place, but he had finally persuaded her to take a chance on them. A second chance though? She really wasn't sure about that and quietly told him so.

"We don't have any choice," he replied. "This morning, the Knoxville newspapers begin running our ads announcing the sale on exotics starting Monday."

"Damn, that completely slipped my mind," she muttered. Then her eyes filled with dismay. "But today's Friday! We can't possibly get more exotics in by Monday morning!"

"We're going to have to try. I'm sure we won't be able to get them delivered on such short notice, so we'll probably have to rent a truck and go pick them up ourselves."

"Drive all the way to Florida and back *after* we close the shop tomorrow night? And get there on Sunday? The nursery won't be open."

"I'll give them a call today and see if we can make some special arrangements. As long as they have the plants we

216

need, we'll work out some way of getting them back here. Don't worry."

"But I am worried," Grace admitted, looking into his eyes. "I mean, maybe it's not worth it to go to so much trouble. Even if we can get more exotics, what's going to stop these . . . these idiots from coming back and destroying them too?"

"We'll figure that out when we have to. If necessary, I'll put a cot up in the shop and sleep out there."

"You're not serious," she exclaimed softly. "I don't want you to do that. It could be dangerous."

"Not to mention uncomfortable," he teased.

She was not amused. "This isn't something to joke about, Dan. What if they break in again and you're out there and—"

"Gracie, try to relax," he murmured, his slight smile fading. "I'm not saying we should be reckless, only that we have to protect our own interests. I know you don't want to knuckle under to these strong-arm tactics."

"No, of course not but—"

"Then we have to replace those plants by Monday. It's not very good business to promise the public something then not deliver."

"I know that, but if—"

"It's getting light out. No use going back to bed now, especially with that mess in the greenhouse to be cleaned up," he softly interrupted, rising from his chair. "I'll go dress, and when Glenn and the print man leave, I'll be able to get right to it."

Still cradling the full mug of cocoa in her hands, Grace watched him walk out of the kitchen to go upstairs. When he disappeared from sight, she stared down at the tabletop, knowing she might as well accept the fact he was going to replace the exotics. He had made up his mind, and maybe he was right about that. But she hoped he'd only been kidding about guarding the new plants by sleeping in the shop, because that was an idea she would never go along with.

After helping Dan put the greenhouse back into some semblance of order, Grace spent the remainder of the morning working on clients' accounts. Then she made a light lunch of soup and salad, ate alone, then went out to relieve Dan in the shop so he could have his meal. He returned in less than a half hour, and the curve of her brow lifted when she looked up and saw him approaching the counter.

"That was fast," she said when he came around to join her. "I hope you remembered to wash the dishes, partner."

"I always remember. By the way, the soup was delicious."

She grinned. "I'll tell Lipton you enjoyed it. It was a mix."

"Still delicious. But I *did* give you homemade when you were sick," he quipped, but as she started past him, he lightly caught her arm, his expression becoming more serious. He looked around and saw their three customers were happily browsing for the time being and didn't appear to need assistance. The roughened tips of his fingers brushed briefly over Grace's bare skin. "If you don't have to rush back to the house, I want to tell you what I've arranged with Goodman's Nursery in Jacksonville."

Looking up at him, she stood very still. "I'm in no hurry. Go ahead."

"If we leave in the morning for Jacksonville, the nursery will have our order ready to be loaded by the afternoon. After we pick it up, we could start back and spend the night somewhere along the way, but I think we should spend the night there. I've reserved a hotel room, and the plants will be all right in the truck overnight."

Grace wrinkled her forehead. "You keep saying 'we.' "

"Right. You're going with me."

218

"I can't do that. We can't close the shop tomorrow. Saturday's our busiest day."

"Yes, but that's not going to be a problem. I was talking to Jim, and he offered to keep the place open himself."

"Jim! Oh, no. No way," she proclaimed, adamantly shaking her head. "I don't want him any more involved in this mess than he already is. And I'm surprised at you for asking a man his age to take such a chance."

"I didn't ask him," Dan brusquely said. "I called to ask if he knew someone responsible we could hire to keep the shop open tomorrow. He wouldn't hear of us hiring anybody. He insisted on taking care of it himself. Frankly, he sounded very eager to do it. I have a feeling he misses dealing with customers since he retired."

"Maybe he does, but he's also got a wife to think about. And I'm sure Dottie's not going to be thrilled about this. She's really frightened something might happen to him, and I can't blame her one bit."

"Jim said he'd be able to convince her she shouldn't be."

"Well, nobody's going to convince me of that." Grace's small chin jutted out. "I won't let him risk it. You go to Jacksonville, and I'll stay right here."

"Oh, no, you won't," Dan responded adamantly, his eyes fiercely impaling hers. "I'm going to request that the deputy patrolling out here tomorrow check on Jim occasionally so he'll be safe. These cowards do their dirty work at night anyway, and I'm not going to let you stay here alone tomorrow night."

"But Buster—"

"Can barely run. Be reasonable, Gracie. With her leg in a cast, she'd only get hurt if she tried to attack somebody threatening you. She can't protect you or even herself. We'll board her and the cat at the vet's while we're gone."

"I'm not going, Dan. If we both leave, God knows what will happen to the shop and even the house. Royce might decide to tear them down before we can get back. I have to stay and keep my eye on things."

"How the hell can you be so cautious where 'things' are concerned and so foolhardy when it comes to your own personal safety?" he growled, keeping his voice low. But his words were harsh, clipped. "I'm not going to let you stay here alone. You're going with me to Jacksonville."

"I am not."

"If you insist on staying, I'll have Eric and Allison spend the night out here with you."

"You most certainly will not!" she whispered heatedly, glancing at the customers, relieved to see no one was noticing their argument. She glowered at him. "I'm not about to impose on them, and even if I were willing to, Allison would be a nervous wreck if she had to spend the night here, after all that's happened. And I don't need bodyguards. I'll be just fine by myself."

"You aren't going to have a chance to find out because either you go with me, or you drive to Jacksonville to pick up the plants and I stay here."

"Don't be ridiculous. I—"

"Take it or leave, Gracie," he ground out. "Those are the only two options you're going to get because I'm making sense and you're just being damned obstinate. So what I say goes this time."

"Just who do you think you are, telling me what—"

"I'm telling you because I'm right and you should listen. We are partners. But maybe you'd like to own a hundred percent of this business."

Grace's mouth snapped shut. With a flounce of her skirt she stepped around him, wondering exactly what he had meant by that remark but unwilling to ask, afraid he might tell her. Was he insinuating he might be willing to sell her his half of the shop to get out from under the responsibility? That would certainly make it easy for him to leave again.

* * *

220

Grace went to Jacksonville with Dan . . . reluctantly. During the entire drive south in the rented truck, she worried about Jim, but in silence. She and Dan said little to each other.

Once, when she relieved him at the wheel, he hunkered down in the passenger seat and observed her from the corner of his eye, wondering what the devil she was thinking. She had no reason to resent him for trying to protect her from possible harm, and he still suspected something altogether different was bothering her, something she was too stubborn to tell him.

Arriving in Jacksonville about four that afternoon, they went directly to Goodman's Nursery. As promised, their order was ready, and after the plants were loaded in the truck, Daniel signed the invoice, thanked Nathan Goodman, and got back in the cab.

"Maybe we should start back now," Grace suggested as he pulled away from the loading dock to head across the parking lot toward the entrance to the highway. "It's not even five o'clock yet."

"But we've been on the road over twelve hours" was his flat answer. "We both can use some rest. We'll go to the hotel."

Later, after dinner in the dining room, they took the elevator upstairs to the room they were sharing. After taking a bath, while Dan had a shower, Grace paced restlessly from television set to bed to desk, nerves stretched as near the breaking point as they could get without actually breaking. She longed to go to sleep, to escape the tension that had been mounting between Dan and her all day. And when he came out of the adjoining bathroom, she rushed forward to go brush her teeth but, not really watching where she was going, nearly stumbled over his shoes placed at the foot of the king-size bed. Regaining her balance, she glared at him.

"I think we would have been better off with separate rooms."

"You're right," he replied, his eyes raking over her. "But when I made the reservation yesterday, we were getting along just fine. Then I told you about Jim, and everything changed."

"I was worried about him."

"But you have no reason to worry about him now. When we called him a while ago, he said nothing even suspicious happened all day."

"Thank God. But I'm still worried about what might happen tonight at the shop and the house."

"It's not just that. Something else is bothering you, something that made you aloof yesterday and grumpy today."

"I'm not grumpy!"

"The hell you're not."

"Dan, you're—"

"Tell me what else is wrong."

"Nothing!"

"Little liar," he gruffly muttered, reaching out to pull her into his arms, his lips seeking the slender column of her neck. "Tell me."

"There's n-nothing to tell," she gasped, struggling to free herself. "Let me go, Dan. S-sex isn't the answer to everything."

"No. It isn't," he murmured, stripping off her robe as he lowered her onto the bed. "But when we make love, I feel like I know all your secrets. That's how I want to feel right now."

"*Daniel!*" she moaned as the tip of his tongue wandered down from the base of her throat to the uprising curves of her breasts. She trembled violently. He shed his pajama pants, and while his fiery hands roamed all over her, he parted her legs. He entered her, thrusting tenderly yet deeply, and she ecstatically whispered his name. Tomorrow she might be sorry but tonight she welcomed him, love conquering all her doubts.

CHAPTER FIFTEEN

Fortunately, when Gracie and Dan returned home, they found everything in order. Their enemies had missed a golden opportunity to make mischief during their absence, and Grace was able to breathe a little easier. It was good to be home again, but she did regret the fact that they had arrived back too late to pick up the animals at the vet's. It wasn't their favorite place to be, especially overnight.

Monday morning, Grace dug into the bottom of her purse for her car keys while walking toward the shop. Twirling the key ring round and round one finger, she glanced up at the bright blue sky dotted here and there with fluffy puffs of pure white clouds. Pale sunlight lay in dappled patches beneath the overhanging boughs of the old oak trees, and the air was scented with the fragrance of honeysuckle. In a lilac bush, a mockingbird imitated the cheerful warble of a cardinal, as if celebrating the cat's absence. It was a lovely day, although it promised to be another hot one before it ended. A light breeze stirred tendrils of Grace's hair, but she knew the air might feel like a blast furnace by early afternoon, and she wanted to finish her errands long before then, come home, and get into a cool pair of shorts and a halter.

She found Dan in the greenhouse watering a potted pampas grass, and he didn't notice her when she came in. She went over to him, lightly touched his back.

"I'm going to rescue Buster and Little Bit," she told him. "I'll pick them up on my way home from the doctor."

"Doctor?" he repeated, frowning. "Are you sick?"

"No, no, it's just a checkup, but I just wanted to tell you I might be gone a couple of hours. Less if I don't have to wait long to see Dr. Brooks."

"I wish you'd told me you had an appointment so I could have arranged to go with you. I really don't want you going anywhere alone."

"You can't be my bodyguard everywhere I go," she quietly said, flipping her palms up in a gesture of acceptance. "It's too inconvenient for both of us. You have to open the shop, and I have to keep my appointment. And maybe we're being too cautious anyhow. These people can't be watching us continuously; they'd be wasting their time because we're both almost always here."

"True," he conceded. "But—"

"I'll go straight to the doctor's office, then to the vet's from there, and straight back home," she promised, starting to move away. "And I'll keep my eyes open."

"Gracie," he murmured, catching hold of her arm for a second, gazing darkly down at her. "Be careful."

Nodding, she slipped away, his words making her feel good inside. He was truly concerned about her safety. Encouraging. Or was she merely grasping at straws in an attempt to convince herself that his feelings for her had become much deeper than they had been two years ago.

After no more than ten minutes in Dr. Brook's waiting room, Grace was called. The gynecologist's examination was over soon, certainly not a pleasurable experience but one that was a yearly necessity for her own peace of mind. After she had dressed, the doctor talked to her for several minutes in his quiet friendly manner, then moved on to another patient. Grace paid the receptionist and left, driving back out of Alpine Springs to the vet's.

Dr. Walsh's assistant, Ray, led her into the back room

where Little Bit was sleeping in a roomy cage but a cage nonetheless. Grace softly called the kitten's name, and her eyes opened to narrow slits, then widened. She mewed mournfully as if to say: "How could you desert me for so long?" Trying to compensate a little, Grace scratched the cat's furry little chin, carrying her while Ray took her to the run where Buster was loudly lapping water from a bowl. At the sound of Grace's voice, her ears perked up, she began to wriggle all over, and her tail quickly wagged back and forth in wild exultation. If not for her cast, she would have bounded out of the run and might have knocked Grace down in her excitement. As it was, however, she simply pressed her nose against Grace's thigh, whimpering an emotional "Hello. Thank you for getting me out of this place."

"Grace," Ed Walsh called when she walked out of the back room and past his office. His door was flung wide open, and he motioned her in. "I want to talk to you for a few minutes. Got time?"

"Sure," she said, going in to take the chair across from his neat desk. The dog plopped down as close as she could get while the kitten curled up happily in her lap. She idly stroked both their heads while asking, "What is it, Ed?"

"Since Buster was here, I examined her Saturday, X-rayed her leg, and it's mending well. But while I was examining her, I discovered something I'm sure you'll find very interesting."

Grace leaned forward, listening.

There were several cars parked in front of the garden shop when Grace got back about thirty minutes later. While Little Bit scampered away across the barnyard to resume her feline pursuits, Grace took Buster into the shop, where the dog greeted Dan with renewed whimpering, then found her favorite place behind the counter and settled in. Before Grace could say anything to Dan, a customer approached him with a question while another followed to wait a few feet away. Pressed into service, Grace offered her assistance.

The exotic plants brought people in and sold so well that it was after one o'clock before Grace could get away to the house and quickly put together roast beef, lettuce, and tomato sandwiches for Dan and herself. After eating hers and having a cooling glass of iced tea, she went back to the shop to relieve him.

By two, business began to get slower. Obviously, many folks weren't willing to come out during the hottest part of the day, and Grace was rather glad. She needed a break, and as she lifted the back of her blouse collar away from the damp nape of her neck, she looked around and saw that he wasn't dealing with a customer either. Although two women were browsing in the shop and a man was in the greenhouse, none of them seemed to be waiting for help. It seemed the perfect time to tell him the news she'd been forced to keep to herself all day because they'd been so busy. She hurried over to him.

"I have some exciting news," she said, her eyes alight. "I've been wanting to tell you since I got back but didn't have a chance."

His responsive smile formed attractive shallow dimples in his cheeks as he met her gaze. She was so exquisitely lovely when she forgot her inhibitions and allowed the sheer joy of living full rein. He wanted to take her in his arms and kiss her, but this was neither the time nor place with those two customers moving around them, glancing their way now and then, so he made no move to touch her. Instead, he simply asked, "What news, Gracie?"

"You're going to be so surprised. I certainly was," she said, practically beaming as she proudly announced, "We're going to be hearing the pitter-patter of little feet around here soon."

His breath catching, he stared at her. "You mean Dr. Brooks told you that you're going to have a—"

"No, oh, no," she said hastily, then had to laugh at the

misunderstanding, although she thought he paled a little beneath his tan. She patted his shoulder. "You've got it all wrong. I guess I should have said the pitter-patter of little *paws*. Ed Walsh told me Buster's going to have puppies. And I thought she was getting a little tubby because she's not getting as much exercise."

Suddenly, Daniel laughed too, shaking his head. "Buster's pregnant. I thought you—"

"Obviously, but how could you think I was pregnant? We always take precautions."

"No method's one hundred percent effective."

"True. Sorry I upset you by saying little feet instead of little paws."

"I wasn't upset, Gracie," he murmured, reaching for her hand. "Mostly just astonished because you seemed so hap—"

"Could somebody help me?" their customer in the greenhouse called out, crooking a finger as he stepped into the doorway. "I want to take a closer look at the rose foxglove on the top shelf."

For a long moment Grace's eyes held Dan's. Then, with an inward sigh, she averted her gaze, and he finally walked away to attend to business.

No more than five minutes later, a middle-aged woman with graying hair burst into the shop, carrying three potted royal purple delphiniums, which she plopped down upon the counter and huffily demanded, "I want my money back."

"What seems to be the problem, ma'am?" Grace asked in a most professional tone. "We don't want any unsatisfied customers, so if you'll just tell me what's wrong, I'll—"

"I'll tell you exactly what's wrong! I bought these because *you* said they were grown organically from seed. Then I heard that's a lie, that these plants are chockful of chemicals no different from the ones I can buy cheaper at Compton's."

"They are very different," Grace calmly but firmly said. "I assure you every plant in our shop was grown organically from seed, without the aid of any chemicals."

"Well that's not what I heard!"

"Maybe you'd be kind enough to tell exactly what you did hear, then," Dan put in, stepping up behind the woman, smiling politely as she spun around. "We'd like to know."

"And I'm happy to tell you, because I don't put up with getting cheated. Not if I can help it, and I heard that you all are saying this stuff is organically grown just to lure in customers but that you really buy everything from the same supplier Thad Compton does," the woman accused, cheeks pink as she turned back on Grace, waggling a finger at her. "I knew your grandmother, young lady, and she was honest as the day is long. I decided to give you my business because you're her granddaughter. Wish I hadn't. She'd be so ashamed of you. False advertising is lying, pure and simple."

"You're absolutely right; it is," Grace agreed. "But you're mistaken. Our advertisements are truthful, and as I said before, everything we sell is organically grown."

The woman sniffed.

Witnessing this exchange, one of the potential customers in the shop marched out the door, a disgusted look on his face while the other remained, observing the dramatic scene with avid interest.

Dan moved closer to the counter, pulling one of the delphiniums toward the edge. "Would you let me show you something, Mrs. . . ."

"Morton. Lily Morton." She shrugged unenthusiastically. "Well, I don't know."

"Please."

His earnest expression and natural charisma thawed her a little. "Guess it won't hurt to look," she acquiesced, watching as his fingertips gently moved the soil in the pot, exposing the tops of the roots.

228

"What do you see?" he asked. "Besides the plant and the soil, I mean."

"Nothing."

"Precisely. If this had been treated with chemicals, you'd see white dust, the dust you find around nearly every plant in Compton's Garden Centers."

"I have noticed that before . . . but . . . but what if you sprayed something on, something I can't see?"

"You're a hard lady to convince," Daniel told her, smiling winningly, then looking at Grace. "Would you reach under the counter and bring out the invoice we got in the mail this morning from Goodman's Nursery? Should be right on top." When she quickly complied, he opened the manila envelope and withdrew three computerized sheets that itemized their order for the previous month. At the top of the first page, he pointed out the company's motto for Mrs. Morton: "Natural is better; loving gardeners don't need chemicals." His broad shoulders rose and fell in a shrug. "If you've been cheated, we've been cheated, but I'm sure if you called the Jacksonville Better Business Bureau, you'd discover that Goodman's Nursery has an untarnished reputation."

Lily Morton eyed him, then Grace, then him again, growing uncertainty lining her face. But she still wasn't totally won over. "Maybe I will call them."

"I wish you would," Grace said. "And you might want to go ask someone at one of Compton's centers who supplies them. I can guarantee it isn't Goodman's in Jacksonville."

"Really?"

"Really. Go ask."

"Well, I declare," Lily muttered, shaking her head. "I wonder where such rumors get started."

"Maybe you can help us find out how this one did," Daniel suggested. "Who told you we were cheating our customers?"

"Let's see now. It was . . . No, it wasn't him." Tapping

229

her fingers against her lips, Mrs. Morton thought hard and long, then grimaced. "To tell the truth, I can't remember who it was I heard say it. There were just some people talking about it after church yesterday morning."

Grace groaned inwardly. *Some people.* How many? If enough heard this despicable, totally untrue rumor, Nature's Garden Shop might not be worth a plugged nickel. Business might come to a grinding halt.

"I think I'll take my delphiniums and go home now," Lily murmured. "Sorry I've made such a ninny of myself. When I tell Ernie—he's my husband—what I did, he'll tell me I ought to stop listening to gossip. I'll say I'm going to, but he won't believe me. But I'm going to tell everybody I know that they can trust you, that you're honest, and believe you me, I know lots of people."

That they didn't doubt for an instant, and both of them smiled at her as she loped to the door of the shop, stopping to give them a little wave before she went out. Then they looked at each other, but before they could say a word, their observant customer approached the counter and pointed out two of their largest, lushest, most expensive staghorn ferns.

She smiled warmly at Grace. "I'll take those, please. I'm Maggie Clemmons. I knew your grandmother too, but I also know you're continuing her Christmas Stocking work. So I never believed for a minute that what Mrs. Morton had heard was true."

"I needed to hear that. Thank you," Grace said sincerely.

After Maggie chatted awhile, paid for the ferns, and promised to come back soon, Daniel carried the heavy pots to her car for her. When he returned, he found Gracie leaning her elbows on the counter, her chin resting in her cupped hands. "Thank God Gran was well thought of around here and you are too," he said. "We probably wouldn't have a chance of succeeding if you weren't."

"We might not anyhow. You saw that man leave. How

many people will he tell that we're a couple of cheats?" she asked, raising worry-darkened eyes to meet his. "We're in real trouble, Dan. They could ruin us by spreading lies like this."

"I know that. And I think it's time to counterattack," he stated fearlessly, striding toward the small office. "I'm going to give Richard Michaels a call. Maybe Pete Royce will change his tune a little if our attorney threatens him with a slander suit."

"But we can't prove Royce started this rumor."

"No, but sometimes bluffs work."

That was true. But she wondered if this would be one of those times.

Late the following afternoon Grace sat in front of her computer, the kitten snoozing at her feet, fuzzy chin resting on her sandaled feet, twitching whiskers occasionally tickling her bare toes. She didn't mind. A lazy cat can be a pleasantly quiet companion during a balmy afternoon. Sitting back in her swivel chair, she reorganized by date the debits accrued by Winslow's Dairy Farm during the preceding month, prior to entering them in the computer. When she finished, before she could begin striking the appropriate input keys, someone banged loudly on the front door screen, and she slipped her feet carefully from beneath Little Bit, then shrugged when the kitten's eyes opened accusingly.

"Sorry," Grace whispered, getting up. "Go back to sleep. It's too hot to do anything else."

Leaving her office, she stepped into the hallway, then nearly turned back around when she saw that Pete Royce stood outside on the veranda. Spine stiffening with full-blown animosity, she walked toward him instead, not even bothering to force a semblance of a smile. When she reached the door, she stared coldly out through the screen. "Yes?"

He began badly. "Aren't you a picture?" he said, his

voice dripping sugar as his nastily insinuating eyes crawled over her, lingering obnoxiously long on her long tanned legs and the swell of her breasts. "And don't you look fresh as a daisy in that little sundress?"

Silently, she heaved a disgusted sigh. "May I help you?"

"I just want to have a little talk," he claimed, easing a fleshy hand over his too-sleek pompadour. "Aren't you going to ask me in?"

Not in a million years. She simply stood where she was, exceedingly glad that the screen door was hooked. "What do you want to talk about?"

"Well . . . I had a very disturbing phone call this morning, and there's surely a misunderstanding. I was told you and Dan Logan think I'm spreading lies about you, and that's just not true."

He was such a horrible actor that it infuriated her to know that he actually thought she would believe him. "Don't hand me that line," she drawled. "Dan and I know exactly what you're trying to do. I thought we made that clear the last time we saw you."

His mood changed in an instant. All the pseudofriendliness disappeared. His nostrils were pinched, the set of his mouth cruel as he glared at her, eyes malevolent. "I don't like getting calls from lawyers," he hissed. "Especially when they threaten to sue me for slander."

"Then stop lying about us, and you won't get any more calls . . . from our attorney, at least."

His face went scarlet with fury. "You're making one big mistake, little lady. I've got power behind me, and you and that boyfriend of yours are going to lose."

Enough was enough. Temper flaring, she slapped open the screen door hook and stalked out onto the veranda. "Get off my property. *Now*," she commanded. "And if you ever call me 'little lady' again, you're going to get a swift kick where it hurts the most."

He started toward her but was stopped in his tracks when Buster came round the side of the house, moving fast as an express train despite her leg and slightly bulging belly. She instinctively seemed to realize Grace was in some sort of danger, and it took nothing more than her curled-up lip and growling snarl to convince Royce to back off down the steps. Yet, he still did so with the bravado of a fool as he eased toward the safety of his car when Grace called Buster off.

"You're going to be sorry about this," he threatened out the driver's window after falling in beneath the steering wheel and slamming the door shut, his beady eyes darting from Grace to the still alertly tensed dog as he added, "Try suing me, and you're going to find out what real trouble is."

And as he sped away in his long, gaudy sedan, she believed him. He was just stupid enough to try something else, something more drastic.

CHAPTER SIXTEEN

"What exactly did he say?" Dan asked Grace as he stirred the ingredients of the omelet he was preparing for dinner. "Did he threaten to hurt you?"

"Not in words, but he was coming toward me when good old Buster saved the day. I don't know what he was planning to do," Grace said honestly, tearing tender lettuce leaves into a wooden bowl, disdain tightening her lips. "But I wouldn't trust him as far as I could throw that big flashy car of his. Such a thoroughly obnoxious man."

"And a coward too. He could've come to the shop to see me, but instead he talked to you because you're a woman and he thought you'd be more easily intimidated."

A sudden impish grin lighted Grace's delicate features. "I wonder if he still thought that after I told him what I'll do if he ever calls me 'little lady' again."

"What did you tell him you'll do?"

Grace explained, her grin remaining.

Dan grinned back. "At least he knows you have spunk now."

"I have a feeling he doesn't admire spunky women."

"I'm sure he doesn't. I wonder if he's married."

"I pity his wife if he is," Grace murmured, shaking her head. "He must be a sweetheart to live with. Wonder what makes him such a bully."

"Probably the belief that he can get away with being

234

one," said Dan. "Power corrupts, and he's obviously had things all his own way for so long without any competition that he thinks he has a right to do whatever he pleases to hold on to control. Our shop's an inconvenience, and tyrants don't like to be inconvenienced."

"Or talked back to. He was steaming mad when I told him to leave. All that gushy so-called charm of his disappeared, and he showed me he has a violent temper. How . . . far do you think he might go to try to drive us out of business?"

"He's already gone further than I expected him to. I thought he'd give up once we opened the shop. But . . ." Daniel left the statement unfinished, but his meaning was clear. A man of Royce's caliber was practically unpredictable. He might hatch any kind of plot in that pea-sized brain of his. And that was an uncomfortable realization but one that Daniel had to accept. "Since we don't know what he's capable of doing, I want you to be more careful, Gracie. If he comes here again, don't talk to him. Call the shop and I'll walk over and he can say whatever he has to say to me."

"I could sic Buster on him again. He wasn't at all eager to mess with her. She deserves a special treat for coming to the rescue. I'll give her a bowl of milk. It'll be good for the puppies."

Smiling, Dan looked across the kitchen at Buster. Lying on her pad, she acted as if she knew she was being discussed. Her ears were perked up, her brown eyes bright and alert. "Since you're going to be a mother soon, I guess we know that you weren't chasing rabbits all those times several weeks ago. And I doubt there's much chance of your puppies being full-blooded Irish setters."

"I guess we just didn't raise her right," Grace pretended to lament. "She probably got involved with a dog who was just passing through, one of those who loves 'em and leaves 'em. A vagabond."

"Could be. Vagabonds are mysterious," Dan agreed,

playing along. "Sometimes they can have a powerful appeal."

Tell me about it, she was tempted to retort but didn't as she looked closely at his lean face and saw no evidence that he remembered she had once called him a vagabond.

Later, when the grandfather clock in the parlor struck eleven times, Dan gathered up the pages of the manuscript he'd been working on, covered the typewriter, and slipped his chair back from the antique secretary. Slowly, he stood and for a quick moment laid a hand against the small of his back. "Guess it's time to call it a day," he announced. "Might as well go on out to the shop."

Grace raised her eyes slowly to meet his, shaking her head. "I thought the backache you got sleeping on that cot last night would be enough to put some sense in your head. You winced just now when you got up, and I've seen you rubbing your back several times today. Last night, you were just too stubborn to listen to me when we argued about this. Don't be a ninny again tonight. Unless you want to wake up with a sore back in the morning too. Do you?"

"No, I'd rather not."

"Then forget about sleeping in the shop. It really isn't necessary."

"You said that last night but—"

"Don't go," she murmured, putting her sewing aside, leaning slightly forward on the sofa, and beckoning him. When two long strides brought him closer, she gazed up, her ash-gray eyes soft, glowing. "You don't have to. Stay with me."

Some unfathomable emotion flitted across his face. "We don't want the place torn apart again, Gracie."

"I don't think it will be. These people haven't pulled the same thing twice yet," she said, although uncertain herself what hoodlums might do. Yet, she was unwilling to let him go. Knowing he might be in danger in the shop had given her bad dreams last night, frightening dreams she

236

didn't want to experience again. She wanted him with her, to know he was safe, and to feel safer herself. She needed him to hold her in his arms and to tightly hold him. "Stay, Daniel," she repeated, reaching out to hook her thumbs beneath the side belt loop of his jeans. Pulling herself to her feet before him, she slid her arms around his waist, stretched up on tiptoe, and danced her soft lips across his, murmuring, "Don't leave me."

He didn't.

Early the next morning in the shop, Daniel took the first of many enraging phone calls. The moment the muffled words were spoken by a crude, raspy voice uttering vile explicit threats against Gracie, fury exploded in him, a fury further fuelled by a sense of helplessness. He couldn't fight an unidentifiable voice that uttered intimidating messages less than a minute before the line abruptly went dead. Slamming down the receiver, he raked his fingers through his hair, then led Buster back to the house. Every time she wandered over to visit him thereafter, he immediately took her back to the kitchen, but quietly, not wanting to make Grace suspicious. He didn't want to tell her about the phone call or to admit that he considered Buster the first line of defense whenever he himself couldn't be in the house.

After receiving five such nasty calls in as many hours, Dan contacted Deputy Glenn Watson.

"What exactly did he say?" Glenn asked, and listened in attentive silence before adding, "How long does he stay on the line? We might be able to get a trace."

"Never more than a minute," answered Daniel. "I doubt that's long enough. Is it?"

"No way." The young deputy commiserated but could offer no official assurances except to say that he would talk to the sheriff and request that officers patrolling that area keep a very close watch on the shop and house on a round-the-clock basis. Then he promised that he personally was keeping an eye on the situation.

After expressing his sincere thanks for Glenn's cooperation, Daniel hung up, but in less than thirty seconds the phone rang, and when he answered, the raspy voice repeated previous threats and started to elaborate on them. Unwilling to give the degenerate caller the satisfaction of knowing he was listening, he replaced the receiver in its cradle, noticing his hand was shaking.

At four fifteen Thursday morning, Grace was rudely wakened by the shrill pealing of the phone beside her bed. Heart thudding in swift staccato beats, she reached over to snatch up the receiver, eager to stop that irritating ringing. As Daniel stirred beside her, she placed it to her ear, sleepily muttering, "Hello."

Silence at the other end.

"Hello," she repeated.

Nothing.

Once more, impatiently, she ground out, "*Hello.*"

Then came the sound of deep breathing, punctuated by coarse groans.

"Oh, you must be kidding," she snapped. If this was a practical joker, he had no taste at all, and she didn't appreciate being jarred awake by such an imbecile. "Just who the devil is this?"

More exaggerated groans.

As she started to hang up, Dan propped himself up on one elbow, frowning, muttering, "What's going on?"

She raised her eyes heavenward in sheer disgust. "Would you believe a heavy breather?"

At once he was totally alert, moving with the swiftness of a pouncing tiger to take the phone from her hand and growl into it, "Hello. Who is this?"

A loud clapping pop was his answer as the connection was immediately and violently broken. Uttering an oath, he reached across Grace to lay the receiver beside the base of the phone. When she started to replace it in its cradle, he stilled her hand.

"Leave it off the hook," he softly commanded. "They'll probably call back if you don't."

"Oh, I'm sure that was just a fluke." Stifling a yawn, she shook her head incredulously. "What I don't understand is how anybody has time to waste dialing numbers at random just to aggravate people. Lord, I hope I'm never that bored."

Turning her onto her side toward him, Dan searched the coal-dark depths of her eyes, knowing he must tell her the truth, at least part of it. "It probably wasn't a fluke," he said, his features tightening even as he gently smoothed the back of one hand across her right cheek. "I don't think this number was picked at random because I've been getting threatening phone calls at the shop for the past two days."

"Th-threatening calls? Why didn't you tell me?" she exclaimed bewilderedly, curving slender fingers round his wide wrist. "Why?"

"I didn't want to worry you."

"But all I heard was heavy breathing. Y-you said you were threatened, so maybe there's no connection."

"I think there is."

"Wh-what kind of threats, Dan?" she asked, believing he was right, although she didn't want to. "What did they say to you?"

"The man just made vague threats," he lied, unwilling to admit they had been made against her specifically. She didn't need to know that. He meant to protect her. She need never know the whole truth. Bending down, he lightly kissed her forehead. "It's going to be all right."

"You think either Compton or Royce is behind this, don't you?"

"One or the other. Who else? Maybe both of them."

"Did you recognize the voice of the man who's been calling you? Was it Royce?"

"No. But he always has somebody else do his dirty work for him."

"Oh, damn," she whispered thickly, burying her face in the side of his neck. "I'm beginning to think this is never going to be over."

"It will be, I promise. And in the end, we're going to win," he vowed, pulling her nearer. "Just try to go back to sleep now."

And after a long time, as they held each other close, she did.

In the week that followed, as the calls to both Grace and Dan continued, they solved the problem for her by having the house phone number changed to an unlisted one. At the shop they couldn't do that; the public had to have easy access to the number there because people often phoned to inquire about prices or ask whether or not they stocked this or that. Daniel simply had to tolerate the threatening calls. He listened to only the first few words each time before hanging up, but the situation remained highly disturbing nevertheless.

To make matters worse, business had fallen off a little. Obviously some people believed the untrue story that their plants were as full of chemicals as Compton's. Luckily, threatening to sue Royce had apparently nipped his devious plan in the bud, that particular plan anyway. But Dan was quite sure he'd come up with something else soon. Having someone make menacing calls wouldn't satisfy his nasty streak for long.

Dan wouldn't have been nearly as tense if Gracie hadn't been involved, but she was. The man who called him three or four times a day issued his threats against her, which infuriated Dan and also made him rather reluctant to leave her alone, even in the house. It was always a relief when she helped him in the shop, and when she couldn't, he had convinced her to keep Buster close by at all times. Although the setter's belly was lower to the ground with the weight of the puppies she carried, she could still move with astonishing speed when the need arose, and of course her growling bark always spoke volumes. And the dog was very protective of Gracie; that eased his concern to some extent but certainly not altogether. He found himself staring into space on occasion, considering ways he could be certain Gracie was absolutely safe. Some options weren't feasible; a few had possibilities, but he knew his best bet was to keep a close eye on her, which he discreetly did.

After a satisfyingly busy Saturday at the shop, Grace and Dan were about to close when Eric and Allison arrived.

"You can't close your cash register yet," Allison said excitedly, bustling into the greenhouse and coming back out with two African violets in full bloom. "I have to buy these. You know the other one I bought? I took it to my mother this afternoon—that's where we've been—and she loved it. Couldn't believe all the blossoms on it. And since we're going to Eric's mother's tomorrow, I want to take her one too and his great-aunt. So how much do I owe you?"

"Nothing," said Dan. "They're yours, with compliments of the management."

"Oh, no, I couldn't do—"

"Oh, yes, you can and will," Grace interceded, smiling. "We insist."

As his wife nodded, Eric stroked a velvety leaf on one of the plants, saying, "Getting these isn't the only reason we dropped by here. We have reservations for four at Chase's and expect you two to go there with us for dinner."

"It's nice of you to ask," Grace said, but a note of resignation entered her voice as she glanced at Daniel and added, "But I guess we'd better stay here and guard the place."

"But—" Eric and Allison said simultaneously before Dan quietly interceded.

"I think we should go, Gracie," he declared, looking at her, a slight smile forming those attractive half dimples in his cheeks. "It's like you said—we can't allow ourselves to become prisoners here."

"I should say not," Allison agreed, vehemently shaking her head in unison with her husband. "Come on, Grace; you must need a night on the town."

"Probably," she conceded, a glimmer of excitement sparking in her eyes as they met Dan's encouraging gaze. She quickly examined Allison's ice-blue dress and tossed up her hands. "Okay. Sounds great. Just give me a few minutes to get out of this denim jumper and into something else. It won't take me ten minutes."

"Maybe less," commented Dan. "She can get ready to go somewhere faster than any woman I've ever known."

"And he's known plenty of them. Just ask him," Grace lightheartedly teased. "He'd love to tell you about all his conquests."

"Not in front of Allison," he retorted, his tone as teasing as hers had been. He reached out to tweak a strand of her hair. "You women stick together, so I know when to keep my mouth shut. Besides, I want to change clothes too." He smiled at the Kingstons. "I'll lock up here, and then you two can have brandy in the parlor while we dress."

Less then fifteen minutes later Grace and Dan followed the Kingstons into Knoxville in her car so the other couple wouldn't have to drive them back to the farm when the evening ended. They found Chase's crowded as usual, but the number of people didn't detract from the subdued charm of the restaurant. Conversation was muted, rarely loud, but the atmosphere was subtly invigorating. Everyone there seemed so animated, while knowing how to have a quiet good time.

Comfortable in her black skirt and ivory silklike camisole, Grace relaxed while sipping wine before dinner. And the meal itself was delicious. With a hearty appetite she thoroughly enjoyed stuffed flounder and asparagus tips after a fresh garden salad with a particularly tasty dressing that was the house secret recipe.

Coffee was accompanied by idle conversation until soft music began and Dan arose from his chair in silence to extend a hand to Grace. Without hesitation she took it as he excused them both and led her away from the table. His arms went lightly round her waist; she slid hers around his, and they swayed rhythmically together to the slow, pulsing beat.

After a while he murmured close to her ear, "You don't feel at all tense tonight, Gracie."

A faint smile touched her lips. "It's kind of nice to escape our problems for a while."

"Yes, very nice."

"You're tired of all this, aren't you?"

"Who wouldn't be?"

Indeed, who wouldn't? Leaning back against his powerful arms, she avidly searched his face for an answer. But to what? To a question her mind couldn't quite formulate into words. Silently, unable to express her vague misgivings, she held him nearer.

When the music ended, they returned to the table at the same time Eric and Allison did. Conversation recommenced but soon became uncomfortable for Grace when Eric asked, "How's business been lately?"

"Not bad," Dan replied. "The lies about us seem to have died down."

"What about those awful phone calls?" Allison inquired, turning toward Grace. "Are you still having to listen to nasty obscenities?"

"I never had to. Whoever called me never said a word. All I heard was a lot of heavy breathing. And since we've had an unlisted number at the house, nobody's bothered me at all."

"What about you, Dan?" Eric questioned. "You were getting calls at the shop too, weren't you? Have they stopped?"

"I wish I could say no," Daniel murmured, unwilling to lie, especially to Gracie. "But I can't. I'm still getting several a day."

"What fun," Allison muttered, smiling grimly as she looked at him. "Isn't the business world beginning to get you down, Dan? Aren't you ready to come back to the lecture hall where you belong?"

"No" was his flat answer. "Because that's not where I belong."

Grace's eyes moved over his tan face. She believed him; he didn't think he belonged in the lecture hall. But did he think he belonged in a garden shop either? That was the precise question that had evaded her earlier, but it was suddenly clear. During the past few days she had often noticed the faraway look in his eyes. Had he been thinking of faraway places? Was he about to leave her alone again?

And what if he did? It would hurt, badly. She knew that. The very thought of him going made her heart ache. Yet, she knew herself and was aware of her intrinsic strength. She would survive, no matter what. She could keep the shop going even if he left. She was too damned stubborn to let Compton and Royce defeat her. And even more importantly, the garden shop was a venture she and Dan had shared. She would keep it going because of that, if for no other reason. In the end it might be all of him she had left.

CHAPTER SEVENTEEN

Late Monday afternoon Brian Price visited Grace. She was surprised to see him. It was the first time they had gotten together since the morning he had turned down their loan application, although he had phoned her once about a week later. That conversation had been brief. Neither of them had known exactly what to say. Wondering if they would be any less restrained this time, she walked toward the screen door.

On the other side of the fine silvered mesh door, Brian smiled at her with some uncertainty and a hint of sheepishness. Craning his neck a little awkwardly, he straightened his tie.

"Hello, Brian," she said, unlatching the door, opening it to silently invite him in. "What brings you out this way?"

"Just thought I'd stop by and say hi. It's been a while, hasn't it?" he murmured, stepping into the hallway beside her, straightening his tie again, quite unnecessarily. His eyes met hers for an instant, then fell away. "I wanted to find out if you're still mad at me."

She shook her head. "I'm not mad, Brian."

"Disappointed then?"

"Not even that now. I understand how important your career is to you and that you felt you had to make the decision you made."

245

"But you think I should have shown more backbone?"

"I think you did what you felt you had to do. And your actions are your business, Brian, not mine."

His gaze finally met hers for an extended period. "I've missed you," he declared. "Have you missed me too?"

"Come into the parlor and sit down. I'll get us some iced tea," she evaded, unwilling to tell him the unvarnished truth, that she hadn't missed him at all. During the past weeks her clients, the shop, and Dan—especially Dan —had pushed all thoughts of him right out of her mind. Yet, she was a tenderhearted person; she couldn't possibly be blunt enough to tell him that. Better to slowly but surely ease him toward that realization so that when he left later, it wouldn't be with wounded pride. After he settled down at one end of the sofa, she excused herself and went into the kitchen.

When she returned to the parlor several minutes later, she carried an enamelled tray bearing two glasses filled to the brim with clear amber tea over loads of sparkling ice. Sprigs of mint peeked out over the rims. She smiled kindly at Brian as his face lighted with enthusiasm.

"I could sure use that," he said, taking the glass she handed him. "It's a hot one today, isn't it? A scorcher."

"And humid."

"I'll say. Stepping out of the bank was like walking into a steam room."

She nodded.

"Wonder how much longer it's going to last," he added. "I can stand the ninety-five-degree temperatures, but the humidity kills me."

Realizing this prolonged and very trite discussion of the weather was soon going to become ludicrous, Grace took a sip of tea, then asked, "What have you been up to lately?"

"Oh, the usual. My duties at the bank keep me busy. How about you? Obviously, you and Dan were able to secure a loan for your business. I'm glad. And I hear the shop's a success although you've had some problems."

"Yes," she said. "But how did you hear about them?"

"The grapevine. In a town as small as Alpine Springs everybody knows everybody else's business. I heard about everything that's happened out here within twenty-four hours, maximum. These acts of vandalism—do you think Thad Compton or someone who works for him is responsible?"

"There's no concrete proof of that."

"But you think so anyhow?"

Grace looked squarely at Brian. "What do you think?"

He averted his gaze, unwilling to answer that question. "I heard the lie that was going around a couple of weeks ago too," he muttered instead. "And I told the person who repeated it to me that I know you personally, and if you say all the plants you sell are chemical-free, then they are, no doubt about it."

"Thank you for that, Brian," she said, softly smiling at him.

At the same time, in the shop, Daniel stepped out the front door to look toward the house, a habitual check he made at approximately fifteen-minute intervals. A swift frown furrowed his brow when he saw the strange silver Corvette parked in the shade of the magnolia trees. Someone was there with Gracie, and he had no idea who, but he intended to. After quickly telling two browsing customers he'd be right back, he sprinted into the house.

In the hallway a few moments later, he caught the tail end of a request—". . . take you out to dinner tonight?"—and recognized the voice as Brian Price's. He was relieved though not particularly pleased, yet he smiled as he strolled into the parlor

"Brian, good to see you again," he said, going over and extending a hand. "You've traded cars. Enjoying the Corvette?"

"She's got great pickup," Brian enthusiastically an-

247

swered, sounding almost awed. "And handles like a dream."

"It's a beauty."

"Thanks."

"I didn't know who it belonged to, and since a few people have been giving us some trouble, I wanted to make sure everything was all right. Now I have to get back to the shop," Daniel explained, then unexpectedly leaned down over Grace, lifted her chin, and touched his lips to hers. It was a brief kiss but certainly not a quick peck, and he thought it adequately conveyed the message he wanted to get across. His long finger lingered on her jaw before he straightened, his gaze imprisoning hers. "See you in a little while, honey." He turned to Brian. "Sorry I can't stay to talk."

Then he was gone.

"Very protective of you, isn't he?" Brian murmured.

"Yes, well, we've been getting some threatening calls. We're both kind of edgy."

"Obviously the two of you are more than just friends and business partners now. Aren't you?"

"Yes. We are."

"In love with him?"

"Hopelessly in love."

Brian smiled humorlessly. "Guess that means you won't go out to dinner with me tonight, doesn't it?"

She nodded. "But thanks for asking me."

"That damned loan. If I hadn't had to turn it down, maybe—"

"It has nothing to do with the loan," she told him, lightly touching his arm. "Even if you'd approved it, I'd still be in love with Dan right now. Some things are inevitable."

"You sound a little sad about that."

"No. Not sad at all. Maybe a bit insecure, but then being in love makes most people feel some insecurity so at least I'm normal."

248

"Well, it's certainly made Dan possessive," Brian remarked somewhat peevishly. "That kiss he gave you was a signal to me to steer clear."

But being possessive didn't necessarily mean he was in love, Grace thought, slowly twisting her pearl ring round and round her finger. It could simply mean he was still satisfied with their renewed intimate relationship and didn't want to have to bother with the attention Brian might give her.

"I think I'd better be on my way," Brian mumbled, interrupting her reverie as he quickly got up.

Grace accompanied him to the front door and walked out onto the veranda with him. She looked at his brand new shiny Corvette. "That's a really nice car, Brian," she said. "You must have a great time driving it."

His expression lightened. "Oh, I do. She's a magnificent machine. I got her up to nearly ninety miles an hour on the interstate the other night, and it was like riding on a cushion of air."

"Ninety! Brian, that's crazy. You'll get yourself killed doing things like that."

"You sound like my mother."

"Good. I don't mind being compared to a woman with common sense."

Brian glanced at the Corvette then back at her. "I was hoping to take you for a ride."

"Thanks, but no thanks, not if you hit ninety on the interstate."

"Besides, you just don't want to go."

"I think it would be best if I didn't," she candidly admitted. "And you understand why."

"That doesn't mean I have to like the reason," he muttered, thrusting his hands in his pockets. He walked down the stairs onto the flagstone path, then looked back up at her. "I'm glad you're not mad at me about the loan, at least. I guess that's as much as I should have hoped for in the first place."

"Will you forget about that loan?" she insisted, smiling warmly. "And it was nice of you to drop by to see me." She looked up at the bank of ominously dark clouds chasing across blue sky, eating it away little by little. A rising wind swooshed through the trees around the farmhouse and turned up the paler undersides of the leaves. She shivered slightly. "Looks like a bad storm brewing. Be careful driving home."

With a rather resigned smile and a good-bye, he went to get in his car and rev up the powerful engine. And even though she did like him, he was almost completely forgotten by the time he sped out of the driveway. She went back into the house, remembered to latch the screen door, and continued on to the kitchen to begin dinner, all her thoughts concentrated on Dan. Why had he kissed her in front of Brian in such a deliberate manner, as if he did indeed want to warn the other man off? The kiss had caught her by surprise, although it wasn't odd for him to kiss her. He did so often, yet she knew he knew Brian had some romantic interest in her, so why hadn't he allowed her to handle the situation gently, discouraging Brian in her own way? He had interceded purposely. Why? Was mere possessiveness his motivation, or could it be that some deeper emotional consideration had prompted him to act? Question after question after question bombarded her mind, but she had no answer to any of them. Only Daniel knew what had motivated him to do what he had done. If she wanted to know, she'd have to ask him, and she intended to do just that.

At six thirty-five, when Daniel came down to the kitchen after taking a shower, he joined Grace in the kitchen, where she was putting the finishing touches on dinner. Artificial light filled the room because, outside, the sun had been shrouded in a black cloak of tumbling, swirling clouds as the storm gathered around them. Lightning flashes were becoming brighter. Previously rumbling thunder became sharp jarring claps. A wild wind rushed

250

through the trees, swaying the evergreens, making the leaves of the oaks, maples, and magnolias do a rustling dance. A few fat drops of rain started plopping loudly onto the ground, and the fresh clean smell of the earth drifted in through the opened windows.

"Looks like we're in for a rough one," Dan commented, raking back his still damp hair as he looked over at Buster and Little Bit curled up together on one cozy pad. "I see you came to the rescue and let both of them in."

"They were scratching at the door. What else could I do?"

"Tenderhearted Gracie."

"Umm, maybe, sometimes," she said, looking over at him, her heart seeming to burst with warmth as he smiled. *Could he love her?* That tiny hope was trying to open full-blossom in her soul, and she had to suppress it. Hopes raised only to be dashed cruelly later are one of life's most painful torments. And she didn't want to fool herself into believing in something that might never be. There were so many questions for which she needed answers, but this was not the right time to ask them. *Later.* She took the London broil from the oven and started to slice it diagonally. "I hope you're hungry. Everything should be ready soon."

Suddenly, without any flickering warning, the electricity went out, plunging them into semidarkness. She sighed. "Come to think of it, everything's ready now. I wanted to give the broccoli a minute or two longer, but it should be all right. Would you get the kerosene lantern out of the pantry so I can see what I'm doing? And would you light the candles on the dining room table, please?"

Dining by candlelight was an exciting change as torrents of rain lashed at the windowpanes, gusts of wind buffeted the house, and jagged streaks of lightning were immediately followed by explosive bangs of thunder, which seemed to shake the rafters of the old house. Yet, Grace felt safe and cozy inside. The broccoli was fine, the

London broil tender and delicious, and the potatoes au gratin perfectly browned. Conversation was upbeat. Business in the shop had picked up again, proving that the untrue rumors had done them little actual damage. Terrific news.

It was when Grace took her last sip of rosé wine then declined more when Dan offered to pour it that she gathered the courage to turn the discussion around to a very personal topic. She had to swallow hard and take a deep breath but finally asked, "Why did you kiss me the way you did in front of Brian?"

"Because I wanted to," he drawled, resting back in his chair, the flames of the candles reflecting in his mysterious eyes as they held hers. "Do you wish I hadn't?"

"No. It's just—"

"Then why do you ask?"

"Because I think you had some other reason to kiss me besides just waiting to do it."

A slight smile moved his carved lips. "You're right. I did."

"What . . . was your other reason?"

"I heard Brian ask you out to dinner, so I thought I'd better remind you you couldn't go because it was your night to cook."

Sucking in her breath, Grace jutted out her small chin, appalled by the insulting insinuation. "You actually thought I might go out to dinner with another man when you and I are . . . are . . ."

"Sleeping together," he finished for her with near-infuriating calm. He shrugged. "Some women wouldn't think twice about doing that."

"I'm not *some* women! And you should have known I would never do that."

"Should I?"

"*Yes!*"

"Maybe so, maybe not. How can I tell what you to think when you're keeping secrets from me?"

252

So that was it. He was playing a game with her, one in which she stubbornly refused to participate. She turned the tables on him. "I don't believe you kissed me in front of Brian to remind me it was my turn to make dinner. There was some other reason."

"Maybe there was. Maybe not."

"Dammit, you're acting like a little boy."

His wide shoulders rose and fell in another shrug. "All men act like little boys sometimes. This is one of my times."

"But—"

"And if you can have your secrets, I can have mine."

She thought she had turned the tables, but he still had the upper hand. She had hoped for the truth from him, but he was being as evasive as hell. She couldn't stand it. In the glowing candlelight, her eyes flashed. "How many times do I have to tell you I don't have any secrets?"

"Don't you? Then I don't have any either."

"You're impossible," she muttered, standing up fast. She had been seeking words of love, and here he was, giving her a comedy routine. She didn't have to put up with that and wouldn't. Picking up her plate, she reached for his. "Absolutely impossible. There's no use trying to talk to you."

With incredible quickness he caught her right wrist, took both plates from her, and put them back down while asking, "What's for dessert, Gracie?"

"Nothing," she answered, the glitter in her eyes growing hotter with each passing instant. "I didn't make anything."

"You'll do, then," he murmured provocatively, pulling her toward him. "You can be sweet when you want to."

Grace drew back, was hauled forward, and began to struggle more violently. *Useless effort.* She was no match for him physically, yet she tried to get free even after he brought her down onto his lap, his muscular arms wrapping around her. She twisted and wriggled despite their

253

iron-hard strength. She cursed him in no uncertain terms. "Let me go!"

"No."

"Dan!"

"Never," he whispered, his warm firm lips descending upon hers, coaxing them apart with the gently flicking tip of his tongue.

Pushing at his chest, she protested, "If you think I'm this easy—"

"Honey, easy's something you've never been," he answered, his deep chuckle rumbling in her ear. "But I can be a very determined man."

Trying to ignore the tremor that cavorted over her when he nibbled her earlobe, she shook her head. "I'm not in the mood."

"You will be," he promised. "Very soon now."

As his hands spanned her waist, she tried to pry them away. "Dan, stop it."

"Too late. And you don't really want me to. Thunderstorms have always made you . . . hmm, well to put it delicately—aroused."

"Maybe they used to but not . . . not now."

"I don't believe that." His strong fingers curving around her ribcage slightly increased pressure. "Am I going to have to tickle you to get you to tell the truth?"

She squirmed, her eyes meeting his. "Don't you dare!"

"All right," he whispered, his teasing expression replaced by one of passionate intent. "There are more pleasurable ways anyhow, pleasurable for both of us. Like this."

His hands moved up under the cotton knit shirt, unhooked the front closure of her bra with magical deftness, and found the soft wonder of her breasts tipped with taut excited nubbles. He heard her swiftly intaken breath become a steep gasp and relentlessly toyed with her swelling, throbbing flesh.

His touch was heaven, so light and sensitive that resistance immediately began to ebb. Her skin felt as if it were on fire. She could scarcely breath.

"You see, thunderstorms still arouse you," he persisted. "You are aroused."

"You . . . *Dan.*" The balls of his thumbs rubbing over and around her nipples made her tremble as raw desire exploded in a shower of sparks in her very center. Body and soul, she surrendered, softly moaning, "Oh, *Daniel.*"

"Mmmm, Daniel, instead of just Dan," he breathed, a trace of triumph in his deep husky voice. "We're making progress."

"Scoundrel," she called him. "Seducer." Then her parting lips sought his.

Daniel trembled too when she unbuttoned his shirt to trickle her fingers over his chest and sides to the small of his back where they dipped down beneath his waistband. Her tongue played between his teeth over his tongue, velvet-soft and tasting fresh as spring rain. With a low groan, he drew it deeper within, his hands ranging freely over her lissome body as she pressed hard against him, running her fingers through his hair. The storm raging outside, venting its awesome power in jagged streaks of lightning and mighty pops of thunder, was not more tumultuous than the tempest of passion building in him. And desire and excitement seemed to emanate from her. He basked in her warmth, the pace of his heartbeat quickening. The faint fragrance of her perfume clung to her creamy skin, and he wanted to possess her completely and for always. How had he managed to live without her for nearly two years? How many hours of sheer exhilaration and unbridled passion had he missed? Too many. He didn't intend to miss any more of them. Applying a light twisting pressure to her tenderly shaped lips, he dragged off her shirt, then her bra, and rained kisses over her smooth shoulders, finding hollows and fragile contouring bones, delighted as she quivered in his tight embrace.

"Daniel, this . . . is crazy," she uttered unevenly when

his fingers moved to the snap of her cutoff jeans. She stilled his hand. "You can't undress me here."

"We'll go upstairs then."

"The dishes—"

"Can wait. I can't."

"Savage," she accused, leaning back in his arms, half smiling as she looked up into his fiery eyes. She stroked his face. "You're such a savage."

"You ain't seen nothing yet, lady," he vowed, grazing a hand over her bared breasts. "Let's go to bed, Gracie. Make love by candlelight."

"Hmmm, we've never done that."

"And there's a first time for everything."

"Maybe," she conceded, lowering her eyes only to raise them slightly again to gaze provocatively at him through the thick fringe of her lashes. "All right . . . if you promise to give me a back rub. I've always loved for you to do that."

"No more than I love to do it." After allowing her to slip off his lap, he got up and took the candlestick she handed him. She carried another, and as he followed her out into the hall and up the stairs, the glow of both candles shimmered on her porcelain-smooth skin. Her dark hair swung around her naked shoulders. Her lovely bare back dipped in to form her narrow waist, and beneath the denim of her cutoffs, her hips slightly swayed. Her long shapely legs moved with natural grace. She looked like a native girl, and he needed to touch and kiss every inch of her.

On the landing he took her hand and led her to her room, to the side of her bed where she put the candlestick down on the night table. He left her to place the one he carried on the table on the other side, then came back to her, watching as she meticulously folded back the quilted counterpane. Then, without looking up at him, she removed her shorts and lace-edged panties to stand in exquisite naked glory before him, her head slightly bowed, her shining hair falling forward, her irresistible body showing no sign of tension. He stepped toward her.

She looked up, held out a hand. "Not yet. You have to get undressed too. It's more fun that way."

"You're right; it is," he agreed, and quickly stripped. And as she slipped into the center of the bed, he went over to get a bottle of body lotion from her vanity.

Watching him move in the circle of soft candlelight, eagerly exploring every powerful line and contour of his virile body, she had to catch her breath. He was so magnificently masculine; his skin was like burnished copper, and he walked with the stealthy, quiet tread of a stalking tiger. So dangerous and so exciting. An implosion of heat erupted deep inside her, and even the coolness of the sheet beneath her did nothing to cool her feverish flesh as he approached the bed. She turned over onto her stomach, heart hammering when she felt the mattress sink a little as he knelt down beside her.

"The lotion's going to feel cold," he said.

"It's all right. It's a hot night."

"And bound to get hotter," he whispered with wicked intonation. "Hmm, Gracie?"

Her head lying on the pillow, she glanced sideways up at him and had to smile. "Just rub my back."

"My pleasure," he murmured, rubbing lotion between his palms then applying it to her shoulders. "You don't need this stuff. Your skin's like silk anyhow."

"But it feels so good."

"It certainly does."

"I mean the back rub," she informed him with a light laugh. "So don't stop now."

He didn't. His large hands moved steadily down in slow circles alongside her spine, lean fingers kneading and massaging underlying muscle. He smoothed lotion over the gentle rise of her buttocks, along the backs of her thighs, and down her calves to her ankles, his touch feeling almost impersonal.

257

Beneath his ministering hands, she relaxed completely, until without any prior warning, the tip of his tongue ran over the arch of one foot, tantalizing the sensitive sole and tickling like mad. She tensed. "Daniel, *don't!*" she gasped. "You know that drives me crazy."

"Yes" was his only answer as his tongue flicked across her soles, again and again and again until she was giggling helplessly and wriggling. Then without further ado, he turned her over onto her back to begin an upward journey that started when he kissed the tip of each of her toes and proceeded from there, anointing her legs with light lotion then her thighs where his hands lingered. One slipped between, braising upward to brush against compelling feminine warmth, then ease open her long legs. He moved between them and journeyed on with gentle kneading to her waist.

His touch was not impersonal now. His hands caressed as they moved up over her uprising breasts to stroke them, rub them, and mold their rounded shape against his palms. Cupping one then the other, he bent down, his lips pursuing each succulent tip in its turn, his warm, moist mouth closing hungrily around them both over and over, deserting one only to seek the sweetness of its twin. Her giggling had abruptly ceased, and she took breaths in quick short gasps as his tongue feathered circles around her breasts, upward to claim her nipples repeatedly. The sensations he created were nearly too piercing to bear. In sheer self-defense, she linked her fingers tightly over the nape of his neck as her opening mouth found his.

They kissed many times, his lips melding with hers, hers with his as her hands skimmed over his broad back, feeling corded muscle flex beneath her wandering fingertips.

"God, I want you so much, Gracie," he growled, his hot breath filling her ear. "I have to have you now."

"Not yet. Soon," she whispered, slipping from beneath him to reach for the bottle of body lotion. "But first—"

"I don't need that." His glinting eyes impaled hers. "I want you too much already."

"Turn over," she softly commanded. "You had your chance to drive me crazy, and you succeeded. Now it's my turn to do the same to you; it's only fair. Roll over, Daniel. You're going to enjoy this."

"Gracie, I—"

"Roll over."

At last he did but with a smile. "You know, I think the sexual revolution is the nicest thing that's ever happened to men. It's very exciting for the woman to be the aggressor sometimes. I like it when you act like a tigress."

"You ain't seen nothing yet," she whispered, giving his own words back to him. A sensuous smile playing over her lips, she knelt beside him, her hair falling against her cheeks as she leaned down to apply unscented lotion to his back, moving her hands in slow circles to rub it in. She loved touching him and delighted in the very texture of his skin.

At first her touch was light as the brushing flutters of a butterfly's wings, arousing his every nerve ending to the ultimate in receptivity. Then her strokes became firmer, probing the flesh and bone structure of his shoulders and spine, defining bands of muscle and working over them. Tingling warmth spread through him.

"You're good at this," he murmured with a satisfied sigh. "Ever think of turning professional?"

"Are you saying you think I should get a job in a massage parlor?"

"Just try it," he growled, despite his grin. "I'll make you sorry you did."

"Oh? And what would you do to me, hotshot?"

"Believe me, you'd rather not know."

"Such big talk," she retorted, laughter bubbling up in her voice.

"I meant you could be a *respectable* professional masseuse."

"Ah, then thank you for the compliment." She bestowed a lingering kiss on his nape, but when he started to turn over, her hands on his shoulders pressed him back down. "Be still. I'm not through with you yet."

Indeed, she wasn't. She proceeded to massage his thighs and the backs of his legs before moving astride him and bending down to graze her lips all over his back, her tongue etching erotic patterns on his skin, her teeth teasingly nipping his flesh.

"*Gracie,*" he groaned.

Smiling, she fluttered her fingers over his ribs, then began tickling him. "You see, I'm not the only one who's ticklish."

With incredible quickness and little effort, he flipped onto his side, and hauling her down next to him, joined her in muted laughter. "So you want to play games. Okay, but this is one I'm always going to win because I'm bigger than you are," he warned wickedly, but as his hands encircled her waist while he looked into her eyes, the game abruptly ended. He pressed her down upon the mattress, his mouth swiftly covering hers, his tongue pushing inside when her lips parted with the sweet eager sound she made. Then her arms were around him, holding him closer, her taut round breasts straining against his chest as she laced kisses along the column of his neck and whispered amazingly provocative messages for someone normally so reserved. Whenever they made love she was free, unrestrained, and so warm and giving that he wanted the loving never to end.

"Sexy Gracie," he murmured in her ear. "Do you know how good you are in bed?"

"Why don't you tell me?"

"You're fantastic. Wanton. Imaginative and never shy, and I love everything you do to please me."

"This, you mean?" she whispered, moving down to trail her lips over his chest and midriff and across his abdomen. "And this?" Her tongue danced over his skin and her hair fell forward in a light cascading swirl against him, further inflaming his senses. "And this?" Touching intimately, she stroked and caressed, delighted by her ability to excite him as she felt the potent power of aroused masculinity. Her breath drifted over his superheated flesh.

Great thrumming sensations plunged through him. His hands moved feverishly over her shoulders and breasts, his palms braising the hard nubbles tipping her nipples until her daring caresses nearly snapped his self-control and he had to clasp her upper arms and pull her quickly up into his again. "Woman, you're driving me crazy."

"You taught me how."

"Yes," he muttered, tracing the precious bow of her lips, looking up at her, his eyes holding hers prisoner. "And you've learned all your lessons well."

"Thank you, Professor," she said, her smoky gaze steady. "Does that mean I pass the course?"

"You did that long ago. Everything now just gains you extra credit."

She kissed his chin. "And I'm having fun doing it. How lucky can—"

His lips took possession of hers with swiftly graduating pressure, silencing her, his arms tightening around her waist. Turning, he drew her beneath him and leaned over her. Her uprising breasts beckoned the touch of his fingers, and he explored every inch of the resilient slopes and at last scaled the roseate summits, which he languidly played with, enchanted by the lovely firm tips he aggressively yet gently fondled.

"Daniel," she gasped when his lips left hers to follow the exact route his fingers had taken. "Oh, *Daniel.*"

He closed his mouth around one succulent crest then the other again and again, curving his tongue against her flesh and drawing hungrily upon it, needing to extract every ounce of her honeyed sweetness. But even though she moaned softly and moved ecstatically in response, his satisfaction wasn't nearly complete. He had to touch and taste all of her, and his tongue journeyed everywhere while her delicate hands roamed as thoroughly over him and every touch they exchanged was electrically charged. Her breathing was as rapid and shallow as his in the savage heat that enveloped them both. In their exclusive realm of blazing ever-intensifying need, they murmured endearments and wildly evocative words that rushed him toward the brink. His knee gently pushed down to part her legs. His hands glided up her thighs, thumbs seeking the most secret juncture to feather over most sensitive feminine flesh. He felt her tremble and trembled himself as she boldly caressed him. His feathering fingers opened her, and he lowered his head to whisper against her lips, "Yes?"

"Oh, yes," she breathed, lost in the keen sensations he was evoking. "Daniel, now."

She held him closer, and he pressed against her, looking into her drowsy gray eyes as with a tender thrust he entered the most exquisite warmth he had ever known, warmth that bloomed open to receive him. She trembled again, and he kissed her once, twice, many times.

"Gracie, you feel so good," he whispered at last, seeing the bliss that lighted her features, enthalled by it, by her, by his own feeling of supreme tenderness. He stroked back her gloriously tousled hair. "So very good."

"You do too," she whispered back, lovingly cupping his face in her hands. A faint but lovely sensual smile graced her lips as he settled more deeply within her and she wound her limbs around him.

Bathed in candlelight they moved in perfect synchronization, and she met each of his slow, rousing thrusts as the rapture they gave each other heightened from plateau to ever keener plateau, making her feel nearly faint, making him ache for release. But he held back; it was happening too fast, and the ecstasy was too exquisite for him to let it end so quickly. Even when Gracie's arms tightened around him and he knew she was close to fulfillment, he ceased moving, then laid a silencing finger against her lips when she started to speak.

262

"Wait; let me wait," he implored, touching his lips to the racing pulse in her throat. "I want to make it last."

And he did, sweeping her and himself up toward the pinnacle again a few minutes later only to stop moving once more.

"*Daniel,*" she softly cried, the deep, piercing flutters he had created within her not abating in the slightest. Her fingernails raked lightly down his spine. "Take me, love me."

"Soon."

"Now," she insisted, taking the initiative, arching closer to him, rotating her hips, her rhythm slow and sinuous and utterly irresistible.

Daniel groaned. Unable to stop himself, he took what she so sweetly offered.

His long masterful strokes deepened, quickened, and as they spun upward together to the piercing, finely honed pinnacle of ecstasy, her entire body was set ablaze as she felt his hot essence erupt within her, and she was suspended for a breathtaking moment on the very spire of ultimate bliss. Then sensation abated only to peak again, and she clung to him, confessing before she could stop herself, "Oh, Daniel, I love you."

"I love you," he said gruffly as together they spiraled down into warm physical contentment.

It was only later as she lay in the circle of his arms, head resting on his shoulder, that her contentment began to ebb a little. Tilting her head back, she looked up at him. His eyes were closed. His breathing had slowed to a steady rhythm, and she knew he was asleep. *Had he meant it? Did he really love her? Or had her own words of love prompted his? Or had he merely said them in the heat of the moment, not really meaning them?* So many questions, and she didn't have an answer for any. Snuggling closer to him, she tried to cast all her doubts aside, no easy accomplishment, but finally after a long while she did fall asleep.

263

Just after dawn the next morning, Grace awakened with a start, still in the grip of a dream, an unhappy dream in which Dan had left her alone again and horribly lonely. Blinking her eyes, she tried to shake off those residual feelings of loneliness. After all, Daniel was next to her in the bed. She could reach out and touch him. And last night he had said he loved her. But she still wasn't at all sure he had meant it. She had said it first and needed him to do that before she could even begin to believe him.

Rising up on one elbow, she gazed down at him. She smiled, drawing a fingertip along the line of his jaw, not minding the light stubble of a day's growth of beard. Bending down, she kissed his cheeks, his temples, the lobes of his ears, then his lips, meaning to wake him, which she soon did. His eyes opened, and she looked deeply into them.

"Morning," she said.

"Morning," he murmured sleepily. "What time is it?"

"I don't know exactly. The clock's all out of whack because the electricity was off. But it's pretty early." Her lips touched his again.

"Hmmm, this is better to wake up to than an alarm clock," he admitted, cradling the back of her head in one of his large hands. A slow suggestive smile quirked up the corners of his mouth. "What do you have in mind, Gracie?"

"Guess," she challenged, bestowing another tempting kiss, one that lingered.

As he kissed her back with impassioned demand, his arms went around her, and he pulled her over atop him. Lost in the joy she always experienced with him, she quickly forgot that she had started this seduction in the hope that he would tell her he loved her without any prompting. But, considerably later, in lovemaking's warm afterglow, she realized he had never spoken the words.

264

CHAPTER EIGHTEEN

It was a lull before the storm. Daniel felt it. Although he continued to receive threatening phone calls, nothing else had happened, yet he knew something was going to sooner or later, probably sooner. And that was a logical assumption to make. Pete Royce, with or without Thad Compton's blessings, had already taken some fairly drastic steps to try to put Nature's Garden Shop out of business. There was no reason to believe he no longer wanted to do that. More likely, he was simply biding his time for some unknown reason. Trouble was, Dan had no idea what Royce might try next in his effort to crush the competition, and the uncertainty was making him edgy.

On a Thursday afternoon when he saw Gracie being pulled by the hand by a burly man toward the back of the greenhouse, he came close to attacking before realizing he was simply an overzealous customer who needed her assistance in picking out a suitable exotic plant for his wife's birthday. When Dan got close enough to hear the conversation, he stopped dead in his tracks, but not before Gracie glanced back over her shoulder and saw him coming. A few minutes later, wearing a puzzled frown, she sought him out in the tiny cubicle they laughingly called their office.

"What was that all about?" she asked. "For a second

there you looked like a stalking tiger ready to pounce on Mr. Knight and me. What on earth was happening?"

Dan flipped a palm back and forth. "It just looked like he might be trying to drag you to the back door of the greenhouse and out of the shop."

"Don't you think I'd have been screaming to high heaven if he'd been doing that?"

"Of course, I realize that now. I overreacted."

Grace stared at him speculatively, her expression somber. "Something's bothering you. What's happened that you haven't told me about?"

"Nothing's happened."

"Dan—"

"That's the truth, Gracie," he said firmly, then raked his fingers through his hair. "I guess I'm just a little uptight because of the calls that—"

"The threatening calls? You're still getting them?" she exclaimed softly, dismay shadowing her features. "But I thought . . . You never mention getting them anymore, so I assumed they had stopped. Why haven't you said anything?"

"Because I saw no reason to bother you by complaining about what's become an everyday nuisance."

"The calls must be more than just a nuisance or you wouldn't be uptight about them."

"They're annoying," he answered evasively, peering around her out the office door. "Ah, there's a customer at the counter. Don't want to keep her waiting. Excuse me, Gracie."

Saying nothing, she watched him walk across the shop, but her frown deepened as she strummed her fingers upon the neatly stacked first draft of his half-finished manuscript lying on the desk. And she strongly suspected there was something he was trying to keep from her.

The remainder of the afternoon was busy. A greatly satisfying influx of customers drove Gracie's suspicions to the back of her mind, and they had no time to revive after they closed the shop at six. Needing to replenish their supply of trowels out front, she went into the dark storeroom to get some, and when she turned on the light, she saw Buster in the far corner, pawing at rye straw, then meticulously arranging it to make what was obviously a bed. Grace's eyes lit up with excitement, and she quietly called Dan.

"Look," she said when he joined her in the doorway. "She's fixing a place to have her puppies, so it won't be long now. When Ed Walsh took her cast off yesterday, he said he thought she'd have them by the beginning of next week."

"But why out here?" Daniel asked. "I thought she'd have them in the whelping box I built."

"Me too, but maybe she doesn't like where we put it. She might not feel safe in the hall beside the staircase."

"Then we can move the box somewhere in the house where she'll feel more secure."

"Oh, why bother, since she seems to want to have them out here?"

"Because I want her to have them in the house."

His adamant tone made Grace stare at him incredulously. "I know you put some time into building the whelping box, but—"

"For God's sake, Gracie, that doesn't have a thing to do with it," he said sharply. "I want her to have her puppies in the house so she'll be there with you when I can't be."

Suspicion blossomed full flower again. "Why?" she asked tautly. "Something's wrong, and I know it, because this isn't like you. You'd be glad to let Buster pick any place she wanted to have her puppies if nothing was bothering you, and I want you to tell me exactly what is, right now."

He'd tipped his hand; he knew it. No amount of bluffing on his part was going to convince her he was withholding nothing. She was too intelligent to buy that, so he presented her with the truth, taking both her hands in his, lightly squeezing her slender fingers. "All right, I'll tell you. Those calls I get—the man who makes them always makes specific threats . . . against you."

"Me?" she breathed, her face going a bit pale. But she recovered quickly, although it was with some bravado that she added, "Oh, he's just trying to use me to get to you. You know what I mean. He considers me the 'weaker sex'; that's the kind of people we're dealing with, and he hopes he can make you back down just to protect me. We can't let him get away with it."

Looking down at her, Daniel said nothing.

And his silence was absolutely unnerving. After swallowing hard, she took a deep breath. "Okay. What's he threatening to . . . to do?"

"Nothing specific, Gracie," he murmured, lifting a hand to touch her hair. "Just vague threats."

"Such as?"

Daniel sighed. He might as well tell her. He knew only too well how stubborn she could be, and she was determined to hear the truth. So he told it. "I usually hang up on him, but once in a while he has enough time to say that it would be a shame to have to terrify you by grabbing you sometime, someplace, and taking you somewhere to teach you a few lessons."

"L-lessons?" Her eyes widened. "You don't think he means—"

"Hell, I don't know what he's actually threatening to do. We're dealing with a bunch of goons, and they seem to have no morals, so who the hell knows what they are capable of doing?"

"I don't think they'll do anything, Dan. They're bluffing."

"I'm not so sure, and if anything were to happen to you—"

"Nothing's going to. I'm keeping my eyes open and being very cautious. Even if Buster has her puppies out here, I'll be safe in the house. If anything happens, I promise I'll scream loud enough for you to hear me. But nothing's going to. These people never do their dirty work during the day, and you're always with me at night. Besides, I don't think Buster's willing to let us choose where she has her puppies. Some instinct made her pick this place."

"Looks that way," Dan conceded, but he didn't like the situation at all. The thought of Gracie being alone in the house without even the dog to protect her was totally unacceptable, and there was an uncompromising glint in his eyes as he added, "All right, but if Buster stays out here, you have to work in the shop every day."

"Well, I always do as much as I possibly—"

"I mean all day, every day, Gracie."

"But, Dan, I'll have to spend some time in the house, keeping up with my clients' accounts."

"We'll move your computer into the office out here."

Her gray eyes widened. "Don't you think that would be going a bit far? I'm sure I'd be safe in the house."

"Gracie, let's not make an argument out of it," he murmured, a hint of appeal in his voice. "I have a feeling something's going to happen, so indulge me. Just this once, go along with me for at least a little while. Okay?"

"O-okay," she agreed at last. How could she refuse when he felt so strongly about it?

Tuesday afternoon Grace quietly entered the storeroom, unable to resist taking another peek at the three-day-old puppies. They had arrived late Saturday night, and she and Dan had stayed with Buster in case complications arose that might make it necessary for them to call in the vet. Luckily all had gone well and the setter had come through it like a trouper and all the puppies proved they were healthy by going after their first meal within minutes of being born.

When Grace walked over to the bed, the dog awoke from a light snooze, and her tail swished back and forth, stirring straw around. Bending down, Grace stroked her head. "Hello, mama," she said softly, then gently picked up a puppy that began to move out of the little pileup composed of his brothers and sisters. Brown eyes trusting, Buster watched Grace pet her baby and didn't even show any alarm when Little Bit strolled into the storeroom and over to the bed. Dan and Grace had expected sparks to fly if the cat ever got near the pups, but Buster had only given a halfhearted growl the first time Little Bit approached, and now she seemed a welcome visitor if she didn't get *too* close. Wisely, the kitten gave the pups only a curious glance, then curled up on a bale of pine needles a few feet away.

Holding the puppy in both hands, Grace smiled. He was a cutie, and although his eyes were still closed, he was a wiggler, and his roly-poly belly proved that he got his fair share of his mother's milk. When he whimpered a little, Grace put him back down, and he immediately nestled up to Buster for a refill.

"Thought I'd find you here," Daniel suddenly spoke up from the doorway, smiling indulgently when she turned round to face him. "I told Glenn you couldn't keep away."

Young Deputy Glenn Watson stepped into the storeroom, smiling too. "Dan says you're thinking of moving in with Buster and her new litter."

Grace wrinkled her nose. "Dan exaggerates."

"Mind if I take a look at 'em?" Glenn enthusiastically asked. "Never seen a litter of purebred Irish setter puppies."

"I hate to disappoint you," drawled Dan. "But you're not going to see one now either."

"None of the puppies is even russet," Grace said. "All of them are a light brown, but they're good-looking anyhow."

"They sure are," Glenn agreed after speaking soothingly to Buster as her ears perked up alertly the moment he came near. Making no attempt to touch, he simply looked the pups over carefully. "I've got a niece who sure would love to have one of those. Any chance of me getting one when they're old enough to leave their mother?"

Grace and Dan exchanged glances. He flashed her the victory sign. "One down, five to go," he wryly said, then nodded at Glenn. "You can have your pick of the litter as soon as they're weaned."

"Hey, thanks, I appreciate it," the deputy said with a comical grimace. "I guess it's a good thing for me Buster found herself an unregistered boyfriend. I wouldn't have been able to afford a purebred pup."

"You'll certainly be able to afford one of these. We're going to give them away," Grace told him, then qualified, "if we can be reasonably sure they're going to get good care and lots of love."

"No need to worry about my niece. She loves animals and will probably spoil a puppy rotten. Wants to be a veterinarian when she grows up."

"Perfect. Sure you wouldn't like to give her all six of them?" Daniel asked jokingly. "We need a guard dog around here, but Buster is able to handle that job by herself without us keeping five of her offspring as assistants."

"Yeah, see what you mean," Glenn murmured, suddenly solemn. Eyes downcast for a moment, he fidgeted with the uniform cap he held in his hands. Finally he looked up at both Grace and Dan. He made a quiet cough-like sound. "Er-uh, there's something I have to tell you folks. That's the reason I dropped by."

Grace's stomach did a quick little dip. He had bad news. She had no idea what it could be but knew she dreaded to hear it. But trying to ignore trouble rarely, if ever, made it disappear. And she had to face it, whatever *it* was. She spread her hands in a resigned gesture. "What's wrong, Glenn?"

"Why don't we discuss this in the office," Daniel calmly suggested after glancing back into the shop. "We have a customer who seems to want some help, so I'll join you two in a few minutes."

The few minutes stretched into several. In the small glass-enclosed cubicle, Grace and Glenn chatted for a time about puppies, then fell silent, both of them tense. Finally, Daniel came in, his expression seemingly placid. But his eyes were rather darkly grim, almost flinty. He sat down on the edge of the desk, long legs outstretched. "All right, Glenn, let's not beat around the bush," he said flatly. "What do you have to tell us?"

"Something's about to go down," the deputy blurted out in law enforcement jargon. "I don't know exactly what or when, but I got it from a reliable source that plans are being made that'll mean trouble for you two again."

"And just who's planning to make this trouble?"

"My source didn't know their names."

"But you're sure he's reliable, this source of yours?"

"Always has been," answered Glenn, scrunching up his face. "You see, there are some people in this county who get around and know just about everything that's going on."

"An informant, you mean?"

"Yeah, a snitch. They aren't all in the big cities; we have a few of them out in the country too, and they can be a big help sometimes. Like now. At least I can warn you something's about to go down."

"But you don't know what?" Gracie inquired. "Or when it might happen?"

"No. My man was in a tavern; it was noisy; he only picked up snatches of the conversation at the next table, but he heard enough to know this place is going to be hit again soon."

"How soon?" Daniel asked, the planes of his tanned face hardening. "Do you have any idea, Glenn?"

"All I can do is give it a guess."

"But it'll be an educated guess, so go ahead. Tell us what you think."

272

"I think something's bound to happen by the beginning of next week."

"Damn," Gracie muttered, shaking her head disbelievingly. "This is all so crazy."

"But not unexpected," commented Daniel, looking at the deputy. "Any chance of picking up these men your informant heard talking?"

"Not much. He's sure they aren't locals. When they left the tavern, he tried to follow them to get a make on their car, but it was so crowded that by the time he got outside they'd disappeared."

Dan nodded. "I see. Well, Gracie and I are going to have to be extra careful during the next few days."

"Wish we could post a deputy out here round the clock, but we just don't have the manpower," Glenn muttered apologetically. "But I've talked to the sheriff, and you can be sure we'll be patrolling this stretch of the road more often than usual day and night. That's a promise."

Dan nodded again, and Grace produced a weak smile as she said, "Thanks, Glenn. It helps to know you and the other deputies will be around."

"Just wish I could do more. I'll stop by early in the morning," he said, slapping his cap against his right thigh with obvious frustration as he stalked out of the office.

Rising to his feet, Dan went over to Grace, took her hands in his, and drew her up before him. Their eyes met.

"Oh, hell," she whispered.

"Couldn't have said it better myself," he whispered back, slipping his arms around her as she laid her forehead in the hollow of his shoulder and released her breath in a deep, long sigh.

The following three days crept by, rife with tension. With every second that passed, Grace felt more on edge, and she had gotten to the point where she even eyed unfamiliar customers with suspicion, and she noticed a couple of times that Daniel was doing the same. Although they talked about the dilemma they were in, discussion never seemed to help. Both of them were poised on a razor edge, jumpy, waiting for something to happen.

Friday evening Grace puttered around the kitchen, assembling the ingredients needed for the spaghetti she planned for dinner. Using her own secret recipe, she prepared sauce to pour over browned ground beef and set the stove to simmer. She went into the pantry to get a box of vermicelli and promptly dropped it.

"Fumble fingers," she muttered, uttering a curse as the thin long stalks scattered like pick-up-sticks on the floor. She got the broom and swept up the mess, still muttering beneath her breath. Luckily, there was another, unopened box of vermicelli on the shelf, and she carried it into the kitchen, laid it on the counter, then started a pot of water boiling. Her hands shook. She hated that. She was a person who needed to strictly control her life, yet here she was, her day-to-day existence influenced by a bunch of thugs. She looked around the empty kitchen; Daniel was upstairs taking a shower, and she wished he'd hurry and come down so she'd be able to talk to him, to tell him how she felt.

Restlessly, she moved to the window overlooking the side porch and peered out. It was nearly dark already; they had needed to restock some shelves in the shop and had left later than usual. The automatic vapor light overlooking the shop, triggered to come on as twilight gathered, shone brightly down on the parking lot and building. And if not for that high intensity lamp, she would not have seen what she saw—the spiraling plume of dark smoke wafting up to disappear against the black, moonless sky.

Her heart stopped. "Oh, my God!" she gasped, snatching the shop key off its hook and starting out the door onto the porch. She stopped short, spun back around, and raced out of the kitchen down the hall and up the stairs, bursting into the bathroom. "Dan, the shop's on fire!" she cried out loudly enough to be heard over the steady spray of water in the shower. "Call the fire department."

She heard him urgently call her name but didn't hesitate an instant as she dashed back down the steps, out the front door, across the veranda then the barnyard, her thoughts exclusively on Buster and her puppies. *Why hadn't Buster barked the moment the fire broke out?* she wondered, then knew the answer when she saw the dog loping across the field back toward the shop. The setter had needed to go out, but now she was coming back, and as two shadowy figures darted out of the shop, she chased after them, erupting in a frenzy of ferocious barking.

"Come back! Buster, here girl," Grace called. Seeing the smoke was pouring out the back door of the shop, she sprinted to the front. It had been broken open and left ajar to create a draft, and dropping the key she no longer needed, she sped inside.

Flames licked at the counter, and sheer instinct led her to the fire extinguisher located on the south wall. Hefting it up, she sprayed foam on the outlicking fingers of fire but couldn't douse them completely, and when she glanced toward the greenhouse and saw another blaze had been ignited there, she flung the extinguisher down and ran into the storeroom, the safety of the pups foremost in her mind, and was relieved when Buster galloped past her to pick up one of her babies by the scruff of the neck and run outside. Grace gathered up three more and followed suit, depositing them gently on the grass some distance from the shop. Everything after happened so fast, she never remembered all the details. But in that moment she knew two puppies were still in danger, and she ran back inside, Buster close on her heels. The dog took one whimpering pup. Gracie snatched up the last, coughing harshly as the thickening smoke filled her lungs while she stumbled toward the exit. She passed the shop, remembered, then stopped short. She had to go back. Daniel's manuscript was in there on top of the desk. *All that work.* She couldn't just let it go up in flames, despite the choking heat gathering in her throat.

Even when she turned back, the faithful Buster

wouldn't leave her. She followed Grace into the office and back out again after she had swept up the manuscript. Together, each carrying a puppy, they moved through the suffocating smoke to the outside door.

Sirens pierced the quiet of the night, but Grace hardly noticed. Then Glenn Watson appeared out of nowhere, and she tried to smile a welcome as she thrust both the puppy and manuscript into his hands. She tried to suck in great breaths of the fresh air, but her lungs burned and ached, and suddenly, her knees began to crumple beneath her and everything went dark.

When the blackness receded some time later, she was lying on the ground and mercifully breathing much easier, though the burning was still in her lungs. Opening her eyes, she found a fireman bending over her, administering oxygen. Behind him stood Dan. She reached out a hand, and when he came forward, knelt down, and took it in both of his, she pushed the oxygen mask away for a moment.

"The puppies?" she asked, her voice raspy. "All okay?"

"Fine. Buster moved them all over by the shed, and I'm going to find them a safer place in just a minute."

"Good." She smiled faintly. "And your manuscript? Did Glenn give it to you?"

Eyes narrowing, he nodded.

"You can talk later, miss," the fireman insisted, moving the mask back toward her.

But she started to sit up. "I think I'm all right."

"Let him be the judge of that, Gracie," Daniel commanded. "Now's not the time to act stubborn."

"Just one more thing, Dan. Turn off the spaghetti. We don't want the house catching on fire too," she said, then willingly allowed the fireman to replace the mask over her nose and mouth. Truth was, she didn't feel too great, but inhaling the pure oxygen helped.

She was taken to the hospital, treated for smoke inhalation, and released two hours later. While driving her home in the van, Daniel gave her the good news.

"The men who started the fire have been caught. Glenn met them as they were making their getaway, radioed their direction to the other patrol cars in the area. There was something of a chase, but they lost control of their rust-bucket truck and ended up in a ditch, got a few bruises and scratches," he explained. "According to Glenn, they're a couple of punks who suddenly stopped acting tough the minute they were arrested. Being charged with arson scared them, and they're talking hard and fast. They've already implicated Pete Royce, saying he's been paying them to harass us."

"Well, thank God. Maybe this will be the end of the whole mess," Grace said hopefully, but she didn't really feel relieved. "Unless . . . Oh, dear, I'd feel much better if they had implicated Compton too."

"I doubt they can. Probably never met him. But if he's directly involved, Royce might spill everything. And even if he doesn't, I imagine Compton might decide not to push his luck any further."

"In other words, leave us alone finally."

"Yes."

"Oh, I hope it is over," she murmured, crossing her fingers, then asking the question she had dreaded to ask: "How much damage was done to the shop, Dan?"

Taking his eyes off the road for a moment, he glanced over at her. "The fire department got the flames under control before there was any structural damage. But the water and smoke took their toll. It's a mess, Gracie; we're going to have to close for at least a week, probably longer, to clean up. As for the plants . . ." His shoulders rose and fell in a rather weary shrug. "I don't know if many or even any of them survived the smoke. But the insurance will cover all our losses."

"Yeah, but if anything else happens, the company's going to designate the shop a high-risk area and up our rates," she said with dark humor that failed to elicit even a flicker of a smile from Daniel. Lighted by the glow of the dashboard, his profile was stern, as if carved from stone. Afraid he was wishing himself anywhere besides this place and involved in this latest predicament, she looked out her window for several seconds, pressing her fingertips against her forehead as she watched the uneven and shadowy line of trees flash by along the side of the road."

"Head hurting, Gracie?" Dan abruptly asked.

"Oh, a little," she admitted, turning back toward him. "But not all that much. Tell me, where did you put the puppies?"

"Buster seemed content to let me leave them in the whelping box near the stairs in the hall."

"I guess beggars can't be choosers. At least all her pups are safe."

"Yes. They are," Dan said tonelessly while turning at the farmhouse and passing the shop, deserted now with the fire truck and patrol cars gone. "And you helped Buster save them. But why—"

"Will you look at that?" Gracie gasped as the van's headlights picked up the long black Cadillac Seville parked under the magnolias at the end of the drive. Her mouth very nearly fell open. "That looks just like Compton's car. We saw it when we went to see him. Remember? My God, he's here! Can you believe the nerve of the man?"

His jaw rock-hard, Daniel braked to a stop, cut the engine, and as he got out from beneath the steering wheel, Gracie was already out the passenger door. Together, they walked up the flagstone path and the steps to the brightly lit veranda where Thad Compton sat rocking back and forth in the wooden-slatted swing suspended from the ceiling. He actually had the audacity to smile.

Which cut no ice with Dan. He glared at the older man. "What do you want?"

"To talk to you both," Compton answered too smoothly, getting up to walk over to where they stood, the heels of his hand-tooled western boots thudding on the wooden flooring. His put-on smile became simpering. "I just heard the news, and I am shocked! Completely shocked! When Pete called me and said he'd been arrested, I couldn't believe it."

As if bored, Daniel shifted his weight from one foot to the other while thrusting his hands into his pockets and maintaining a cold silence that forced the other man to continue to babble on.

"Pete's been a loyal employee for a lot of years, so when he asked for help tonight, I naturally gave him the name of a good attorney. But I want you two to know I had nothing to do with any of this."

"Really?" Grace drawled. "Why should we believe that?"

"Because I say so," Compton snapped. He was a man who had had too much power too long, and he didn't like anyone questioning him. Yet, after a second he regained his composure and tried to sound nice and grandfatherly as he went on with his spiel. "Listen, the reason I came here is Pete. I don't agree with what he's done, but I think I can explain it. You see, the profits for the shop he manages for me have been dropping off for a couple of years, and when you two opened out here, he got real scared. That's why he's gotten himself in this mess. I just wanted you to understand that. I'd like for you to drop the charges against him."

"That's out of our hands," Daniel replied curtly. "He's been charged with conspiracy to commit arson by the authorities. And even if we could have the charges dropped, we wouldn't."

"I'm sure he didn't mean to get in so deep," Compton persisted, that vacant smile still on his face. "I'd like to make you understand that."

Grace raised her eyes to the heavens, unimpressed. Compton was such a fraud. He couldn't even put on a

279

good act, and she felt sure he was more worried about being implicated himself than he was about Royce.

"Well, maybe you can't get the charges dropped now," he conceded, but with all the overconfidence of a nitwit. "Still, if you'd put in a good word for ole Pete, it—"

The short fuse of Daniel's quick temper ignited before he could do a thing to prevent it, and he roughly grasped the lapels of the man's sport jacket. "Listen up, Compton," he uttered between clenched teeth. "Royce deserves anything he gets. He paid to have the shop set on fire, and Gracie went in there to rescue some helpless puppies. She might never have come out. And you expect us to put in a good word for Royce! Forget it. If you're afraid he's going to implicate you, you'll have to find some other way to keep him quiet."

The man's eyes bulged. "But I didn't have anything to do with any of this."

"Yes. You did. Maybe you weren't actively involved, but Gracie and I told you what Royce was doing, and you refused to talk to him," Dan said, his voice deceptively soft as he abruptly released the lapels. "He's your employee; you're responsible for his actions. You need to put a plaque on your desk, one that says: 'The buck stops here.' And you need to read it every chance you get until it's memorized."

Jerkily smoothing his jacket, Compton stood blustering incomprehensively.

Inside the house, obviously hearing the angry voices, Buster whined and scratched at the front door.

"Go," Grace told Thad Compton, the menacing glimmer in her eyes at variance with her delicate features. "You're upsetting the dog, and you're just not worth it."

"But I'm telling you, I had nothing to do with any of this."

"And I think you're lying. I just hope all the truth comes out," she tersely replied, then turned her back on him and glanced at Dan. "Let's go in. I've had about all the bull I can take for a while."

Taking his keys from his pocket, he unlocked the door, and soon after Grace and he stepped into the hallway, they heard Compton's car door slam shut, then the low rumble of the Cadillac's engine. Grace turned up her nose. "What a nerd."

"He's a bastard."

She couldn't disagree with that assessment and simply inclined her head. Then she hurried over to the side of the stairs where Buster's pups were all fast asleep in a haphazard pile.

Daniel watched as she gently touched every one of them as if to assure herself they were truly safe. When she stood up straight again and gave him a lovely, relieved smile, he started toward her, his expression solemn. "I want to talk to you, Gracie."

"You'll have to wait. My clothes smell like smoke and so does my hair. And I feel sooty all over," she said. "All I want right now is a shower and shampoo."

"Okay, my question can wait," he said, his dark green eyes following her as she walked up the stairs.

Twenty minutes later Grace left the bath and went into her bedroom, securing the tie of her terry robe round her waist. She had wound a towel in a turban around her head, and as she loosened it to begin rubbing her hair, she looked up and saw Daniel sitting in the easy chair by the bed, slapping a rolled-up sheaf of paper against his right thigh. She gave him a little smile.

His narrowing gaze swept over her. "Feeling better?"

"Umm, yes. Very much," she said, squeezing the excess water from the ends of her hair, then going over to stand in front of the vanity mirror to comb out the wet strands. All the while Dan was silent, and after she finished, she turned toward him with a questioning frown. "Okay, what question did you want to ask?"

"Why?" he muttered, leaning forward in the chair, allowing the roll of papers he held to open up and be revealed as the pages of his half-finished manuscript as his eyes captured and held hers. "I can understand why you went into the shop to rescue the puppies. But why this? Gracie, why?"

"Because I saw it on the desk, and I couldn't just let it burn. You've worked so hard on it."

"But, dammit, your life's worth a hell of a lot more than a hundred or so typed pages!" he snapped, tossing the manuscript on the floor as if it meant nothing to him. "I can't believe you risked your life for that. Why did you do it?"

"Why do you think, you big idiot? Because it's your work, and I love you," she snapped back, her own temper suddenly as volatile as his sometimes was. Balling her hands into tight fists at her side, she glowered at him. "And if you ever leave me again, Daniel Logan, I swear I'll come after you and I'll . . . I'll . . ."

"Does that mean you'd go with me if I decided to leave?" he asked, his voice lowering to a husky whisper as he reached out to catch her hands in his and pull her to him. "Is that what you're saying, Gracie?"

"Are you saying you're thinking of leaving?"

"Would you go with me if I did?"

"Yes! I'd go," she reluctantly confessed. "But I don't know how long we could make it last. I'm just not the wandering kind, Dan."

"And I've been trying to tell you for weeks, I'm not either, anymore."

"Are you really being honest with yourself about that?" she had to ask. "When you talked to me about Maine, you said you wished you could be there through all the seasons, like you wouldn't mind going up to spend a whole year."

"I'd like to see Paris in the springtime too, but that doesn't mean I'm going to pack up and move there. Just because I said a few things about Maine, you—"

"It isn't just that. Lately, you've had a faraway look in your eyes, and I've noticed it often."

"Gracie, you can blame the threatening phone calls for any faraway looks I might have had," he said, moving his hands up her arms to her shoulders. "The threats were against you—I've told you that. I've been worried and trying to think of ways to keep anything from happening. That's why I've seem preoccupied. And I am being honest with myself. I don't want to go anywhere. I want to stay and run the shop and be with you. Even if I had the urge to travel again and you didn't want to go with me, then I'd stay because I don't want to lose you. I love you, woman, for God's sake."

Looking up into his clear green eyes, she longed to believe him, and part of her did. Yet another part still had lingering doubts. She laid her hands against his chest, her fingers plucking at his shirtfront. "If you do, then why do I always have to say I love you first before you say it back?"

Heaving a sigh that became a low groan from deep in his throat, he shook his head. "Because I'm a nincompoop, I guess. Maybe men don't remember to say the words as often as they should, but the feeling is still there. And I'll try to do better, I promise, because I do love you, love you, *love* you." His hands on her shoulders tightened, and he shook her gently. "I love you so much that I still feel like putting you across my knee and giving you a few good wallops for saving my manuscript by risking yourself. My God, honey, if something bad had happened to you tonight, I would've gone out of my mind. That's how much I love you."

Joy engulfed her in warmth as she believed him at last with all her heart and every fiber of her being. Yet . . . Slipping her arms around his waist, she rested her head against his shoulder to ask, "Do you love me enough to marry me, Dan?"

For an instant he was silent, then low laughter rumbled

up as he tilted up her chin. "You crafty wench," he murmured, loving amusement in his eyes. "I think you manipulated this conversation just to sneak in a proposal of marriage."

"No, it just worked out this way. But you haven't answered my question."

His darkening gaze swept over her upturned face. He brushed the hair-roughened back of his hand against her cheek. "Do you want us to get married, Gracie?"

"Yes, I do," she told him outright. "I'm old-fashioned, maybe even a stick-in-the-mud, like you've called me sometimes. But I need the commitment, the words on a certificate that'll prove we believe we'll be together forever." Suddenly a tiny grin curved her lips. "Besides, that certificate will make it more difficult for you to get away if the wanderlust ever comes over you again."

"Well, all right." He pretended to agree with great reluctance despite his answering grin. "I'll make the supreme sacrifice—my freedom, since it means so much to you."

She pretended to try to pull away from him. "Never mind, if you feel that way about it."

"Now, hold on just a minute." He pulled her closer, wrapping his arms loosely around her. "I can see how beneficial marriage would be to me too. At least it would keep young swains like Brian Price from trying to put the make on you."

"He never had a chance after you came back," Grace admitted freely, linking her fingers over the nape of his neck. "Can I assume you're accepting my proposal?"

"Might as well. I was planning to propose to you soon, anyhow. You just beat me to it."

"I wonder if I should believe that."

"Will this help?" he asked, dropping down on one knee before her to plead theatrically, "My dear Miss Mitchell, will you do me the great honor of consenting to become my wife?"

"Oh, get up, you crazy man," she insisted, laughing, pulling at his hands until he rose effortlessly to his feet again to look down at her. She gazed up adoringly at him, dancing a fingertip over his finely chiseled lips. Then she rumpled his hair. "I'm surprised at myself—I actually proposed to you. Wonder what Gran would've had to say about that."

"She would've said 'More power to you.' After all, she was a very feisty independent lady," Dan replied with a fond reminiscent smile. "She might very well have proposed to your grandfather."

"She might have wanted to, but when she was young, everything was so different."

"You're right. And I'm very glad some of those things have changed . . . for the better," Dan murmured, following the line of her jaw with one finger. "I like for you to be bold."

"Like this?" she whispered, scattering kisses upward along his neck. "And this?" Her parted lips played over his. "And this too?" The tip of her tongue flicked against him.

"Exactly like that," he growled, his warm mouth taking passionate possession of hers as he pushed her robe off her shoulders, unlooped the tie belt, then removed the garment completely. He gave it a careless toss, his gaze reverent as she stood before him naked without any sign of self-consciousness. She moved toward him, took him by the hand, and led him to the bed. She pulled back the covers, then unbuttoned his shirt and unbuckled his belt. Lying down, she watched him shed all his clothes, and they exchanged sensuous smiles when he came down beside her, propped on one elbow. Her hands floated over his back as he moved one of his hands upward from her abdomen across her midriff and allowed it to dwell upon her breasts. While she touched him everywhere, his fingers played over her nipples, tenderly squeezing and caressing the firm aroused nubbles of flesh. He tasted their sweetness.

The delights they experienced together were more exquisite than they'd ever been. Their words of love freely spoken and whispered endearments heightened all sensations as they merged together as one. He immersed himself in her, giving and taking with loving tenderness. She surrounded him in warmth, as eager to take and give as he was. A sweet hot-blooded temptress, she ardently met his every masterful stroke, revelling in his gentle possessive power and happily consumed in the fire of their mutual desire. When they could no longer wait for completion, it came in a sunburst of searing ecstasy so supreme and splendid that they trembled together on the finely honed pinnacle and were trembling still when they spiraled down slowly into contentment.

"Well, how did I do?" Daniel inquired several minutes later, lifting a tendril of her hair back from her right temple, smiling into her eyes. "Better this time?"

"You were wonderful. But you've never given me any reason to complain," she answered honestly. "You're always a terrific lover."

"I know. That goes without saying," he retorted, his gaze teasing. "I meant did I tell you I love you often enough?"

"Ummm, there was improvement, but there's room for more. You can't say it too much. I'll never get tired of hearing it."

"Demanding woman." Nuzzling his lips against her ear, he murmured, "I love you, love you, *love* you."

She believed him. Grazing her fingertips across his cheek, she murmured back, "And I love you, Daniel, so very much."

He drew her closer, but when he started to kiss her, Little Bit meowed plaintively outside the closed bedroom door, raking her sharp little claws over the wood. He smiled. "She obviously wants something."

"Probably hungry."

"Speaking of hungry, are you? I am. We missed dinner, you know."

She wrinkled her nose. "I doubt we can salvage the spaghetti. But we have cold cuts."

"Sounds terrific. We'll make big, thick sandwiches. And we'd better eat hearty because we've got our work cut out for us tomorrow. Got to start cleaning up the shop."

Gracie groaned, stretched lazily, and trailed a finger over the bridge of his nose. "This whole situation's been so crazy. But then, when you came back here, I knew that if I got involved with you again I'd be asking for trouble."

"Ah, but love is the best kind of trouble, isn't it?"

"Yes, and you're worth it," she said softly, winding her arms around his neck, urging him nearer. "You make me happy, Daniel."

"I'm glad, because you make me happy too. I love you so much."

"Ummm, say that again," she murmured.

And he did, over and over between long leisurely kisses. He was back to stay, and he didn't intend ever to let her doubt that again.